BHABANI BHATTACHARYA (1906-1988), remains one of the most celebrated writers of his time, widely admired not only as a novelist but also as a translator, scholar, cultural historian, biographer and a short story writer.

Bhattacharya's achievement as a novelist lies not only in the choice and handling of themes, narrative technique and art of characterization but also in shaping the English language as a suitable medium to convey Indian sensibilities.

> *'Think of the wonderfully embroidered rhythms of Joseph Conrad, who wrote in English though some part of his mind was still thinking in Polish... so it is with Bhabani Bhattacharya. He writes in a language which is not English, yet all the words are English...,'* wrote the prestigious *Saturday Review*, New York.

One of the striking features of his novels is the prominence given to women characters. Women are usually presented by him as highly significant if not central characters and in no way inferior to men.

He was honoured with the Sahitya Akademi Award in 1967.

Music for Mohini is outstanding among Bhattacharya's novels for its charm, warmth and artistic economy.

'Bhattacharya paints every emotion with ease and dexterity of the seasoned artist that he is.'

Nagpur Times

LIBRARY OF SOUTH ASIAN LITERATURE

Library of South Asian Literature is an ongoing endeavour to publish in English an eclectic selection of some of the finest writings from the rich diversity of South Asian Literature. It attempts to bring together books regarded as landmarks in their language, for having won literary awards or critical acclaim, or having been a major influence in their genre, creating a new narrative style or simply representing an outstanding writer's art.

Readers are invited to recommend books to make this more truly representative of the vigorous literary tradition of South Asia. These maybe sent by mail or email to Editor, Orient Paperbacks, 5A/8, Ansari Road, Darya Ganj, New Delhi-110 002. Tel: +91-11-2327 8877, 2327 8878 email: mail@orientpaperbacks.com

MUSIC FOR MOHINI

BHABANI BHATTACHARYA

Orient Paperbacks
DELHI | MUMBAI | HYDERABAD

ISBN : 978-81-222-0616-6

Music for Mohini

Subject: Fiction

1st Published 2019

Published by
Orient Paperbacks
(A division of Vision Books Pvt. Ltd.)
5A/8 Ansari Road, New Delhi-110 002
www.orientpaperbacks.com

Cover design by Vision Studio

Printed at Thomson Press, New Delhi

MUSIC FOR MOHINI

one

'**Mrs. Silverthrone,** Miss Peabody, Mrs. Longstreet, Miss Whiteleather, Dr. Goodnight, Miss Vile, Colonel Birdwhistle, Captain Rainbird,' Heeralal droned on, reading from his collection of odd English names, 'Miss Wardrobe, Mrs. Stammers, Major Kneebone, Dr. Death, Dr. Blood, Dr. Slaughter, Mr. Still, Miss Stiff, Mrs. Quickly.'

He paused; his eyes narrowed, wondering; he repeated, 'Mr. Still, Miss Stiff, Mrs. Quickly!' and broke into a giggle.

His sister, Mohini, perched on a table strewn with books, was swinging her long legs and nibbling a pencil end. She was three years older than Heeralal — she would be a full seventeen soon, on the day of the Festive Lights — entitled to superior knowledge. She was not to be outdone in the collection of names.

'Captain Borntired, Miss Sheepwash, Mrs. Midwinter, Dr. Cakebread,' she read proudly, with an edgeways tilt of her head, 'Misses Freeze and Frost, Major Tearsheet, Captain Shivers. And these, my latest: Lady Godsland, Mrs. Manhood, Miss Coffin. Miss Coffin is very strange, *nah?*'

She turned her face from her notebook to watch the effect of that last name on her brother.

'Miss Coffin!' Heeralal was tempted to steal his sister's new find and add it to his own list. He disguised his eagerness with a casual air.

'Call that odd? Why, heaps and heaps of English folks are Coffins. Where did you pick it up, though?'

'Crossword winners,' the girl said. She had looked through back numbers of *India Weekly* and come upon lists of names, pages full, many of them English people.

'Miss Coffin!' Heeralal felt the name stick to his tongue. 'Exchange it, Mohini?'

He leaned back in his narrow chair and eyed his sister, fearing her sharp refusal. She was freshly bathed and looked cool and bright, thick wet black hair awash to her hips. She bent and caught a dripping fistful and pressed the water out on the floor, while she weighed her brother's offer. Coffin: black-clad figures, iron heaviness in the air, the flowers stiffening. Mohini, who loved the warmth, the colour of life, could not bear images of decay.

'What will you give me in exchange?' She bargained with Heeralal in her soft voice with its slight drawl. 'Not that I aim to part with Miss Coffin, an old name, say what you will, but since your heart is set on it, *Bhai,* and you could make it into Dr. Coffin, and add it to your Dr. Slaughter series —'

'Miss Coffin!' Heeralal's anxiety to possess the name grew as he repeated it. He, too, was a hard bargainer. 'Why make a coconut out of rice? What d'you see in that name? If we collected stamps, I'd say Miss Coffin is a commemorative. You pick up that sort here, there, everywhere. See?'

'Mother Ganga!' the girl invoked the holy river with a forced sigh of complaint. 'To haggle like fishwomen in the market place!'

'Fishwomen!' said Heeralal, and in that instant he had an idea. He would hate to part with any name in his slim list, but his sister, unawares, had suggested a new one. Why not Fish? It sounded likely, even if he had never seen it in print. Let it be. Miss Fish!

'Take it or leave it.' The roundish, gay face pretended indifference. 'Miss Fish. Don't tell me, Mohini, it's in your book.'

A tiny wrinkle between her light, faintly arched brows rebuked him.

'Miss Fish? I said fishwomen, so you made up Miss Fish, didn't you? Fast work. Do you deny this, swindler? Miss Fish is mine. Don't be unfair.'

'Unfair?' Heeralal grimaced his disgust. 'Unfair? When we started our collection we agreed, didn't we: a new name belongs to the one who finds it first. Well, then, who found Miss Fish? And you can't have it unless I trade it to you. Rules of the game.' The voice sounded solemn. 'Miss Fish for Miss Coffin. Take it or leave it. Please yourself. *Hoon!*'

'All right, *Bhai,*' Mohini yielded quickly, lest Heeralal, young hothead, withdraw his offer. Miss Fish was tempting enough. But then, was it genuine?

'Who was ever named Fish?' Mohini challenged Heeralal.

'Miss Fish,' said Heeralal brightly, cheered by his bargain. 'Heaps and heaps of English folks are Miss Fish and Mrs. Fish and Mr. Fish. Why not, if there're so many kinds of fish — Herrington, Whiting, Salmon, Pike? If you doubt this, ask father. Just ask him.'

Heeralal jerked his thumb at the dark brown wood partition which ran from floor to roof and separated their little room from father's more spacious study. Father had visitors with him.

'What're they saying? Mohini, let's listen!'

The boy, with sudden interest, cupped his hand back of his ear. There was a crack in the partition which he had diligently enlarged with a pen-knife to a peephole.

'No!' Mohini answered sternly. 'How you love to eavesdrop on your elders. What do they teach you at school?'

Dashed, Heeralal made faces. 'This and that.'

Her smile mocked him. 'A monkey could do better. No — o?'

Heeralal, a little shamed, twisted his arm to scratch his back. 'Oh my spine won't stop itching!' and he scratched again. 'It's an omen, you know. I'm in for some beating today.'

Heeralal had an instant vision of his algebra teacher, eyebrows and moustache rigid with anger, and he wished he could wear an extra pair of khaki pants over the pair he wore to school. But Mohini would surely notice. She always saw everything.

'An ear-pull will do you good,' said Mohini, with a sudden uneasy feeling that she had made a bad bargain.

Why had she thrown away Miss Coffin in such a rush? Heeralal was keen on it — he had a fancy for that kind of name — and with patience she could have had something better out of him.

She suppressed the unwelcome feeling with a question: 'The time, *Bhai?* The right time by your three new watches?' The large black pupils that seemed to fill her eyes slanted a little, while she swung her legs and bit the pencil end. No pencil or penholder in the house was unscarred by her teethmarks.

New watches! Heeralal, touched on a sore spot, made a wry, helpless face. Three weeks back he had read the curious notice in a Calcutta English periodical:

> Our superfluous-hair remover will take off unwanted hair from the body and make the skin supple and smooth like velvet. Hair will not grow there in your lifetime. Used by leading stage and screen stars. Price per bottle, Rs. 1.75. Three bottles at a time, Rs. 5.
>
> To make this wonder lotion popular, we are giving away a fancy wrist watch with every bottle as a FREE PRESENT to the first twenty thousand buyers! This watch is strong and beautiful and guaranteed for seven years. Buyers of 3 bottles will get 3 watches.

Heeralal had acted quickly. He had taken a loan from his sister to add to his meagre savings and had sent for three bottles of 'superfluous-hair remover' — so he wrote with unconscious irony. Would there be luck for him? Would he be among the first twenty thousand? Why, all India would seize this chance, and there would be at least a million applicants. Day after day he had stood on the balcony waiting for the blue-turbaned postman, Ram Singh, watching tensely as he walked in through the gate. At last, yesterday morning, Ram Singh had looked up at the anxious face and nodded as if to say: 'Yes, yes, I have it here.'

Heeralal gave a shout and rushed down the stairs. When the postman had left, Heeralal untied the parcel strings with frantic fingers. There were the three watches! But the boy sat stupefied with anger and dismay. The watches were tin and cardboard with the hands painted on the disc!

Mohini often asked him with sweet mockery: 'The time, *Bhai?* The right time your three new watches?'

'Why do English people have such eccentric names?' Heeralal asked by way of escape, as though he were really puzzled.

On his sister's lips hung a dim smile. Poor boy! He had been tricked into parting with the few rupees he had saved by denying himself peanuts and candy. Behind her brash fun was a latent sympathy, and even while she delighted to tease, she sighed for him.

'Eccentric? They may not sound eccentric to English ears. What about our Indian names? Heeralal Ray, Diamond Red Chief!'

Diamond Red Chief! She fitted the protesting image to its funny name. Mohini loves to laugh and she needed only a slight excuse for an outburst. Heeralal in helpless alarm, watched her put her hand to her mouth in a familiar gesture. Her mouth when she laughed was much too wide, and her eyes half-closed, the smooth skin under them crinkling. Yes, once she went off into fits of laughter, she wouldn't stop, Heeralal knew. Father would hear her across the partition, and that would mean trouble. It relieved him to see her hand move off, her lips tighten.

'Father is Butter Boy Chief!' Heeralal grinned.

Her brows drew together in protest. 'Don't be disrespectful to Father.'

She would not let her father be mocked or spoken of lightly. How could she bear it? Was there ever a father like hers?

'And you?' Heeralal went on. 'Mohini, Heaven-land's fairy. Why not put on your wings and fly about — whish!'

Mohini, the *apsara,* the peerless beauty of heaven handed her its magic mirror; her eyes lit; her lips half-parted in an absent way; she was grace itself.

'Whoever is your *apsara,* Heeralal,' she said, 'keep your friend Buba, who is all of eleven years old, in reserve.'

'Twinkle, twinkle, movie star?' chanted Heeralal, teasing in his turn.

In an unguarded moment Mohini had once confided to her brother her secret dream to be a cinema star.

With a jump she was on her feet. She grabbed her sarcastic brother, and shook him soundly. She pulled his snub nose.

'Tongue clever! Am I not your elder? Bad enough that you so often call me Mohini and not *Didi*. Elder Sister.' She swept back a loop of hair, damping her brow. 'You should knock your head on my feet at every sun-up and beg my blessing.'

'All right, then: *Didi, Didi, Didi.* Pleased? Satisfied? *Hoon*! How fitly Old Mother calls you image-of-golden-grace! Huh!'

Slim and undersized for his age, Heeralal was unlike his tall, well-shaped sister, except for the jet black eyes with their thick lashes.

Mohini pulled his nose again. She did this often raising the snub nose alarmingly skyward, and as she pulled, she picked up the thread of names: 'Mr. Pitcher, Miss Jug, Mrs. Napkin. What about the trio? Tell me.'

His ears were pricked for sounds in the corridor.

'S-sh!' he said, and the ink on his warning finger stained his lips. 'I heard ankle bells, *Didi*. Bindu's out there, listening. If she finds out we're doing names, not homework, she'll rush to Old Mother and tell her. That Bindu —'

'Bindu, we can hear you,' Mohini called out merrily. 'Your ankle bells betray you every time. Why wear them?'

Mohini sat perched on the desk, her legs crossed, her feet in blue suede slippers under a white cotton sari with blue-flowered borders. She turned a bright face to Heeralal.

'Talk of homework? Your Ananda Babu will do my homework. I only copy it out. You know.'

Yes, he knew, and he pulled a long face. Mohini had no tutor. She didn't need one, being a grown-up girl, it was said. Heeralal had his Ananda Babu, a stern taskmaster, who made his pupil work like a slave. But let Mohini come and ask him to write an essay for her, as though she were doing him a favour, and Ananda Babu, meek as a mouse, would do it. And while he wrote the essay, he would keep Heeralal buried in an absurd pile of arithmetic. He would lift his eyes often in a stern watchful glance. Mohini would step into the room once in a while to ask, as though she were his tutor: 'Ananda Babu, how are you getting on?'

'You know!' said Mohini stressing the point, a prideful smile curving her mouth.

She felt very happy. The fact was that Ananda, a post-graduate student and a favourite pupil of her father, loved her. Of course, he was not the only one to love her, but a woman could not tell this to a child of fourteen! And what if the lovers were very much her invention — pawns in her game of make-believe? They made her happy. They occupied her thoughts and illumined her fancy.

'Father's having great fun,' said Heeralal, with a pointed glance at the partition. *'Didi,* let's look,' he begged.

She, too, had heard the loud laugh across the partition, and tingled to know what it was about. Only her father's dignity restrained her. At last, beaten by curiosity, she gave a toss of her head, rose, and moved over to the crack. Heeralal forestalled her with one swift bound.

'Turn for turn,' said Heeralal, his eye to the peephole, his nose flattened against the woodwork.

Strange people sometimes came to see Father. The girl who was here last Thursday, for instance. The thought of her made Mohini purse her mouth with scorn: plain-looking, eighteen or so, she had apparently sat for the internal assessment examination, fared badly in Father's paper, history, and, because she thought she would fail, had come begging for a passing mark.

'You'll get the marks you deserve, no more, no less,' Father had said, staggered by such a bold request from a student.

When she found he wouldn't be moved by her pleading, the girl had burst into hysterical weeping.

'Oh, don't, please don't, please go,' father had said. But she had sat slumped in a chair and sobbed, her face buried in her hands.

'Why don't I kill myself?' she had moaned, utterly wretched.

Poor, helpless, easy-going father!

'Listen, I'll do what I can,' he had pleaded. Yes, now he was the one who had pleaded.

'Why don't I throw myself in the lake?' she had moaned.

At last father was hit by panic. 'Don't,' he had said, desperate. 'You'll get passing marks, I promise; let me have your roll number.' Then he added a bitter touch: 'I hope there aren't many like you in our Universities. Don't repeat this blackmail — ever. It isn't worthwhile.'

The girl had looked up then. 'Sir, you have saved my honour and my life. Sir —'

Melodrama at its worst! And Mohini had felt so sorry for father.

'What do you see? What sort of people?' Mohini demanded. She nudged Heeralal with her elbow.

'S-sh!' said Heeralal, intent. 'Wait.'

Some wicked imp in the girl urged her to action. Heeralal had an arm raised, clutching a rail. Mohini tickled him in the armpit.

'O-u-ouh!' Heeralal squealed with laughter.

'S-sh!' warned Mohini in her turn. 'Father heard you. Rush back.'

Yes, the Professor had heard. He paused in his talk with the visitors. He was middle-aged, rather heavy of build, with a wide brow fringed by long greying hair.

'What mischief are those two bent on?' he asked, frowning.

The door of the little room opened with a jerk. The children were at their desk, as though deep in work. Heeralal, shoulders hunched, entered figures in an exercise book. 'Seven into seven is forty-seven.' he droned. And Mohini, a scowl of concentration on her brow, mumbled: 'Reaching Benares, Gautama Buddha delivered his first sermon on the Noble Eightfold Path leading to peace. The second sermon stressed the need of detachment from the world's affairs as the means to freedom. The third delivered on a mountainside —'

'What are you about, my boy?'

Heeralal gave a start, jolted out of his absorption, and gravely answered. ' 'rithmetic, Father.'

Slowly he turned his head, weighed with knowledge and enlarged by uncut, unruly hair.

'Your pencil —'

The boy looked down, and his face fell. The pencil had no point. Uncanny, how father had caught him! Heeralal glared at his sister. Her all-chewing teeth had been busy sawing off the point. Father leaned over the desk and examined the page and smiled.

'arithmetic, seven into seven is forty-seven!' His hand sought his son's ear. Heeralal, alert, ducked. No use. He kept his eyes focussed on the tip of his nose as he resigned himself to the inevitable.

'And you, studious girl?'

The studious girl had paid no attention to her brother's punishment, it appeared. Her eyes and mind were buried in her work.

'*Ancient India,*' she said in prompt answer, as she looked up at her father. A tiny smile showed at the corners of her mouth, but she kept her face grave.

Her eyes rested on the large rip at the neck of the grey wool coat she had knit for her father's last birthday. The rip had grown much larger; she had neglected to mend it, for shame! Father! She yearned toward him with all her quick warmth, for the ripped wool coat somehow gave him a helpless air. What would he do if he had no daughter? To mend and stitch and sew buttons on vests and shirts which came back maimed after every wash? How pleasant she felt to be important to her father.

Father fumbled for his glasses with a knowing *'Hoon!'* and prompted again by an uncanny sense, he leaned over her desk. There lay the book she had hurriedly opened to pore over in a mindless way,

The Poisoned Kiss, a Bengali novel she had borrowed from Reba, her school friend.

'*Ancient India*, my studious girl?'

Beige ear lobes peeped from under wings of black hair. Thick fingers took hold of an ear above its gold, bell-shaped pendant and shook it gently. '*The Poisoned* — er — so!' And the other ear. 'So!'

Her mouth dropped open. She was startled, pale with confusion. Then the colour came back to her face in a warm flood, her nostrils dilated with quick drawn breaths. Her eyelids fluttered and then were still as she looked up for an instant to meet her father's glance. She lowered her eyes, which fluttered again.

Voiceless, motionless, frozen. She bit her lip lest tears come. To be caught reading *The Poisoned Kiss* of all books, and to have her ears pulled — the disgrace was unknown in all her experience. Her breast heaved.

Father stared in bewilderment, at the pain in her eyes, the veiled reproach, her stillness. This was so unlike Mohini. He hadn't meant to hurt her feelings: he had pulled her ears almost playfully, without thought. Oh, he would love to pet the child, to soothe her and make her smile. He lifted his hand tenderly to his daughter's head, rested it there a moment and quickly withdrew it. Shyness had come over him. Tucked inside his rather stern-looking body was a man of strong affection. Suddenly, without a word, he turned and shuffled off, his thick eyebrows moving up and down in his agitation.

As soon as father had left, a plump dark-faced girl about Heeralal's age slipped into the room with a jingle of silver ankle bells. She was Bindu, daughter of the cook-woman who had grown old in the service of this house. The cook-woman had been engaged first by Mohini's mother. She had seen the children born, and her mistress die when Heeralal came. Her husband, a night watchman in a Calcutta bank, called her Spitfire because of her tongue lashings. But she had spoiled Bindu, her only child.

'Oh, *Didi*, jewel-faced one, what terrible sadness is this? Such a fond father! How could he pull your ears in hot anger? Mother Kali!

Oh, *Didi*, jewel-faced one!' Her eyes and voice seemed to pour sweet sympathy.

But Mohini gave her a furious glance. Bindu had been spying from the doorway. She had enjoyed the sight, the hypocrite! Nothing could happen in this house unseen by her prying eyes. Mohini, her face livid, stepped toward her. Bindu, watchful, caught the meaning of her look and spun round to the doorway.

'Old Mother will hear this tale. Oh, *Didi*, jewel-faced one!' she said, and fled.

Mohini sat down, a lump in her throat. How would she lift up her head — ever? That mischievous monkey would carry the tale to the servants' quarters. All the world would know, and — Mohini bit her lip at the hateful thought — sympathise!

Heeralal, meanwhile, was puzzled at his sister's frown, her tight-lipped silence. Such gentle pulling of ears, nothing at all. Even her novel had not been forfeited: father had put it back on the table before he had walked off. Strange!

Heeralal attacked the tension in a tactful way.

'*Didi*, five queer names I offer you for your Miss Coffin,' he spoke as though nothing had interrupted the delightful pursuit of their game. 'Miss Egg, Dr. Finefrock, Captain Curry, Major Pickles, *and* Professor Careless. There! Oh, luck! A little ear-twisting and the ill omen of my back's itching is fulfilled. Easy escape, *nah?* Now, I'll be safe at school' — he paused, his face merry — 'the three little sparrows cheeping in my throat!'

Three little sparrows. Mohini's tight face relaxed, and the hard line of her lips yielded to their accustomed smile. Heeralal, as a baby, had hated the sight of milk and old Mother had had to coax him. 'Drink it up, child. Three little sparrows sit inside your throat and they want the milk — they're so hungry that they can't cheep.' The baby would drink the milk, and the sparrows would resume their cheeping. The baby seemed to hear the bird voices, and he was happy. Heeralal was a grown boy, but the sparrows were a cherished memory.

In a moment Mohini's face was grave again.

She could still feel the pressure of a hand on her head, the tender pressure, conveying more than words, soothing her, begging forgiveness. How well she knew the gestures characteristic of her father! Old Mother must not take him to task on her account. Yes, he needed her protection. Mohini sprang to her feet.

She paused at the door, spun round to her brother, and called: 'Try and catch up with me. I'll get ten odd names before Swing Festival Day.'

two

THE NOON MEAL the professor ate by himself. Mohini and Heeralal had an early morning meal, then tiffin at school, unless it was a week end. After Old Mother had served her son, the Professor, she squatted in front of him on the red cement floor, and waved a satin-frilled, palm-leaf fan in front of him, mindless of the electric fan whirling overhead.

Each course of the noonday meal seemed to have an extra seasoning — gossip: the bitter *neem* leaves fried in mustard oil with slices of egg fruit were often piquant with the reported chitchat of neighbours; the heaped white rice eaten with lentils, dry potato curry and prawns bore perhaps the pickle of current household affairs; rice again, and a pond fish bathed in gravy with several vegetables — this rich course went well with the chili pungency of delvings into the past. Later there was a bowl of curd and the Professor, if pleased with the meal, would talk of the good things of life. If the food was not to his taste, he might speak of old age, the body's growing infirmities and the latest pranks of undergraduates in his college.

He sat cross-legged on a square yard of bright rug in whose centre puffed lettering spelled out the invitation. *Eat more. Eat again.* He was forced to listen to Old Mother's complaints about steepening household expense; he countered with a lavish serving of curry which was not chili-hot enough.

'Tight-fisted in this house with chili,' he grumbled. 'What good is curry, Mother, if it won't bite your tongue? Tell me, what sort of economy is this?'

Out flipped a sheet of paper.

'Look at this cut-throat bill from the power company: 87 units in a month. All saving on chili, Mother, an anna-worth, no more, and here's money thrown away to buy light, 87 units!'

An absurd idea struck him and made him smile. It was so ridiculous it would surely impress her old world spirit!

'Why not use bean oil, Mother?' he went on. 'Bean oil is cheaper than electric current.'

'True, true,' Old Mother agreed at once. 'Why not use bean oil as our wise forefathers did? Often enough I have asked: is it a good thing to trap lightning from the sky-world and hold it in big iron machines in the powerhouse and make it your bond servant? One day that lightning will break free, I tell you, and your powerhouse will be blown sky high.' She paused a moment and added with a nod, 'True, true. Bean oil is cheaper than current.'

'Why, Mother, darkness is cheaper even than bean oil!'

The bland smile now grew across his face. He had almost played into his mother's hands and must pull himself out!

'Why not use darkness?'

But Old Mother gave him a long keen glance. She mused awhile, and then said sternly: 'Where's your sense, childling? Have you gone back to babyhood?' Old Mother never called her son by his name except when she was very angry with him. In all his forty-seven years she had fondly called him childling. 'You let the girl's voice be caught in shiny black discs. You let her songs be sold in the bazaar for a few rupees apiece.'

Her son looked up quickly from his food, an eyebrow lifted in honest amazement.

'Mohini? It's a matter of pride, Mother, that Mohini gets her songs recorded. Indeed, she has made a name for herself in the world of music, that girl of ours. She has a contract to sing for All-India Radio once a week. Why' —he smiled fondly — 'as her father I'll soon be a celebrity myself!'

'True, true,' Old Mother's voice was almost a wail, 'You are in your early infancy. All these years you have not grown. Why do you not get this plain fact in your stomach? A fellow, good or bad, saint or lout, can go to the gramophone shop and buy a shiny black disc for Rs. 3, and it is as though he buys a little of our girl, for her voice is truly a part of herself. Terrible! Even her name is printed there, on the disc, for every eye to feel.'

The Professor cleared his mouth of curry for one hearty laugh. Old Mother lost her temper.

'No, you cannot laugh it away,' she spoke sharply. 'I won't have this family disgraced. Rogues and roughs and scamps, all the vagabonds and cut-throats in the four bazaars mouthing the name of our girl with a leer, befouling it, and they make her sing at their bidding —'

He stared at her.

'Girls of the most respectable houses and ladies of the highest social status have put their songs on gramophone records. Why this fuss?'

'Fuss? As if at my age I do not know what is good for the girl or for you! Fuss! No, such things must be stopped. Those black discs in the shops must be broken up. Fuss!'

He swept her words aside with mild ridicule.

'But, Mother, what you demand is just impossible.'

Old Mother's eyelids fluttered fast, her thin lips quivered, and out came her arch weapon: 'Send me away to the Holy City. Let me not take one more mouthful of your food or even drink one sip of water in this house.'

That threat to go away to Benares, to the city of Siva, where ten thousand Hindu widows lived in self-chosen exile, dedicated to grim austerity, had seldom missed its mark. The son could not bear the thought of Old Mother going away, giving herself to the rigours of penance. Better let her have her own way in the house. He drew the line firmly, however, where Mohini was affected. Over Mohini developed a clash between mother and son, even though on many points of orthodox living they had reached a fair adjustment.

Old Mother, too, knew the limits of her power. Years before, her son had decided to send Mohini to an English convent school. Old Mother had sternly opposed him: let Mohini be trained at home; let her learn classical Sanskrit, the language of the gods, the precious vase that holds the essence of true knowledge and wisdom. Her son would not back down. He would mold the girl in a modern way, which was his way. And when his mother used the familiar threat, 'Send me away to Holy City,' he had merely shrugged his shoulders, and murmured coldly, 'Please yourself. Mohini has no mother of her own. You know what she means to me. I must do what I think is best for her. There can be no retreat, no compromise.'

Old Mother had accepted defeat, though she had not spoken a word to her son for weeks. She had moved about the house like a pale ghost, sighing brokenly, with a pinched face and always near tears.

Today she was using her weapon again, woeful because of the disgrace to the family name, to the girl who was truly the darling of her soul.

But a counter-thrust came from an unexpected quarter. The son pushed his plate away with a firm gesture.

'First of all, let *me* go hungry. I will have to stand upright for three full hours — just try it — lecturing boys till my tongue aches, all on an almost empty stomach. Let this be my lot. God!'

He pulled himself to his feet.

'Childling!' Old Mother forgot her grievance, rose quickly, and took hold of her son's arm. 'Childling!' she begged. 'No more of my silly talk. Eat in peace. My lips will be sealed.' And her left hand beat her forehead in self-deprecation. 'Well past my seventieth year — why wonder dotage has come?'

'No, Mother, my appetite's gone.'

'Childling, eat my head.' There was a break in her voice.

'But —'

'Eat my head.' Old Mother was almost in tears.

Relenting graciously, he sat down on the rug. Pleased with himself. Tact! He ate in silence for a time. Old Mother watched him, wordless, and waved the palm leaf with great energy, fanning away the heat and his anger.

'One more bowl of curd?' she coaxed.

'A little more, just one chunk. What lovely curd you make. Mother.'

Old Mother peered at him with joy in her eyes.

'Eat,' she coaxed again.

But now that the meal was nearly over, she felt easier in her heart and came out with one more complaint.

'Why are you so thick-sighted? Why don't you see the girl's of age? To lift an angry hand to a grown daughter and put her to shame! Where were your senses? Are you truly in your infancy?'

Taken aback, he saw the image of his daughter's face, flushed, full of startled pain. The brightness of her eyes threatened tears. She was a child no longer. She was sensitive, self-conscious, because she was growing. Poor, gay-hearted girl, why had he thoughtlessly made her unhappy? But fancy poring over a page of *The Poisoned Kiss*, and mumbling: 'Reaching Benares, Gautama Buddha delivered his sermons on the Noble Eightfold Path leading to peace — detachment from the world's affairs...'

Old Mother watched him with a steady gaze. 'You cannot smile it away,' she cried sternly, seeing his gaiety.

'Mohini?' He spoke solemnly. 'She is a child, what else, even if she reads books like *The Poisoned*... er...'

He caught himself lest Old Mother, shocked to hear that Mohini read such trash, scold the girl severely. He could not give her away. Besides, he did not believe in censoring the books a young girl wanted to read.

'Books like?' queried Old Mother with swift suspicion.

'Books,' he said, noncommittal.

Old Mother pressed her hand to her cheek in utter amazement.

'Mohini, a child? Mohini, a woman for four whole years, a child?' She paused a moment, recalling that her Mohini, spare of build though not thin, had not too feminine a figure. Many a younger maid looked riper than she for marriage.

'Seventeen!' Old Mother resumed in a moanful tone. 'And no horoscope made for her yet.'

'Horoscope, Mother? In this age of microscope, who needs a horoscope? Eight stellar beings controlling the life story of every man, woman and child! Everything worked out in advance. And a good astrologer sees it all in the position of the stars at your birth hour. Our ancestors who devised this amazing joke on their pigheaded progeny — all credit to them!' He chuckled and shook his head. 'No, *we* aren't as benighted as all that are we. Mother?'

Old Mother took one good look at the slim gold chain on his neck with its pendant amulet. He mocked many of the old beliefs, but the amulet was there to shield him from the Evil Eye. He had firmly refused to wear it until she had wielded that weapon of hers. 'Send me away to the Holy City.' It was, indeed, one of her major triumphs.

Old Mother felt soothed and moaned on: 'Not even a horoscope! The sun and the moon will surely stand witness that I have poured a hundred cries in your ear, childling: "The daughter of the house will be the laugh of the town unless you find her a groom." My hundred cries you let pass with. "Wait, wait, she's still a child!" Talking to you about this is like pouring milk into a cracked pitcher!'

'I plead guilty,' he said, subdued, for he saw again the vivid flush on his daughter's face, and with wonder he mused: 'Mohini fit for marriage?' Aloud he said: 'Look, Mother. I pull my own ears in retribution. Is that not enough?' This was the surest way to appease her.

Old Mother's thin brown fingers took hold of his plump arm again.

'Indeed, you are in your infancy. If you insult yourself, the sour fruit of sacrilege will be for Mohini's eating. Listen, words won't tie the air into knots and make a groom for Mohini. Bear this in mind, night and day, asleep or awake: our Mohini is of marriage age.'

Mohini of age. Mohini, born on the night of Festive Lights and herself a light. Find her the likeliest groom in Bengal.

'Give up your worries on Mohini's account,' he said brightly. 'And, Mother, set your mind on planning her trousseau and her marriage jewels. Let's see — what's the market rate of gold today?'

~

Mohini sat languidly during the noon hour in a wicker chair on the front balcony, holding her knitting needles, a smile on her lips. The light, the savour of life, she mused, is love.

The front balcony with its green tiled floor and wrought iron railing pushed out of the yellow-washed two-storey house and overhung a narrow width of lawn fringed by scraggly flowers and a low brick wall. Beyond the wall ran a tree-shaded asphalt road connecting two main thoroughfares. Small, semi-detached middle-class houses with flat roofs stretched away on both sides of the road. Washing, saris in vivid colours, hung on the balcony rails. A few of the houses boasted strips of walled garden; the rest were flush with the pavement. And overflow of traffic had of late been pushed into this residential street which was now swollen for hours with rickshaws, cars, pedestrians.

At noon the peddlers came, long-tongued peddlers proclaiming their various wares. The utensil dealer who would replace cracked brass plates and pitchers with new ones, half their weight, bawled, basket on head: 'New brass for old here goes. Mirror-shine in metal shows!' The rag and junk collector rang a small bell and sing-songed: 'Sell all rags. Sell old shoes and scraps and bags. Sell all waste. Take silver, be cleansed!' The vendor of toy balloons painted with bloated human faces lured children with: 'Little ones, hey hey! Meet wrestlers from Bombay!' The pavement barber, his scissors poised, planted himself in front of the corner-house cookshop named *Glutton's Inn,* and yelled in a shrill voice; 'Head four pice, chin two pice, armpits gratis!'

A life without love, Mohini mused with an unaware smile, a life without love is like jasmine without scent, so wrote Dhruba, her poet cousin, in a lyric that fascinated her, *Hail, Eternal Woman Thou!* No, the poem went on, it is like a tree without leaf, grass without green, clouds without rain, the bowl of the night sky stripped of stars, empty, funereal, needless.

But she was not empty, funereal, needless. The sky bowl of her life had two bright stars, if only Dhruba, who was at college in neighbouring Calcutta, just across the river, and who visited this house off-and-on, knew as much! Thralled satellites, he called them. Thralled satellites of the Eternal Woman... No, Mohini shook her head, ruefully, she could not tell him the facts. Though he was a poet, what if he laughed at her? What if he tattled? One never saw the Eternal Woman in one's cousin, that was the trouble.

Love between tutor and girl pupil was a foregone conclusion, or so it appeared from the story-books. If it did not happen, something was wrong with girl or tutor or both. If you failed to arrange a match for your girl, change your tactics and look for an eligible young bachelor as her tutor, people said, half laughing, half in earnest! But Ananda was not really her tutor, and that gave the affair added stature. How eagerly, joyfully, he did her homework for her! That shy, self-conscious young man hadn't the grit to stand up to a woman's unjust demands!

And there was the other young gallant, Somir, the tall, handsome elder brother of Reba, her school friend. They lived three streets away, near the Jamuna Jute Mill. Great luck, indeed, that Somir was a programme director at the Calcutta station of All-India Radio, or else she would never have faced the microphone and sung for all Bengal. Her first singing, lines from Tagore's *Gitanjali,* was such a success that she was now asked to the studio every month and her work was paid for. The way Somir fussed over her was enough to make other girl artists heartsick. He even felt sure Mohini could be a film star, with her cinematic face and sensitive voice, or was it the other way around? A film star! How she glowed with his admiration!

Mohini did not know that the young, handsome programme director had a way of fussing over every pretty girl who stood before the studio microphone. He invested them all with the aura of glamour. He made each girl believe she was the best singer in Bengal; that she lent the studio grace by her presence, and that with her sensitive face and cinematic voice, she could one day be a film star.

Yes, these two, Ananda and Somir, were her true admirers, but there were others of a lesser order. Arun, the young cavalier, would cycle up in his green-striped college blazer, announce himself with his bell, and ride headlong downhill, hands folded over chest. This feat was to impress her as she watched from the balcony. Actually, it only made her laugh! And Vishnu, a freshman at the engineering college, a halfback on the football team, used a well-worn trick: he befriended Heeralal — Mohini made a slight grimace, thinking of it — so that he could come to the house with gifts of peanuts and toffee. Mere boys! Years had to pass before they grew up, grew fit for experiences of the heart.

Her mind, eager to deceive itself, would not recognise her admirers as wish phantasies. Her dream world of romance had to be peopled to become real. These admirers served her purpose, for she gave them, mixing a little truth with much fiction, gestures and impulses to suit her liking.

A red and green paper kite was fluttering by, trailing two cubits of tail. A furlong down the street was the kite flier, a lean boy with a keen, pock-marked face. Mohini's knitting slowed as she watched. He was an admirer of her neighbour, Khuki, who was a year her junior at school. Mohini saw the kite sail toward the rooftop where the short, slim Khuki was bending over the low parapet, following the kite's progress. A letter for Khuki, Mohini knew from observation, was tied to the kite's tail. Presently, it would be manoeuvred over the terrace; it would rise and dip, rise and dip, while Khuki tried to catch the tail. Letters by private air mail! And careful parents might watch the regular posts for letters, but in vain. The kite wheeled and hovered once more. Khuki hopped nimbly, her braided hair slapping her spine, her bare, glass-bangled arms twinkling in the sun. She seemed all eyes and arms, and yet she missed the kite, and missed again. A gust of wind dashed the kite against the spreading *bokul* tree. Khuki screaming in alarm, stood still. Her admirer eased it into the wind, calm skilful, unhurried. Once more the kite fluttered over the roof, once more the eager girl rushed breathless and flung up her arms to catch it. Mohini was big-eyed, pale with the strain of those moments of suspense. She was no longer herself: she had become one with

Khuki. Finally, the kite dipped like a gull, and lay clutched in Khuki's hands. She tore off the tail, and raising her arms tossed the kite back into the air and rushed indoors.

Mohini clapped her hands, her face alight. Young men and their girl friends could always count on her good will. She felt happy, though somewhere in her was a secret ache because no man sent her love letters. That air-mail letter — what was it like? Fancy had often given her longings a taste of fulfilment: when food was bad, for instance, she would fly to a marriage feast and eat lobsters; when a rainy evening was long and dreary, she would imagine herself a cinema star. So, now, self-deceived, she went over the air-mail letter conveyed by a carrier-kite, and was warmed by its outpouring of love, unaware of its likeness to passages she had read in a letter at school last Tuesday.

It had happened in the history class. While the teacher recounted the battle of Hastings, Reba had secretly stuck her fingers down into her blouse and drawn out a pink sheet. With an arch, meaningful glance she had given it to the girl next to her, and Shanti had put it between the leaves of her book while she read and re-read it with great absorption. Then she passed it on. From hand to hand, the pink sheet travelled. The history hour was almost through. Miss Sen, eloquent on the ruse by which William had routed the Saxons at Hastings Hill, suddenly fixed her beady eyes on a girl in the second row. She paused for barely a moment, spoke on as before, and then stepped down suddenly from her foot-high, lecture platform. With three brisk steps, she snatched at the letter. Sunk in it, careless, the girl had given herself away. Miss Sen took the trophy to her desk. She poured over it, while the class waited tensely. The letter had a fancy salutation: 'Dawn-star-of-my-heart's-horizon, oh Thou!'

'Yours?' The teacher's clouded face looked up from the pink sheet.

'Oh no, Miss Sen,' the culprit promptly answered. 'I found it on top of my desk. Just here.'

'Really? Does anyone claim this thing?' Miss Sen flourished the letter in her hand.

'No, Miss Sen, no,' chorused many voices, among them Reba's, loud and clear.

'All right,' said the teacher. Firmly she put the letter in her black handbag. 'Now to the battle of Hastings.'

Later, outside the classroom, the girls crowded around Reba with words of sympathy for her loss, but Reba curled her lip.

'Why worry? What does it matter? I get a letter almost every day, don't I?'

Mohini, listening, caught her breath.

'A letter every day, Reba?'

'Almost. There are so many of them: Monu, Pankaj, Borun, Sukumar, Premendra. It's hard to keep count!'

Reba, lucky one, Mohini had thought with a sigh. Then she wondered: Miss Sen had not torn up the letter; she had put it in her bag. Why? Plain-looking Miss Sen had been twenty-nine last birthday. Perhaps no one wrote her. Perhaps she would read that letter again in the privacy of her room and enjoy the sweet words. Well, let her hungry heart have its fill.

But no one wrote Mohini either. She, too, must read the words of love addressed to her school friends. Mohini grew sad remembering all this in her wicker chair. The knitting needles darted and stabbed, and the wool coat lengthened. 'Eight — nine — ten —' Mohini counted the stitches, a spare red needle tucked in her huge bun of hair. Then she looked up again. Down on the streets a gourdpipe sounded its high shrill notes, the familiar music of the snake-charmer. He came almost every day and squatted awhile on the pavement in the small shadow of the flowering *bokul* tree, facing the house. He was smart, vulgar, common. He had a lean, erect figure, very tall, and he was dressed in a bottle-green velvet vest over a white tunic and a dhoti worn like baggy trousers. His bare, dark-brown arms were tattooed with red-eyed snakes. Sarpa and Darpa, his two pet cobras, were coiled up in the baskets he carried on the ends of a bamboo pole. He put the baskets down and flung them open. As he played on his gourd, the four-foot cobras crawled out. Sarpa reared up and listened with a slow shiver of its sleek head, dull bright with hoof-like markings, and Darpa listened with a hard glitter in its lidless eyes. Both flashed their forked tongues while a crowd gathered and copper pieces clinked in the snake-charmer's tin bowl.

And now, in a moment, ankle bells would jingle through the rooms, and Bindu would arrive. She would stand at the balcony rail, and lean over. The snake-charmer would lift his deep-set eyes often to glance at her. He came as much for her sake as for business, that was plain. Bindu had gone out a time or two and stood among the crowd, sidling up to the snake-charmer, but her mother, the cook-woman, had seen her.

'Let me see you leave the front door when the snake-man's about,' she said sternly, 'and, lazy pumpkin, I'll break both your legs with an iron bar.'

So the wily Bindu watched from the balcony, her arms on the blue-painted wood rail. Only fourteen she had a mind as grown as her plump, high-bosomed figure. She preened herself like a woman.

'Bindu, don't stand there gaping,' Mohini had said one day.

'Oh, *Didi,* I'm looking at the snakes. What horrors! What beauties!'

Brass-mounted red glass gleamed on her ears.

'You see them every day. Haven't you had your fill?'

Bindu evaded the question. 'They're married, *Didi,* they're husband and wife, those two cobras, did you know? They —'

'Enough. Your eyes pop out so, they'll drop someday right on the street, into the snake-charmer's bowl!' Mohini lifted her voice in sharp anger. 'Have you no shame at all?' She had seen Bindu exchange glance for glance with the snake-charmer.

Bindu stood silent, heedless. More glances passed between street and balcony.

'All right, then. I'll speak to your mother. You want your legs broken, do you?'

Bindu turned round quickly. Her voice was subdued and sweet.

'Oh, *Didi,* jewel-faced one, why do you hate me? I not wish you well — always? Why, our Ananda Babu writes clever words for you to take to school. Have I told Old Mother? No. Ananda Babu —'

'Stop, unless you want a slap,' Mohini was red with fury. This Bindu was a scorpion!

'Oh, *Didi* jewel-faced one, why do you hate me? What have I done to you?' Bindu whined. "Let Ananda Babu please *Didi* and make himself useful", I tell myself. What harm if he helps her with school work? Why, indeed, he would be a worthy match for any girl of his caste. So fair, so handsome, so —'

Mohini sprang from her chair. Bindu turned and fled. But the victory was Bindu's. She reappeared after a while with a wide, pink ribbon looped in her hair, and took her place on the balcony as if nothing had happened, her oil-sleeked head bent over the rail. Mohini left the balcony in disgust. And ever after, when the snake-charmer came, Bindu had the balcony to herself.

But today there was no sound of ankle bells, no Bindu in sight. Perhaps the cook-woman had given her work. Or Old Mother had asked her to smear herbal oil on her gouty legs. The snake-charmer's eyes roved in vain.

But he had a hold on Heeralal who had been tricked by a promised offer of snakeroots which cured ills, and a snakestone which sucked the poison out of wounds. Heeralal, inquisitive monkey, was out to probe the man's secrets. Mohini had warned him, in vain. Too sure of himself, that boy, born with an old head, Mohini told herself. When he was three he had loved to drag himself around in his father's big shoes. He had stuck a cigarette holder in his mouth, as though smoking, and he had covered his face with shaving soap. A small boy's way of seeming manly.

The snake-charmer had tried to make use of him one day. What folly to accept sweets from that man! But, then, food was Heeralal's one great weakness. Even plain food made him ecstatic. At supper he would look down on his large, shiny, brass plate with its inch-high rim, and cry with delight: 'Uhhuh, vegetable cutlets tonight!' ...

'Fried fish, don't they taste good!' … 'Shrimps — what luck!' The candymaker had been out hawking that day when the snake-charmer stopped him and bought a palmful of spun sugar animals. He had given the lot to Heeralal: 'Here, man, eat.' Heeralal had grabbed them — trust a fly to refuse an invitation to a honey-pot! The snake-charmer had then bought another palmful. 'Here, man, take these to the fair maid who's Bindu by name. Bindu.'

Fair maid, indeed, the dark-faced owl! And Heeralal, foolish boy, had come up with the sweets, but before he delivered them, Mohini had stopped him on the stairs and ordered him sternly to return both portions. Heeralal had returned them with unwilling hands and a mournful face. The snake-charmer was so angry that he dashed the dainty horses and elephants and birds-on-a-bough on the ground to be trodden underfoot!

Mohini sighed. Even fourteen-year-old Bindu had an admirer — a common, swaggering, vulgar man, but a man to please her heart. And Mohini had satellites who did not count. Mere shadows. She was 'empty, funereal, needless.' The 'Eternal Woman' in her was unseen, unwanted, always unsated.

Mohini stopped knitting and closed her eyes, as though sunk in utter misery.

'Do you never tire of this wool knitting, girl?' The voice of Old Mother startled her. 'The same tale every week end?' Old Mother came bustling through a bedroom door and stood on the balcony. 'And now the household has wool coats enough for many winters! Look, her hair's all awry, a bird's nest decked with a red pin! Ankles, arms, face, chalky like a foundling's. Come, girl, I'll rub the fair skin with a spoonful of oil. Let not the gold bloom fade from lack of care, or else, when you're wed' — the aged eyes lit with some thought, half joy, half fear, 'your fond mother-in-law will feel only scorn for me:

> "She let a dew-holding lily become an inkpot,
> The Old Mother, oh the Old Mother!" '

three

News of the frozen gleam, the wonder gem, was the snake-charmer's gift to his young friend, Heeralal, after some months of queer association.

One day the snake-charmer had watched Heeralal standing by, hands in pockets, wonder on his face, and he had called gruffly, 'Come closer, man, and see our pet beauties.'

Man! Heeralal had at once warmed to the stranger. Later, he followed him to his lodgings.

The snake-charmer stayed with a beggar woman, old and infirm and harsh of tongue, who had passed her life in temple yards, holding her eyes closed and crying to the devotees, 'A price for the eyeless, oh godly ones!' Her begging bowl had been filled daily, year after year, decade after decade, until, with age, she had retired from the trade. Then, on the river side, beyond the rim of shabby dwellings at the edge to town, she had built a two-room hovel under a spreading tamarind: sun-baked walls of mud, palm-leaf thatch, split-bamboo shutters. Since she had no one to call her own, she lives in one room and let the other to a lodger. Her hoarded copper coins she buried in the earth floor of the room, but not before she had made a record of them on a mudwall — each copper was represented on the wall with a small circular chalk mark. Barely half the wall was marked, and it was her dream to cover the whole area before she died. In her idle hours she crouched by the bare area of wall and fancied its greyness whitened with circular chalk marks. This would make her hoary head wag with pleasure, the creased bark of her face gleam a little as she chuckled.

But though she scraped and hoarded and clung, leech-like, to the meanest copper, she could not resist some secret urge in her, some starved mother love, to buy sugar plums and nuts and fried grams for one young visitor. Heeralal never refused her gifts until one day she offered him a luxury dish of curried pork. Heeralal knowing the caste injunctions Old Mother had taught him, would not touch the forbidden meat.

'Eat, man, eat,' cried the snake-charmer, scornful of such taboos. 'Why, a pig's a pig.'

'And a Brahmin's a Brahmin,' snapped Heeralal. His temper rose. He felt the inside of his nose itch. Defile caste? Never. Not for the Nizam's treasures. Not for the Governor of Bengal's powers.

When the vase of this friendship was about to crack, the worried old woman rose, and bending on her stick, hobbled out.

In a few moments her hoarse wailing cry poured from the kitchen: 'Gone — gone — every morsel gone. Oh, the swine, the owl-faced father of a mule —'

'Gone, what?' yelled the snake-charmer.

'The meat, what else? All the extravagance of pig, sliver, thrown away, and now the tongue won't hold meat soft and juicy as melon.'

'Who ate it?' asked Heeralal, visibly relieved.

'That pig of a pariah dog, who but he?' croaked the old one.

Heeralal felt grateful to the dog, but the snake-charmer, with a fat chuckle, yelled: 'A pariah dog!'

His teeth flashed, his eyes mocked the old woman as he yelled again: 'Indeed, a pariah dog!'

Heeralal, bewildered, walked across the yard. The old woman hobbled after him and pointed a bony finger at a trail of gravy on the river's edge. Her left eye closed in a wink behind its network of a hundred creases while her tobacco-blackened toothless gums showed in a wry grimace. She laid a protective hand on Heeralal's shoulder.

'Do not loose caste, Brahmin boy,' she said in a quavering voice.

The tension lifted, and the snake-charmer, eased of his anger, started to whistle a sad tune. Suddenly he sang in a soft, mournful voice which was hardly his own:

The hours, the years, the aeons of life so bleak,
    A mate for some moments we seek!
Oh friends, or brethren, oh readers of our heart,
    A mate for some moments we seek!

Heeralal was fascinated with the snake baskets. The snake-charmer had told him once how he had caught Sarpa. In the dead of night he had reached the thick of the jungle in far-off Sikkim and played a siren song on his gourd-pipe. The serpents had come at his bidding, one by one, gliding from thickets and earth-holes and hollow tree trunks. Although he could not see them because it was pitch dark, he heard their hissing. One hiss was like a muffled roar, so he knew a python was in his audience. All night he played his gourd to them and at dawn he bade them leave, all except one, a king cobra, whom he coaxed into his basket.

'The music-mad spirit of snake and man!' he had ended his storybook adventure.

The snake-charmer was a man of swift temper, who was truly fond of his pets. One day his blood rose against Darpa who would not rear up at his bidding. He seized it by the tail, whirled it three times in the air and dashed its sleek body against a well — *shup!* Darpa lay still, as if dead. Heeralal would never forget the violence of the snake-charmer's repentent grief. He called the inert Darpa, 'my sweet enchantress' and other endearing names which only he would pour on a pet snake. Once or twice, by an odd slip of tongue, he called the snake 'Bindu!' At last Darpa woke from its daze, and the snake-charmer, watching, his eyes burning, went mad with happiness. He threw back his head and gave a mighty yell!

The snake-charmer's voice broke in on Heeralal's thoughts.

'Far in the Eyeless Wild of Teesta Valley where day is dyed with the ink of night, dwells Sankhachura, bred of king cobra and python, blood brother of Basuki, the great one who bears this pebble, Earth, on his thousand-fold hood. A wonder gem Sankhachura bears on his crown. Not all the treasures of the earth's seven mighty emperors may buy a ray of that *manik,* that Frozen Gleam.'

The Frozen Gleam!

Excited, goggle-eyed, Heeralal stuttered, 'Why not g-g-get it for yourself, then, and be India's richest man?'

Heeralal had heard Old Mother speak of Sankhachura, but she had treated him as a legend; she had no inkling that he, serpent of serpents, dwelt in skin and flesh.

'*Han, han,* fain shall we seek out fierce-eyed Sankhachura and pluck the gem from his brow and lay it at the Cobra Maid's feet for the asking. Let her mouth, a cleft pomegranate, speak.'

Heeralal scratched his nose. Bindu — fitly was she named Cobra Maid, for her tongue could pour venom! — Bindu wouldn't help him. She had never missed a chance to sneer at him. Those three cardboard watches — Bindu knew of them, she knew everything about everyone in the house — those watches were always on her mocking tongue. Then Heeralal had an idea. Perhaps he could trick the snake-charmer into revealing the secret of Sankhachura's habitation? Some years later, when Heeralal grew up, he would be able to collect a group of brave fellows and lead, an expedition to the gloomy Eyeless Wild and kill the enormous cobra-python. He would then hack away the Frozen Gleam and sell it for a fabulous price. Out of this wealth he would buy a cycle and a wristwatch for himself, books for Mohini, a shiny new motorcar for father, and a good clay image of Siva for Old Mother. The balance, Heeralal hesitated a moment, he would hand over to his hero Jawaharlal Nehru.

The snake-charmer spoke. His face was hard, his voice intense.

'Let us go wandering with Bindu. Bindu will shun her Bengali garb, don a gypsy skirt and dance with Sarpa and dance with Darpa. Her legs will twinkle, and the fat pig cities will rush and cry and lie at her feet. They will goggle with wonder, and their blood will be on fire, and they will clap their hands — so! They will clap again and wag their heads and croak: '*Wah! Wah! Wah!*' And Bindu, the enchantress, fist-waisted fruit-breasted strikes those she charms with the knife-shine of her eye. She kills them with her laugh, and her legs twinkle. She bends, she gives us snake-charmer, her body's fruit and clings so — she, our own, soft and hard and lean and rounded. Lo! She presses her body's fruit on us, and clings so, she who is a limb of us one bone, one blood, one skin!'

Heeralal broke into a giggle but stopped himself. Bindu dancing, Bindu, fat lump! What did the snake-charmer see in her? Why did he make such strange talk? He was keen to give her a pair of red velvet slippers. Madness! Bindu in red velvet slippers! Well, Heeralal wouldn't mind smuggling the gift into the house and handing it over if in return the snake-charmer agreed to tell him the secret of Sankhachura's habitation. A bargain for both. Fair enough.

But the snake-charmer seemed in a curious mood today. He crooned again, in a tight halting voice:

Afire, the body burns, that you know,
  Do you know how the mind can burn
Like wood, like oil?

Heeralal rose. This was no time to tackle him. It had been an auspicious day, anyhow. He had learned of the Frozen Gleam. Could it be that it was no stone at all but radium, a great lump of radium? He had still to absorb the geography of Teesta Valley where Eyeless Wild lay. Such geography was worthwhile, far more useful than what they taught at school — the length of American rivers, the height of Swiss peaks, the exports and imports of England.

Heeralal strode off. 'Hey,' the old woman called after him. 'Wait a twinkling, child.'

Heeralal stopped. The woman hobbled up to him, laid claw on his shoulder, and her world-worn face broke into a wistful smile.

'Step into the kitchen, son. Eat some nice sugar plums.'

The boy felt his tongue moisten for the sweets, yet he shook his head firmly 'N-no. Going home.'

The old woman nodded 'Aye, aye,' and lost her smile. Her twigs of fingers rose and groped over the youngster's cheeks, lips, chin, with a touch as soft as though the face were precious and brittle.

Heeralal shrank inwardly. He would have rushed off, but something in the woman's face, some agony in her caress, held him.

'Bhagwan will pour his bounties aplenty on thee,' the cracked voice murmured. 'Thou shalt write from an inkwell of gold. Thou shalt live a hundred years and become a king.'

~

Back from his ramble just before sunset, Heeralal drifted up the street and round the corner, sniffing a lungful of spicy kitchen smells as he passed the *Glutton' Inn*. He looked ahead at the balcony and saw his sister gesturing eagerly, as if to say, 'Hurry!'

A garage stood at one side of the house, facing the street. Heeralal peered in and saw father twist the nose of his rickety car. The boy dashed off. Mohini slid aside at the foot of the stairs to evade a collision.

'Pictures?' gasped Heeralal.

Every Sunday evening the family went to the cinema, often an Indian film, though Old Mother, with all her orthodox heart, enjoyed English pictures as well — that 'shadow-show' was to her mind a wonder of wonders, the supreme achievement of the Western people.

'You can even hear a dog bark!' she once cried, as though that amazed her even more than the human voices!

But this Sunday happened to coincide with the fortnightly fast of *Ekadashi*, eleventh-night-of-moon, which all Hindu widows must observe, and it would be a strain for Old Mother to sit through the long show. The advance booking, Heeralal knew, had been cancelled.

'Red Earth Palace,' observed Mohini, looking very charming in a peacock-blue sari, that set off her fair complexion, a puff-sleeved jacket to match, a few light jewels. 'Hindustani picture, *Tarzan's*

Daughter. A minute more, and you'd have been left behind.' She skipped off in a joyous dancing rhythm.

Father had managed this, loath to deny the children their week-end treat. Old Mother was to be dropped at the house of some relatives in Calcutta, while he went on to the cinema with the children.

'Keep both your eyes on them,' Old Mother had urged anxiously. 'You know what to do? You remember?'

Yes, he knew. When a love scene unfit for children flashed on the screen, he must ask Heeralal to shut his eyes tight and he must draw the free end of Mohini's sari over her head and face, so that she would see nothing. That was Old Mother's way of guarding the innocence of the young. It had no effect on Heeralal, who had trained himself to see clearly through half-closed eyes. Only Mohini suffered, and she longed to ask Heeralal later, '*Bhai*, what did you see?' Her grown-up dignity held her tongue.

A cinema was not only joy to eyes and ears, it meant a whole evening released from work. Other evenings, just before dark, they had to sit at the desk, poring over their books. Old Mother set a little painted clay image of Saraswati, goddess of knowledge before them, and lit a long, slow-burning stick of incense. The children must study until the stick burnt out entirely. Only then could they have their evening meal. They stared, eager-eyed, at the lengthening ash of incense, and they blew on it to make it burn more quickly.

Father shifted the gears, the car spurted away with loud threats of speed, and pigmy though it was, made din enough for a bus! That annoyed Heeralal but pleased Old Mother who, simple soul, said 'If you wish to glide in silence, to have no one turn to look at your wheels, why not ride a bicycle? Why waste the petrol?'

'Speed, speed and comfort,' Heeralal told her. 'A stout engine does not roar.'

'Then, what about the skyplane, childling? It has speed, comfort and a roar like ten thunders. Everything.'

Heeralal was silenced, but Mohini said brightly, 'Who can argue with Old Mother? Why, if she had read law and set up practice, she could be an Advocate General or even a Judge!'

Old Mother gave her a tender glance and drew a deep breath.

'Two or three months, and our Mohini will be gone — a groom is well on his way. You rear a motherless child for seventeen summers and then, one day she, image-of-joy, is no longer your own. The old attachments count for nothing.'

'Look, there's an American ship on the river,' Mohini cried somewhat breathlessly, gazing at the saffron waters of the Ganga which they were about to cross. 'I know from the flag. Look at the portholes — scores of cabins.'

Her small attempt to turn the conversation would not succeed, she knew, and the talk of her marriage would flow on, as it had flown on often for weeks past, and she would be outwardly embarrassed, secretly pleased. Somewhere within her she would tingle for more and more of this talk, and the vision of her groom-to-be would give her a tremulous thrill.

A great surprise was in store. As father drew up at the *Red Earth*, he announced: 'Listen. I have an engagement. I can't attend the picture show. You'll behave yourself — Mohini? — Heeralal?'

They stared at him, too dazed for words. Never before had they been left alone in a cinema house.

'Let me take you to your seats.' There was a twinkle in father's eyes. Obviously, he had kept this a secret from Old Mother. 'For once you may see your fill!' added father, with a look at Mohini, a twinkle again in his eyes.

Father did not approve of Old Mother's stern injunction. Why conceal the facts of life from a girl soon to be married?

There was only one snag for Mohini. A crocodile! At the gateway of the picture house a giant cardboard crocodile was at grips with Tarzan. For a moment Mohini grew pale because of her childhood fear of crocodiles.

But once inside, she was jubilant with this freedom, and waited eagerly for the empty seat on her left to be filled. Bad luck. A fat-encased man in his middle years, bulging over the armrests of his seat thumped down beside her as the lights were about to switch off. A *bania*, she thought, with a cloth shop in Burrabazar! Her face saddened, but there was Mickey Mouse on the screen, and her eyes were soon full of tears from the spilling laughter. How she loved these cartoons! How happy she felt!

Later, during the feature picture, her fat neighbour made her laugh again. When Tarzan's young daughter was kidnapped by a villain in a long Packard, the *bania* clacked his tongue in sorrow and seemed dejected till Tarzan rode to the rescue on his pet rhinoceros.

'Go on — faster, faster, faster!' the fat man shouted. He waved his heavy arms and wobbled in his seat as if he, too, straddled a rhinoceros. Tarzan raced through a jungle path, a short cut, and jumped on the running board of the speeding car, took his daughter in his arms and jumped to the ground. The fat one, watching, shook with pleasure. 'All is well!' Tarzan's daughter broke into song to express her profound relief. When she stopped, the man shouted happily: 'Encore! Encore!' Suddenly, the fat man remembered that the picture could speak but not hear. He smiled good-naturedly while Mohini smothered her laughter at him with her hand.

Heeralal was a hero. He was Tarzan, but on another screen he was a tall shadow armed with a magic wand, prowling through the green gloom of Eyeless Wild in pursuit of the incarnation of Evil. The spell was broken only when the giant crocodile of the placard appeared. Heeralal turned at once and saw his sister cover her eyes with her hands. Poor *Didi!*

'Encore, encore!' The shout of her neighbour loosened the grip of fear. She opened her eyes and saw the close-up of Tarzan's daughter, now incongruously dressed in shiny satin, a diamond in her left nostril, her bold, bright look fixed on the audience or, as the susceptive *bania* seemed to think, on him alone.

The screen flashed 'Interval', the light came on.

Almost instantly a voice behind her called out with eager pleasure; 'Mohini!'

Startled, Mohini faced round. There sat Somir, in a box seat by himself.

Her eyes lit up.

'Father?' Somir inquired.

She shook her head, half in pride. 'Myself and Heeralal.'

'Oh!' said Somir in some surprise. 'Look, I have a pass for two, and I'm by myself. Why not come and sit in the box?'

She reddened at his invitation and said uncertainly, 'I'm with my brother —'

'I don't mind,' said Heeralal with a generous air. 'Only don't forget to cover your face when —'

'You remember to close *your* eyes, close them full.' Mohini said in an undertone as sho rose and walked quickly to the box. She was excited at sitting alone in a cinema house with a handsome youth.

They talked of this film and of other films till the lights went off again. Mohini's face flushed in the dark; her heart raced. She sat very stiff, staring ahead, twisting a tiny handkerchief with nervous fingers. When, suddenly, Somir took her hand, her heart jumped and she could hear the beat of her blood. Her hand lay limp and warm in his. When he pressed it a little, a tinkling shot through her limbs, and she trembled.

So they sat while the story unrolled on the screen, but Mohini looked at it with unseeing eyes, absorbed in her personal drama, her nerves tight in a wonder of expectation. What would he do? Words and scenes from *The Poisoned Kiss* filled her mind and made her face burn and redden. Once he edged closer and turned his head toward her but she averted her face while her heart beat even more rapidly.

When Somir released her hand he lit a cigarette, and then seemed absorbed in the picture. He was enjoying it. He made a comment now and then, and even laughed at the pranks of Tarzan's pet ape. But Mohini was sunk altogether in herself and her companion. Her hand fretted for his and moistened in her lap. He did not touch it again. As the picture ended, she was utterly miserable.

Father was waiting in the hall. He took the children in the car and when Heeralal, as usual, scrambled to get in first, Mohini snapped at him, her voice strangely harsh: 'Don't stand on my toes, stupid.'

In Subhash Road, a bus came trundling on. As it dimmed its headlights and passed the small car, Mohini screamed. Father, in alarm, slowed down.

'What's wrong?' he cried.

'That bus was dashing straight upon us, didn't you see?' Mohini answered in a low and quivering voice.

'That bus? Why, girl, there was enough clearance.'

Mohini was shamed.

They picked up Old Mother who turned instantly to the girl and said: 'You didn't forget my instruction? You covered your eyes with your *anchal?'*

Mohini burst into tears. She leaned back in the seat, covering her face with her hands.

four

Father was out in his tiny car, Old Mother was busy in the kitchen. Heeralal was flying a kite from the rooftop. This, Mohini saw, was her chance.

She hustled into Father's office, jerked open the desk drawers and hunted through the files until she found a large, brown envelope, blue-pencilled 'Matrimonial' Mohini whistled! She picked up the envelope, and ran to the big sofa in the corner where she lay on her stomach, her face in her palm.

She read the strips of clippings from an English newspaper:

'Wanted, extremely beautiful, tall, slim, really fair-complexioned Brahmin bride, sweet singer and well-versed in domestic duties, for a groom drawing good salary, scion of respectable family. Girl's maximum age 19. Must be a real beauty. Apply under registered cover to Box No. 110.'

'A handsome Brahmin Mechanical Engineer of robust health wants to secure a good post through matrimonial connections. Girl's medium complexion no bar.'

'Bachelor, 27, independent businessman with attractive income invites natural and recent photographs of beautiful, slim maids, about 17, well up in household work, trained in the orthodox way. Apply with horoscope from a reputable astrologer. Only high status families need correspond.'

'Beautiful bride wanted as well as decent dowry, for a good-looking, cultured groom drawing Rs. 250 p.m. plus commission. Send exhaustive particulars, else no answers.'

'Invited correspondence with sharp head-to-foot photos from tall, exquisitely pretty girls, view matrimony, no dowry, by a London-qualified throat specialist serving in a Medical College.'

There were a dozen similar clippings. Mohini gave another excited whistle. Here was one with her father's name:

'Wanted a suitable match for handsome, educated maid of charming disposition. Highly gifted radio singer.'

Her eyes brightened for a moment because of the sweet compliments, but then her face was grave. Why name and address, not a box number? Just like father to be so careless! Someone at school had surely seen these lines — the girls read the matrimonial column, if nothing else — and would probably pass the clipping around. Her friends would laugh. To be hawked in print as though you were toothpaste! Those girls, in their turn, would find themselves advertised, for it was a custom followed by most parents irrespective of caste and social status. Now, however, they would have fun at Mohini's expense.

'Didi!'

Startled by the voice, Mohini slipped the clippings back into the envelope and sprang to her feet before Heeralal rushed in like a gale.

'Burglar!' he hailed her under his breath, round-eyed with excitement, while she restored the envelope to its place, slammed the drawer and spun round with a guilty face.

'Spying?' asked Heeralal in a voice like a hiss.

He came forward. Now, Mohini would surely share the secrets in father's desk with him. But Mohini saw her danger. Heeralal, inquisitive monkey, would find the clippings and read them. Something had to be done.

She dashed to the sofa, seized a cushion and threw it so it landed on Heeralal's head. He gaped in surprise. Pillow fights were not uncommon, but they took place at night and in a bedroom. Besides, the daring of it — fighting in father's office with fat cushions neatly draped in green — lured him, and he rushed to the attack.

But Heeralal was not at his best. He had a weight on his mind:

'Velvet slippers with gold embroidery. Red velvet. He'd send them by hand, so keen!'

The boy spoke abruptly, without explanation. He had decided to take Mohini into his confidence, to tell her about the Frozen Gleam and his agreement with the snake-charmer. After all, *Didi* was reasonable; she had never let him down. This was why Heeralal had been looking for her all over the house when he had found her in father's room.

Velvet slippers? Red ones? Her heart jumped; she saw herself at school with the slippers on.

'How much did you pay for them?' Reba would ask admiringly.

'Pay?' A fine heedless curling of the lip. 'They're a gift from a friend.' A small sigh. 'Those impetuous boys! Hard job turning down their presents, isn't it, Reba? You know.'

Her arms were limp, helpless, for her mind was spinning happiness. Thump. Heeralal brought her back to earth.

'You'd let me bring them?' he asked anxiously. 'You turned down the spun-sugar things —'

Oh, it was different if Ananda Babu wanted to give her velvet slippers, red ones. Or was it Somir? Somir, far less forward than she used to think —

'Bindu, fat lump, velvet slippers for Bindu!' Heeralal grinned.

It was several moments before Mohini grasped what Heeralal said. Her arms went limp; there was a taste of cotton in her mouth. But not for long. Mohini laughed at herself.

She lifted her pillow and flung it at Heeralal with all her might. The cushion split open, and cotton streamed to the floor. The fight continued. Thick white lumps came plopping out of both cushions. Absorbed, they did not see the door open a crack, they did not hear ankle bells jingle down the corridor.

'What more sights will you cast upon these eyes, Supreme Goddess?' Old Mother stood at the doorway, hand pressed on cheek in utter amazement. 'A grown boy, a grown girl, and look, they fight like people in the bazaar! Bindu told me. Have you lost your head, Mohini? Are you training to be a ruffian, Heeralal? Two good cushions — gone! And all this uproar in your father's room.' She strode up and slapped Heeralal on the cheek. 'Don't you know that an elder sister is to be revered, next only to parents? What have you done to her face, her hair? Look.'

'It's ever so. You always side with your favourite,' the boy moaned, rubbing his cheek.

The favourite had started to make a heap of the cotton on the floor. Her face was red, her hair dishevelled. Old Mother watched her, and, appeared in a moment — could she really be angry with her Mohini? — she shook her white head pensively.

'No many handfuls of days will pass before our girl goes to become a lamp in a stranger's house. And then, Heeralal, your eyes will ache for the sight of her. Ever since the day the father pulled his girl's ears, he has known no hunger nor thirst, nor ease, nor peace; from waking to sleeping he has but one thought: a match for Mohini.'

A low whistle flew from Mohini's mouth at news of father's concern about her, but she kept her face down and resumed heaping the cotton.

Old Mother went on: 'Can the tongue relish rice and fish, can the eyelids close in peace while there is a maiden daughter in the house?'

'And she shooting up like a palm-tree!' added Heeralal, recalling a talk in low tones between his elders which he had overheard.

Mohini stood up and leaned against father's desk. 'Grandmother, see how the mischievous monkey nags me. Why is he such a busybody? Why does he not fry his own fish and leave me alone?'

She stuck one end of father's fat penholder, scarred by her previous nibbling, between her teeth.

'You wait,' Heeralal warned her. 'We'll forget you the moment you cross our doorsill.'

Tears of love made Old Mother's eyes misty.

'*Nah, nah,* it is she who will forget us. The house without Mohini will be darkness. All these years she has sung and played about, and her face has never lost its everliving smile. Her pressence has filled the house like a gay festival. Now, there will be utter darkness.' Emotion broke her voice.

'Why, then?' said Heeralal with a wistful glance. 'Isn't my face gay enough?'

She wiped her tears with the back of her hand and gazed lovingly at the boy.

'He gets more skinny day by day, lean as a thread, have you noticed, Mohini? This amulet will guard his health; it will strike the Evil Eye sightless. Come child,' her voice was a caress, 'It's to be worn round the neck.' Out of a knotted corner of her sari, she produced a copper amulet.

'Amulet!' Heeralal stepped back, arms lifted in protest.

It was bad enough that his hair had been dedicated to the daughter of the Mountains, so that he had worn it long for six months. No iron must touch it, so he must not hear the chirp of scissors until the great festival in mid-autumn. How his schoolmates would laugh if he wore an amulet whose string would be visible on his neck!

'Mother Goddess, this, indeed, is the age of darkness. Children making mock of a charm. Do not be a fool, Heeralal. Aren't you ashamed to be a scarecrow? Come, child, I'll give you a half-rupee to spend at the fair.'

Heeralal, in his distress, caught his sister's glance and signalled her, by repeated inflations and deflations of his cheeks, an urgent appeal for help. And Mohini hurried to his rescue.

'It's a wonder what happens to the platefuls of food he stacks into his lean belly. Need we hang the chain round his neck? Why not fix it to his upper arm and let it be concealed from mocking eyes? Come, skinny one, take off your jacket. Strip your mind of shabby thoughts and have faith that the charm will fatten you up and protect you from curses, hobgoblins, and' — the mischief was bright in her eyes — 'snake-charmers!'

Old Mother shook her head with pleasure, seeing the amulet neatly looped on the youngster's right upper arm.

'The cook has gone to the bazaar for the groceries. When she is back with the change, I'll let you have a shiny half-rupee, Heeralal. Now we'll see a cheekful of smile.'

Heeralal gave a whoop of joy.

'And why no half-rupee for me?' Mohini asked, her soft mouth pouting in the accustomed way. 'Don't be one-eyed. All this trouble for your grandson: driving sense into his wooden head and knotting the charm on him — all a waste, *han?* And you tell me callously, in a month or two I'll be out of the house —' Mohini faltered and looked down coyly as she nibbled her father's fat penholder. She was tense with the hope that Old Mother would now tell her all about the advertised match.

Old Mother walked warily by the snare. 'You will brighten another house, child. What use is a lamp, golden and filled with oil, if it has no wick? The house is the lamp, man is like oil, the woman is the wick, Mohini, and happiness the living flame.'

Mohini pressed her lips and arranged her face in a half-mocking smile.

'Yes, but why this fuss about marriage? You can never tell what crumbs fate will throw. You may be digging a canal from the river to your house door and inviting the crocodile!'

'Mother Goodness forbid! Join your palms and make a *pronam* to her, Mohini. So! Once again. So!'

Mohini made one more attempt to draw out Old Mother. She tossed her head and said demurely: 'I have vowed not to marry — ever. Why, I'm going to be a film star. Don't you know?'

'What crooked talk is this?' Old Mother was annoyed now. 'Come, help me peel the potatoes for the fish gravy. Father will be back any moment and he will want his noon meal early today because of a meeting at the University.'

Mohini had no thought for father's noon meal. Star-shine in her eyes, she was making an image of her groom-to-be.

five

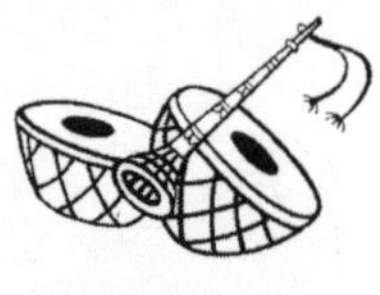

She started this mid-summer day with a propitious omen — a white owl perched at dawn on the *bokul* tree across the street. She gazed her fill, and for once believing, she lifted folded palms to her brow. The owl of fortune blinked as the light grew. With a skirl of alarm it unfolded heavy white wings and flew away.

In the past weeks, rough fingers had squeezed her gay bubble of illusion. The dream postman had come, burdened with his bag, and on father's desk he had piled letters, more than his hands could hold: queries, queries from the parents of bachelor youths seeking a handsome bride. But the real postman, Ram Singh, mocked her dream and brought leaflets and circulars and calendars for the Bengali New Year. Calendar upon calendar. Heeralal collected them all and hung them up on the study walls. An English bathing beauty, frothy with Shipra soap stood next to a Hindu film star who was rubbing her rich black hair with Himani oil. An entire family, young and old, sat feeding their skin with Mira complexion milk. Tuft-bearded Professor Hanuman Singh, India's foremost astral-interpreter and seer, was prepared to read your life free (send a rupee in stamps to defray postage and misc. costs) and tell you your past experiences, your strong and weak points. For another rupee, to meet costs, he would advise you on 'business, friends, enemies, love affairs, lucky times, sickness and childbirth.' Wonder pills to make you taller. A yogi device to make people over sixty, thirty years younger. A charmed fountain pen to teach the aspiring author the tricks of his craft. A world of pinchbeck promises lay among the black rows of dates.

How could the romantic youth of Bengal be so cold to a famous radio artist? A dozen letters had come, languidly interested in the bride's person, greedily interested in her dowry. She had read the letters with resentful scorn. Why had she been photographed, exquisite in the gold-bordered sari called 'Mist of Dawn' since her sepia prettiness must lie unseen in father's desk? Looks were dumb. Only gold spoke, gold.

And the insolence of the two parties which had come to see her and pass judgment! They had been sent by Calcutta Matrimonial Bureau Ltd. ('For quick marriage solutions, please remit registration fee of Rs. 10'), the leading marriage brokers of Bengal, who were a bane to the old-fashioned match-makers, low-down priests and such, whom they had displaced. A product of the hurrying time-spirit. Father, dismayed by the result of his preliminary advertising, had later sent a fee to the Bureau and received a short first list of its Brahmin clients, with income, family connections and other essential details. Two of the matches had seemed set for negotiation. Interviews were arranged.

The first one was an old-fashioned party of elders who would not condescend to bring the groom-to-be with them. (Was he as good a judge as his elders?) They came at dusk, the traditional bride-showing hour, when the soft sunset light painted a girl's face with new grace. Bright gold was looped round her arms and throat; pearl pendants hung at the tips of her ears, and Mohini, in blue georgette, came into the room on slow feet, her heart beating strangely. Old Mother, too old-fashioned to appear before strange men, posted herself behind a screened door.

'Mother Lakshmi!' one of the elders said in greeting, politely using the name of the goddess of prosperity. 'The horoscope is favourable,' he told Mohini. 'Your stars are at peace with the stars of our son.' And then he launched a tricky questionnaire on mythology and religion.

'Tell us, how many divine incarnations have descended on this Earth of ours?'

'The names of the stars that make human destiny?'

'What is *yoga?*'

Mohini with quick wit gave half-answers or kept a discreet silence, staring down bashfully at her feet with red lac dye lines on their edges. With a sidelong look she caught a glimpse of Heeralal sitting cross-legged among the elders, as though he was one of them, his round face puckered in a merry smile. She heard giggles behind the inner door — two of her school friends had turned up unexpectedly! Colour washed her cheeks.

The visitors ate gold-skinned mangoes and pink-fleshed watermelons, and various milk sweets, and an iced *sherbet.* Then the head of the party soothed his hungry nostril with a pinch of snuff and spoke: 'The dowry you offer, sir, isn't enough. We would take your offer if the maid were well versed in our Ancient Culture. She isn't. In the present circumstances, dowry must be the decisive factor. Think it over.'

When they were gone, Old Mother was in a rage, saying: 'Such hypocrites should be thrown out on the street with twenty thrashings of a broomstick. They're like the tomcat who became an ascetic when he was too old and crippled to run after rats. The saying goes:

> "Fish he won't eat, nor meat, rid of greed and wed to religion,
> Rosary on neck and begging-bowl on paw, he makes a pilgrimage to Sri Brindavan!"

The second party came a fortnight later, the groom himself, a young married sister, their old parents. Four pairs of eyes surveyed the girl from foot to head. She had to walk a few steps at the mother's bidding to prove she did not lack grace of movement. They fumbled with her prettily arranged hair and unloosed it down her back to know its length. They rubbed her face with their thumbs to make sure the fair complexion was natural, not of paint. Mohini gulped down her tears of shame. When the women stooped to pull up her sari to the knees to inspect the shape of her ankles and legs, father rose to his feet, his face livid.

'Enough,' he cried, and anger was sharp in his voice. 'You are ill-mannered, vulgar folk, unfit to set foot in a decent house. Get out.'

And the party, too shunned for words, gaped at him for a minute.

'How dare you insult us? It's unheard-of, this atrocity. What have we done?' they asked.

'Go!' shouted father, pointing to the door.

'Are you mad? We'll see to it that your daughter never gets married. We'll —'

Father took three quick steps forward and the party sprang back.

'Come away,' the old man, trembling, called to his brood. 'This is no place for gentlefolk.'

They walked swiftly to the gate and he looked back an instant.

'Ruffian! Madman! We'll see how you get a match, for your daughter,' he shouted.

Then Mohini, with shining eyes, spoke to her father, 'Why must you bear insult on my account? Why must I get married? So many girls these days remain unwed; they work and earn their living. Why can't I do it?'

'True,' father agreed, and his face was now calm. 'I'll not give you away to anyone of whom I do not approve with all my heart. Better not marry at all.'

Mohini spoke bitterly to Old Mother, 'Why don't they set up a monthly fair where girls could be on view? Honest and inexpensive, and much more convenient than this hateful bride-showing. The groom's party could go round the stalls and see fifty girls in two hours, and the girls would be showing themselves to so many people at the same moment.'

Old Mother, hurt by these words of shame and scorn, replied, 'Peasant girl and princess alike bear this ordeal. What other way is there, Mohini? In some modern circles in Calcutta, so, I hear, boys and girls are allowed to mix freely and select their own mates. Are they happier? No!'

'They don't have to give up their dignity,' Mohini flung back, close to tears.

'Dignity? In our Hindu society a maid is addressed as Lakshmi, the gracious goddess. Married, she walks into her new household proud as the Devi.' She paused and sighed. 'Vulgar minds have cast pollution upon the old ways.'

'If we must be old-fashioned, why don't we go all the way back to ancient times? *Swayamvara!*' she cried.

Swayamvara meant a woman had the right to choose her husband. One auspicious day the wooers were all asked to the bride's house. The bride, bejewelled, garland in hand, walked around. She stood a little while before each wooer, looking down at him and then moving on till she found her true husband.

'Crazy one!' Old Mother looked tenderly at Mohini, who was remote, caught in her fantasy. There they sat, twenty, thirty wooers, anxious for her hand. And there she stepped from wooer to wooer, their faces alight with beauty, intelligence, manliness. Godlike images. On whom would her garland fall?

There was not another bride-showing for a month, not until the day Mohini saw the white owl at dawn. This time it was a party without elders. The prospective groom was a modern young man. He arrived with his friends, to make his own choice. They were a gay group who chatted and joked, and were full of courtesy for the bride. They told her how charmed they had been with her pretty voice on the radio, and they paid her many other honeyed compliments.

They were so unpretentious and at ease that when father proudly showed them a sample of her embroidery, a plump white duck on a strip of linen with the lettering 'The Duck' at the top and 'Mohini' at the bottom, they slyly misread the meaning. They turned to her and with a jesting smile asked: 'Is the duck named Mohini, then?'

At this she could not help laughing. They, too, asked fancy questions, however. You play tennis? You dance? Who is your favourite film star? What novels have you read? Do you think Free India should remain in the Commonwealth? Her eager half-answers, ending in a confused gulp, amused them greatly, even if they fell short of their expectations. The groom had an air at once gallant and full of charm, and Mohini, in secret through her lashes lowered over slanting eyes, stole two good looks at his face.

Never had her heart so hurried and pounded as while she waited, breathless, after the party had left, to hear the groom's decision from father. 'They've approved our girl,' he was telling Old Mother presently. 'They said she's graceful and clever and, above all, a gifted singer whose name all radio listeners know.' His voice was joyous and proud. 'Mother, we've found the right match for our girl. Look up the almanac for an auspicious day.'

Old Mother was silent for a time, her face withdrawn and grave.

'Why, surely you approve —'

'No, childling,' she shook her head with quiet decision. 'He is not the right sort for our Mohini. He and his friends have no respect for elders. They smoked cigarettes in your presence, didn't they? And they asked our girl such indecent questions. "Do you dance?" As if she is to be an actress or something. What vulgarity! No. Our girl has not been trained up in their un-Indian way, even if she has read at a Christian convent school. She will be a misfit in that fast circle. Why, they may force her to dance in public, English-fashion, man and woman together, arm in arm. What misery!'

'But, Mother, the groom —'

'The groom belongs to this circle. He has his roots in the soil. They are all alike. No tradition, no true culture. Apes of Westernism!'

His patience gave way. His face darkened. 'Let our girl remain unwed,' he cried harshly, 'rather than be sacrificed to your antiquated outlook.'

Old Mother's face was a picture of rage. Her eyelids flickered and her gentle mouth stiffened.

'Send me away to the Holy City. I won't have no mouthful of your food, or let water pass my lips.'

The son gave her a sharp resentful glance. He cleared his throat as if to speak, then he dropped his shoulders in a sort of weariness, turned and walked away. And Old Mother stood still, a long rich moment. A small smile lifted the corners of her lips slightly. She had triumphed again.

Mohini, too, stood still. Her face drained of colour was like stone till anger made it burn. Then her eyes hardened and her breast heaved. Never had she been so angry with Old Mother. Why must she, who was of another age, have her way against all reason? Why must her antiquated outlook prevail against even father's judgment? With her fixed ideas, her iron prejudice against modernism, how could she expect to know, to feel, to understand the new generation? Misery to dance in public! She, Mohini, would love to dance on a ballroom floor in the English way, in time to lovely music.

Life was hateful. There was neither freedom nor communication between mind and mind. Your own temple housed all the truth on earth. Fantastic. And Mohini, suffering her first real frustration, was mutinous but speechless and helpless.

If only she could set her will against Old Mother's! If only she could speak out her mind to Father who could understand. Had he not urged her often to learn to speak boldly? But the taboo of countless centuries held her tongue.

'Why don't I die?' she said to herself with bitter passion.

The white owl had been a fake prophet. It had not been the herald of a happy day.

Restless and tight-lipped, she flounced around the house, slamming doors as she went. She swept upstairs as though pursued, only to stand on the balcony and watch the carrier kite sail by with a love letter tied to its tailpiece.

Her face hardened. Her feelings, bursting for release, were vented on the stranger and his kite. She spun round and walked down to Heeralal. 'Fool!' she cried. 'A kite flies right by your nose. It mocks you who call yourself an ace flier, yet you take no heed. You sit here in the scullery eating a mango. Don't know? You dare not fight that flier. You are afraid. Braggart! Good-for-nothing!'

'So!' muttered Heeralal, his lips yellow with mango juice. 'Good-for-nothing!'

She turned on him like a fury, shook him by his lean shoulders. 'You think you can trip that kite? Oh no!'

'So!' repeated Heeralal, narrowing his eyes. He wiped his mouth and strode off to fetch his fighter kite, a large all-black structure built for strength and speed. In silence he made it fast to his reel of string, stiffened and sharpened with a special mixture of glue and crushed glass, and, still without a word, strode to the rooftop followed by his sister.

Mohini set the kite in motion while Heeralal held the wheel. The kite's course was away from the enemy: it would be unwise to arouse suspicion. Suddenly, the fighter checked, dipped and pounced like a hawk on the enemy line. Too late the duped message-carrier woke to its peril. The fighter had almost closed all escape lanes. The carrier dodged with caution, seeking a safe lane. Both kites were manoeuvred brilliantly. Then, Heeralal, with a crooked smile, turned his reel sideways and with rapid flicks of his arm, executed a series of jerky movements with the kite.

'So!' he called out to his sister. 'Braggart! Good-for-nothing!'

The sportsman in him was ready to forego the fruit of victory. 'I've stopped that one dead. Look, Mohini! Shall I quit?'

'Snap it!' Mohini's lips tightened into a narrow line. Heeralal smiled again, ruefully. He shortened his line, and let it snap the enemy's. Instantly the message-carrier, cut from its reel, staggered up, flotsam of the air, a corpse of a kite.

The letter was gone and the boy was running hard in the direction of the kite to try to retrieve it. Khuki, leaning out over the parapet, had panic in her face. If she had known that Mohini had done this out of spite!

Spite? Her anger yielded to shame as she asked herself: What have they done to me? How could I be so mean? How face Khuki at school?

The blue-turbaned postman, Ram Singh, one day handed her an envelope with her name in an unknown hand. Puzzled, she tore open the flap. Her eyes grew wide. It was a poem, *Ode to Mohini*, in red ink! Her heart gave little jumps as she read at a gallop:

Ode To Mohini

A soldier would die a hundred deaths
    for thee, sweet-sharp nectarine!
A lover would live a hundred lives
    (Waiting... wanting... waiting... wanting,
In him the sigh of spring)
    for thee, Maid Divine!
Thou peerless being,
    Mohini, Mohini, Mohini,
This bard begs thine bee-honey!

With shining eyes she read this a second time. It was beyond her dreams. Addressed to some other girl, she would have curled her lip in scorn. Sloppy! But addressed to her, it was the tribute of a romantic heart. Proudly, she folded and slipped it through the neck of her jacket, close to her heart.

She felt very happy and sat at her desk to answer her admirer, verse for verse.

The bowl of this heart overflows for thee.
    Come, stranger, cup thy palms, receive!

No, this was no good. Awful. She nibbled her pencil and started again:

Gold seeks fire, clouds need lightning,
    They burn, they become pure;
So dost thou bathe in love's conflagration —

Silly. No good at all.

Her sense of humour came to her rescue. She laughed at herself. Her lyrical spasm was drowned in ridicule. Nevertheless, she wised she were gifted like Dhruba and like him could shape a lovely verse!

Still, what use would it be? Who was he? What was his address?

She thought she knew, and smiled to herself. Yes, she could see him, the handsome stranger at the school. It was at the annual concert, and she had watched him from the stage. He was seated in the front row, a cigarette always between his lips, and he had held his keen glance on her. Something wondrous had flown between them, magical. Surely, he would be the poet.

The next day she waited tensely for the postman. No mail. For three fretful days, the sight of Ram Singh quickened her heart, until she had a second pink envelope.

> No moon has half thy lustre, yet thou art sun-hard!
> Thou soothest yet dazzlest the sight of this bard!
> Lo, the lotus spites thy grace, cloud-mellow, dewy-fresh,
> Thy smile is rain on this heart-wilderness.

How happy she was! All day she seemed to be smiling to herself, and in the English hour at school, when the teacher made the class laugh, she laughed loudest and longest. The girls looked at her curiously.

When would he write? Verses were not enough; they were too remote and impersonal. Every day she leaned over the balcony rail, eyes fixed on a spot, up the street, awaiting the postman.

Days and weeks wore on, but nothing more came.

Tears of anger kept rushing to her eyes. Why had he sent her the verses? His idea of fun? How she despised him. She pulled out the poems nestling under her jacket and flung them into the kitchen fire. For a long time afterwards, the sight of the postman would make her heart beat in secret expectation.

six

MOHINI PEERED through the street door, shading her eyes against the glare.

'Hey, hey, bangale-seller, show me your wares,' she called.

A thin-faced old man came shuffling through the narrow gates, barefoot, a wicker basket on his arm.

'Let Mother Lakshmi cast her auspicious gaze on these beauties,' he said gently. 'What colour in these glass trinkets. They shame peacock plumes! Next to nothing they cost, but lovelier they are than even pure gold!

The heat-bound noon was sticky with dust borne by a warm blanket of wind. The bangle-seller unbuttoned his coarse jacket, and wiped his perspiring chest. The soles of his bare feet were stained by the melting tar of the road.

'A drink of water, bangle-seller?'

His smile of thanks showed his tobacco-stained gums.

'Mother Lakshmi is so young, yet her heart has pity for poor working folk. Live long, Mother. This old man just had a quarter mug of tea from the tea vendor who sold it for a nice lac bangle. There he goes, the pot-belly!'

Mohini turned to watch the fat tea vendor come slowly round the bend of the street, carrying a brass vessel, a brazier of burning coals suspended beneath it. He wore only a loincloth.

'It's not too hot for tea?' Mohini asked.

The bangle-seller, surprised by the question, scratched his chin. Young and ignorant, he mused, looking at her. No vermilion gleamed in the part in her hair, so she was still a maid. But the eyes were full of brooding the gestures restless, the limbs ripe for marriage.

'Heat kills heat,' he told her. 'Tea warms the blood.' He paused 'Your parents need a match-maker, Mother Lakshmi?' he asked after another careful look at Mohini.

Mohini shook her head, blushing. 'I like this gold one,' she spoke hastily, pointing with her slim forefinger. 'Will it fit my arm?'

He smiled again, amused at the fancy of women. Tenderly he pressed her arm and slipped the bangle on.

'Many a comely arm I have seen with these old eyes, but never an arm so faultless in shape. What smoothness! I fear to touch the skin with my claws. Only a groom is wanting. When the groom comes, grace will be added to grace.'

'That red one, too,' Mohini said and quivered a little.

'Of what were we talking? A groom, yes,' he said as he slipped on the second bangle. 'This old fool goes from door to door in this city and across the Ganga in Calcutta, and his seeking eyes rest on many a vessel of learning, handsome as the moon god, calm as a lake. And many an elder begs him to find his young hopeful a beautiful bride. Need there be worry for the parents of a fairy daughter? What caste, Mother Lakshmi?'

'Brahmin,' she breathed.

The bangle-seller nodded twice and started counting on his finger-joints: 'One, two, three, four — is there a lack of Brahmin grooms. In Calcutta city, a half-hour's journey by the ferry? Grooms are sighing for likely maids as maids are sighing for grooms. I have a mind to speak to your revered parents, Mother Lakshmi.'

'Speak, then. Speak to Old Mother.' And his comforting words echoed in her ears: 'Grooms are sighing for likely maids.'

The bangle-seller smiled discreetly with quick understanding.

'Yet we who seek the union of hand and hand are toys and tools of Fate, tied by the writing on the brow. The luckless turn thirsty eyes on a full stream, and lo! the stream goes rock-dry! Who can see what lies round the future's bend? Who can tell when the marriage moth will fly over a grown maid's head? Only one man — Govind Ram, the fortuneteller. He will soon pass this way, a yellow turban on his shaven pate. "A rupee for thy past, present and future!" he will cry.'

She looked up with interest. 'No hoax? Ever had him tell your fortune, bangle-seller?'

'*Bhagwan!* My future? There is only one thing to know: when I may welcome Yama, the Lord of Death. But Govind Ram read my daughter's hand and I paid the old crow with three glass bangles. My Sita is about your age, Mother Lakshmi; looks somewhat like you, too, though not so very fair.'

A voice sounded not twenty yards away: 'Ear-cleaner, ear-cleaner.'

A tall strong-jawed man, a man from up-country strode in, carrying a little wooden case.

'Want thine ears cleaned, fair sister?'

She shrank in the doorway. '*Nah, nah.*' Her hand fluttered to a shapely ear.

'Your brain matter is poor, ear-cleaner,' the bangle-seller sneered. 'Well-bred girls don't have their ears cleaned by folk like you.'

'Let me clean yours, bangle-seller,' he said good-naturedly.

He opened his little box and brought out a long thick needle, twisted and blunted at one end.

'No need.' The old man shook his head vehemently.

'Come, how canst thou have a mind fit to worship thy gods with ears lined fatly with dirt?'

The bangle-seller peered into his bangle basket, his eyes reflecting the glisten of the tiers of trinkets. He shook his head.

'No need, no need.' But his voice was willing.

'Step out of the gate, brother,' he said, 'and wait for me on the street.' And to Mohini he bowed and said, 'No more bangles, Mother Lakshmi?' He took her money. 'My first coins this noon. The chinaman gave me a length of cotton for a dozen glass bangles; the tobacco-seller took a lac pair for a pinch of his snuff, and the tea-vendor, one for some tea.'

Mohini lingered in the doorway. 'If you happen on the fortuneteller, ask him to come and read my hand.' Her face was red.

The old bangle-seller nodded. 'Lo! Here comes the wise crow himself.' He walked to the gate to hail the fortuneteller.

Govind Ram strode up. He was well-built, with good features. He wore the sacred thread on his bare chest. The three white stripes, the emblems of the Lord's threefold aspect as creator, protector and destroyer, were painted in sandal paste on his forehead.

The bangle-seller blinked and smiled.

'A lot of work. Govind Ram. Tell Mother Lakshmi when the marriage god will heed her. And tell this vendor of trinkets — oh, *Bhagwan,* what is there to know but the day when one may close the weary eyes forever in peace?'

Not a full moon-month had passed when it seemed that Govind Ram the fortuneteller had rightly read the marriage line on Mohini's palm.

'Why let thine heart be troubled, daughter,' the kindly voice had almost sung, 'since thou shalt be wed before the Festival of the Rains?'

'Han, han,' the bangle-seller had echoed, 'do I not know the groom?' and he recounted how a young lady in South Calcutta, now wed to a doctor, had ordered armfuls of Suroma bangles (Suroma after the famous screen beauty), and while he slipped them over her wrist, she had said:

'I have a younger brother, a great scholar and master of Behula village. We seek a bride. Dowry does not count, but she should have all the eight luck signs and symbols on her person. All. Mother insists on this. The readings of her horoscope as compared with my brother's would also, of course, count. You sit on many a doorstep with your basket, bangle-seller, on this side of the Ganga and the other, and you bedeck the arms of many a fair one. Will you keep your eyes open for likely Brahmin maid?'

So the bangle-seller was on the *lakshanas,* the eight luck signs and symbols. How could he miss the rare 'lotus' and the 'wheel' on the flat of her thumb as he slipped on the bangles? Govind Ram had seen all the other signs in the scrawl of her palm, all. A rare hand. Yes, he must speak to Old Mother this very day.

'Jayadev... Master of Behula...' Old Mother murmured to herself when the bangleman, squatting at his ease in the inner courtyard, had spoken. Her grey brows were drawn together in thought. All at once she rose, walked to her room and rummaged among some books on a shelf. She was back in the courtyard to look placid lest the bangleman be tempted to ask a big go-between fee.

'This is the will of the supreme goddess.' She lifted her folded hands to her forehead. 'Bangleman, I shall speak to my son about your scholar of scholars. The two horoscopes will be read, compared.'

And the bangle-seller, shrewd enough to read Old Mother's mind, overjoyed because of the fee that would be due to him, walked gay-footed out of the house, looking for the tea-vendor. Surely, now he could allow himself a full mug of tea.

But the Professor was not impressed by Old Mother's eager talk.

'A good match,' he admitted, for he had heard of this brilliant scholar; he had even seen him once or twice at the University.

'A good match from every point of view except one: Mohini cannot live in a village among old-world folk. She would be unhappy, bored to death.'

'Unhappy? Full seventeen years she has lived with an old-world woman, hasn't she?' Old Mother spoke stiffly.

'No, Mother. I can't take the risk.'

'Wait a minute,' she said and walked off to her room.

When she came back, she had a copy of *Maya,* a Bengali illustrated magazine, in her hand.

'Look at this picture,' she cried with triumph. 'That is the youth, Jayadev. The face — would you ask for one more pleasing? Read the lines under the head, *In the Public Eye*. Even at this age, only twenty-five, Jayadev is a writer of rare distinction. Read on. "His monumental work on the culture patterns of East and West through all the ages is to be completed in two or three years. Apart from its value as a work of reference, it will have a message of deep significance for the people of India at this moment of transition, of search for a true way of life."' Old Mother looked up, a gleam in her old eyes. 'Understand? It is too much to expect that such a great man will marry our girl. The luck signs in her palm may help. How strange she has them all! And if, by the grace of the goddess (I'll give her a fat goat-pair as my offering), the horoscopes agree on all points —'

There was a sore cloud on the Professor's face.

'Luck signs. Horoscopes. What rubbish!' His voice was mocking. 'There's to be a cultural synthesis of a horoscope and a microscope!'

Old Mother gazed hard at her son. Then her eyelids began to flutter and her lips to twitch.

'I say for the last time: send me away to the Holy City where people do not laugh at old traditions, where they have faith in ancient wisdom. I'll touch neither food nor water —' She stopped short, tears starting to her eyes, and flung the magazine on the floor and walked away.

Her son stared after her. He picked up the magazine and gazed at Jayadev's picture a long while.

'Pleasing indeed, and an ideal match, but to send away our girl to a village — how risk it?' His eyebrows moved up and down because of his misery, and he sighed.

At the evening meal, though Old Mother sat near him as usual, not a word came from her stiff lips, and he could hardly look at her face, dark and swollen, as if she had cried a great deal. His heart ached for her, but he hardened himself. Was not his girl's future life at stake?

Days of complete silence came between him and his mother till one morning she slipped into his room and said, still very stiffly: 'I want *Maya* back.'

She had looked for the paper, but it was nowhere on his desk.

'Yes, yes,' he cried, fumbling in the scatter of books. Strange! Where had it vanished? The children? It was no secret to him that the children rummaged through his desk.

'Mohini! Heeralal!' he shouted, so that they would hear him in their room beyond the partition.

They came, and Heeralal was about to speak when Mohini gave him a glance.

'Speak out, boy,' Old Mother urged him.

Father had caught the silent message that passed between them, and he smiled to himself and hurried to cover up for Mohini, the meaning of whose look was obvious.

'Mother, now I remember. Someone has borrowed it. I'll get it back soon.'

When Old Mother was gone, he leaned back in the chair and said, 'Heeralal, be off. Mohini, sit down for a moment.'

But Mohini stood by, silent, her face down, her slim fingers crumpling a bit of paper she had picked up from the table.

'What now, girl?' His voice was very tender.

Her face flushed deeper as she looked at him. She gulped and looked away. Her lips parted and closed.

'Good to live in a Bengal village,' she forced herself to murmur. 'The space, the clean air to breathe, the land covered with greenery. Lovely.' She faltered, paused a moment and continued, low: 'What have we here, in the city? Din, dust, hustle. Suffocating.' She drew in the breath sharply.

Startled by her unexpected words, the Professor sat up, and watched her with concern.

'So, you are trying to please Old Mother?'

She shook her hear. 'Trying to please myself.'

He sat silent, agitated, till he heard her murmur: 'You have taught me to speak my heart boldly, haven't you, Father?'

That was true, and his training had borne fruit. The girl could think for herself and could speak with decision. But —

'You don't understand, girl. Space and emptiness could be more suffocating than din, dust and hustle unless you have a mental preparation. Even at my age, I would go mad in the country! And then, consider: no more cinemas, or theatres, or concerts. No singing for A.I.R. What about that? All your talent wasted —'

Her lips curled into a wistful smile.

'Who cares? I'll sing —' She stopped, hung her face.

'You'll sing for "him"!' Father gave her a long glance and burst out laughing. Mohini looked at him swiftly and looked away. Her eyes were shining with happiness.

'The power of a handsome face!' he cried and shook his head as if in disapproval. 'These girls!'

But she hastened to meet his charge.

'A writer of such high distinction — what about that? And at such a young age! Why, in a few years, say ten —'

'Specially with someone to inspire him —' her father put in, on the edge of laughter again.

His heart was easy after many days of oppressive worry. It had been hard, very hard, to reject so worthy a match. Misgivings had pricked him all the time. Now, he felt grateful to his daughter. Perhaps she was right. Perhaps she could see with a clearer vision. And surely there was a chance that Jayadev would leave his village home and take up work in the University.

'Have your way, girl.' He spoke softly and saw the colour spring to her face as she gave him a grateful look. She turned and tripped joyously out of the room. 'Don't forget to hand over the copy of *Maya* to Old Mother, Mohini,' he called after her, chuckling.

He leaned back in his wide swivel chair and began to whirl right and left with the abandon and ease of a youngster!

Word was sent out. Jayadev's married sister, two years older than he, came and saw the bride. When horoscopes were compared, the stars — wonder of wonders! — formed the rare one-in-ten-thousand conjunction of a 'royal union.' Truly, they were meant for each other. And the groom, it seemed, had no need to see the bride. He had her photo; he liked the face; that was enough. Finally, one auspicious day the groom set out from his village home for Calcutta to stay with his sister. There the bride's father was bid for the pre-nuptial blessing-ritual, but not Old Mother — custom would not yet let her visit the relatives-to-be. Holy *mantra* was hymned by a priest while father blessed the groom and betrothed him to his daughter. And as father gazed at this tall, lean youth with the fine tranquil eyes and a dreamy air, he felt reassured. Mohini had chosen well. Pity that she could not yet meet the boy. Jayadev knew the old customs and besides, he seemed shy, reticent.

This was her *swayamvara,* Mohini thought excitedly. If only he would come to this house, just once, so that she could know what he was like. Did he not care to see her? But he must. It was his respect for Old Mother's sentiments that hindered him. Old Mother, he must have thought, would not approve of such 'modernist' ways. Mohini felt grateful, anyhow that he had not demanded a formal bride-showing. At least he had spared her that. And so she sat with her mind-picture of him, more real than reality, for she had lit him with her dream!

'You pretty enough for him?' she asked of her image in the mirror.

All at once she had a great desire to be lovely — till this hour she had not doubted her beauty — and it was as though her body longed to be a gift, fit for offering. It never occurred to her to wonder at this sudden over-whelming urge to give herself, completely to a stranger. For the stranger was, as it were, more an idea than a person. A symbolic inheritance. The Hindu maiden, born and bred in the ancient starlight of Vedic civilisation, washed by the running stream of the centuries, sheathing her limbs and her thoughts in a conventional dress to suit the needs of each passing age, was innately unchanged: she had retained all her ancient hunger to offer worship.

'Tell us how you make that fairy mask on your face,' Mohini had asked Reba, who now moved in a fashionable circle and knew the use of the latest cosmetics.

'Masks are not for beauties like you,' the stylish Reba had answered. 'Who would daub colour on a lily or pour syrup in a beehive?'

But Mohini pressed her, and Reba gave a few hints. The eyes, sparkling with large black pupils, still asked for care; the long lashes and underlids were to be touched with black *kajal*. The mouth, fresh and well-curved, but much too wide in repose and more so in laughter, needed make-up. The smooth luxuriant hair with its neat central parting was not to be pulled back tight and done in so many plaits and then fixed in a flat pancake shape. The new style was to heap the unbraided hair low on the neck in a loose 'carefully careless' way, with an art that concealed itself. A dozen times daily Mohini, for long spells, studied her eager image, touching the eyes with *kajal*, lips with rouge, arranging the hair this way, that way. This became her preoccupation. She could not pass a mirror without looking into it, in her bright wistful way. And while she was so absorbed, self-fascinated as never before, the festive house rushed the hundred details of marriage preparation.

'Strange!' father, beaming with happiness, spoke to Old Mother as she sat planning the girl's trousseau and marriage jewels. 'Where the great Marriage Bureau slips and falls, a mere bangleman trots up suddenly and crosses the stream!'

'True, true!' Old Mother joined her palms at her forehead. 'The word goes: "Horses and camels find the stream bottomless," but the rat squeaks: "Is it knee-deep, then?" Whoever could fancy that the bangleman, like the rat, would really find it knee-deep?'

'The old customs and conventions are not too unsound,' he said. For once the son, out of his heart's fullness, graciously conceded to his mother's wisdom. 'They seem to suit our mental climate. It's as though in Hindu social life there was no room for big business!'

'True, true,' nodded Old Mother, her heart pleased. 'The groom is without a peer, and his is not a large family, the root of many a trouble, for he lives alone with his widowed mother. There lie all the bricks to build a happy home.'

'Yet I worry,' said the son, for doubts were not altogether gone from his mind. 'Will Mohini put up with village life? Will she, impatient one, take to the new rhythm of things? New thoughts, new customs, new tastes, all so very old — will she adapt herself?'

'Childling, we have done our best,' Old Mother's wise lips reassured him for the tenth time. 'We could marry our girl to a city youth, but the risk would be more far more, for city youths these days are wilful and flighty. Village youths are slow and conservative but they have manners, tradition and stability of character.'

Old Mother was thinking of Mohini's mother, who was now a denizen of Heavenland. Wed at fourteen, she had come to Calcutta to keep house for her husband. Old Mother lived in her village home in those days and came to visit her son off-and-on. The newlyweds could not afford servants, not even a cook but her son would not let his bride do all the hard kitchenwork. She was to prepare the noon meal; he himself would do the cooking at night. The young wife was shamed and in tears, but he would not listen to her pleading. And she, deeply moved, gave sacrifice for sacrifice. Daughter of well-to-do house, she bore her poverty with an ever-living smile. Would Mohini be as fortunate as her mother? Would she, impatient one, yield to the complex game, the give-and-take that was life?

How Mohini's mother would have rejoiced on the wedding day of her girl! Why had the gods taken her away in the prime of her life? She would be watching from Heavenland, seeing all, knowing all, sending a benediction: "Daughter, I bless thee. Be happy. Be fulfilled. Be the light and pride of your new household."

Old Mother shed tears for the departed mother and sat and sighed with the weight of her responsibility, for she had decided Mohini's destiny. Her mouth twitched with a sudden stab of misgiving.

'Who knows what music the gods have in store for my Mohini?'

seven

Truly it looked like a house of marriage, the facade covered with flowers and evergreens, the columns gay with bunting, the balustrade festooned with chains of coloured lights, and twenty rows of hired iron chairs on the strip of lawn under a great blue canvas awning.

And it sounded like a house of marriage, with laughter and commotion, the loud biddings of guests and the fanfare of sharp and mellow pipes.

All the neighbourhood watched the festive house from their windows, and balconies, and roofs, and murmured: 'A maid is to be wed.' Many an elder sighed for his own maiden daughter. Many a young woman remembered her marriage day. Mobs of children gazed at the puffy-cheeked *shehnai* players. Even the street beggars, glum fixtures in the festive scene, had a gleam in their eyes, for they were to be fed a bellyful of parched rice, and curds, and a syrupy sweet.

Yet this was not the day of days but the one before, set for the bridal bath, the turmeric ceremony, as it was called, when the girl was to be consecrated with crushed turmeric sent from the groom's house after he had been anointed. With the bowls of yellow paste would come trayloads of gifts: clothes, toilet things, sweets, a hundred knicknacks.

'The turmeric arrives!' rang the cry before the day had aged.

The whole house rushed to the door. Coming past the *Glutton's Inn* were seven men, each with a wicker basket or a shiny brass tray.

'This way, this way,' greeted Old Mother, herself leading them to a hall where they set down their loads, and so on to the kitchen threshold for refreshments.

The men could strut as honoured guests since they were turmeric-bearers and the festive house was not to leave them one chance for casting a slanderous word on it. Old Mother looked after their feeding. She filled them with all manner of delicacies, meats and curries, and richly spiced rice, sweets and jackfruit and curds, until they could hardly breathe.

Meanwhile, the hall was aclamour with scores of women, relatives and guests, admiring the trayloads of gifts. A bright sliver tray held five red velvet jewel cases of different sizes, filigreed bracelets, bangles with a blue-enamelled design in guinea gold, a three-tiered necklace, two sets of earrings and armlets, glittering with sapphires, rubies and diamonds. Another tray, a wide one, was piled with saris, seven silk ones. Benares tissue, and Mysore georgette, and American crepe, each with broad borders in gold or silver. An engraved brass tray showed women's toilet things: four kinds of face cream and powders in dainty plastic cases and vermilion in a small gold casket inscribed with Mohini's name, a silver-framed mirror, and a bottle of red lac dye to stain the edges of the feet. Three other brass trays bore various milk sweets and relishes. And a wicker basket sheltered huge carps, each a yard from gills to tail.

'Rich, indeed!' said a young woman from Calcutta, gazing, fascinated, at the jewels.

'Master of Behula,' said another. 'Lucky girl Mohini.'

'Yes, but to live in the country. Who will see her jewels and saris? They've sent all this lot just for show — what else?'

'Good taste, though. All the saris are the right colour. Country people could not have selected them. Perhaps —'

'Don't you know? The groom has a sister living in our city. Married to a doctor. It's plain enough, she selected the gifts. What will Mohini do with such jewels? She can show herself only to peasant women —'

'And to jackals.'

'Don't forget the mosquitoes.'

'Better far to have a husband in town, even if he's not too rich.'

'S-sh! There's Old Mother coming.'

'The bride is ready for her bath,' announced Old Mother. 'Hurry. The child may not have a bite of food until the ceremony is done.'

Mohini, meantime, was getting ready for her bridal bath. She wore a plain cotton sari, for it would get stained with turmeric, and her hair hung down her back. Bindu stood watching, a pinched look on her face. Mohini knew the reason for her unhappiness: the snake-charmer had jilted her. These days he sat in front of a house three doors off, and the young *ayah* of that house stood by watching while he played gay tunes on his gourd. Deep looks passed between them. The snake-charmer had tired of Bindu's remoteness and was seeking a more accessible victim.

'Bindu, take this powder case. You need one. And a puff.'

Bindu could not believe her ears. 'Powder case?' she echoed faintly.

'Take them, Bindu. They'll remind you of Mohini.'

Bindu forgot her misery. Her face was lighted by a wide smile. In the past she had often stolen into Mohini's room when no one was about and sat at the toilet table, powdering her face, admiring herself. But she had to be careful lest she be caught. That spoiled the fun. Now to have a blue powder case of her own, filled to the rim, with a silk-topped puff!

'And I always thought, *Didi,* you hated me!'

'Oh, Bindu!' Mohini felt a wrench in her heart.

Barely two days and she must leave this house. How she loved the house and yearned for every inch of it! How the house had grown to be a part of herself, its safe familiarity a shield. Bindu, too, was a part of her life, and at this moment she loved the girl.

'Your earlobes are bare, Bindu. Look. Take these gold flowers.'

Mohini picked up a pair of earrings from the table and held them in her palm. Bindu was speechless. Tears came to her eyes.

'Didi, why do you have to leave us?' Her voice was husky.

Tears were pricking Mohini's eyelids, but she quickly controlled herself. The women were coming up the stairs in a rush, calling her name. Mohini stepped out. The women drew her to the centre of the veranda and with shrieks of delight, dipped their hands in the bowls of turmeric and smeared her face and throat and arms, smeared her all over, until she was one bright yellow splash. Then they turned on one another, jabbing, jostling, the timid ones screaming and shielding their flushed faces with their arms, till they were all gold-hued like tulips, their hair down, clothes dishevelled, eyes ashine with laughter.

Laughter and chatter went on into the night, stimulated by the expectations of the morrow, and the morrow came, riding a blue-black cloud of rain, so that daylight was a sickly shadow. The festive house watched the cloud and anxiously cried:

'Lo! Monsoon bearers! What if it pours and spoils the festive night?'

But the long black cloud passed on after an hour's drizzle. The rain-rimmed sun showed at noon, and the cleared sky smiled.

The bride, too, was smiling when Heeralal saw her in mid-afternoon and brought her fried fish, large crisp pieces on a plate, and whispered:

'Didi, eat. You're famished. Old Mother's away on the terrace.'

Mohini had not eaten all day. A bride was not to touch food till the marriage was over — that was the practice.

'Foolish practice,' father had cried in scorn, hating to see his daughter go hungry on this day of joy. But Old Mother was insistent. It was her day. Who was more versed than she in time-honoured ways?

Mohini looked at the fish, smiled and shook her head.

'Not hungry?' Heeralal was perplexed. *Didi* had never lacked appetite when delicious food lay close to her mouth. 'Will you starve the whole day, *Didi?* Such good cooking, and everyone in the house has eaten three stomachfuls.'

'Such is the Law, *Bhai*. Do you know its real meaning? Fasting makes the inner heart pure. This day the bride may not stoop to the tongue's coarse needs.' So Old Mother had explained it to her. 'He also fasts.' Mohini added and after a silence, looking at the fish, she wet her lip with her tongue, 'How did you get it?'

'Grand fun!' he answered her in his bright voice. 'I've been tasting food on the kitchen yard where they've put up three big ranges. I have to tell the cooks if there's too much salt, or a dish is underdone, or it's not spicy enough. What a job! Fish, and meat, and prawn rissoles, and curried lobsters, and sweet rice with almonds —' He swallowed, to ease his watering mouth.

'Enough, enough.' Mohini gently tweaked his nose. 'Why tempt me? Is the lobster juicy and well-cooked then?' Her voice had a plaintive tone.

Heeralal licked the roof of his mouth as though the exquisite flavour still clung to it.

'What cooking! Lobsters, as fat and long as cucumbers! I'll bring you one. Nobody will see.'

He watched her gulp and he made his final assault: 'How do you know Jayadev *Dada* has not eaten? Won't he be tempted by city delicacies in his *Didi's* house in Calcutta where he's put up?'

That settled the point. Old Mother receded mistily in defeat. Heeralal slipped fish into his mouth in excited joy and dashed away.

After star-rise the *shehnai* music came thick and sweet: fireworks cracked and blazed, and the street was lively with paper bombs bursting, Catherine-wheels darting. There was a traffic jam, for the passers-by paused, sharing the gaiety of the festive house.

Mohini was now wearing a sari of vermeil-pink, and her marriage jewels. Pearls caressed her throat, their chaste lackluster complimenting her complexion. Rubies glistened from her earrings, armlets, hair ornaments. Her forehead was decorated with simple grace, with a flower design in white sandal paste.

The festive house, the hustle and commotion upset her. She was weak with excitement. She needed rest. As she sat at her bedroom window watching the sky grow restless with rockets, a new Pontiac wrapped with flowers turned at the street corner and crept up in a moving pool of light. Then, the firecrackers spoke and rockets filled the air with painted rain.

There was a burst of voices: 'The bridegroom! The bridegroom comes!' The bedroom door was flung open, and laughing, gaily dressed women, among them her school friends, passed by swiftly to the front balcony to give the shrill traditional welcome expressive of great joy: *'Ulu-ulu-ulu-ulu-ulu!'*

Mohini would have rushed after them but she saw Old Mother hurry by, and out of modesty she had to restrain her impatient feet.

Old Mother watched intently from the balcony and saw Jayadev for the first time. She smiled to herself. Her son was not wrong. Moon-fair! Old Mother joined her palms on her brow, offering all the gods and goddesses her grateful *pronam.*

The schoolgirls returned soon to their friend. 'Handsome, truly!' said Reba in her gushing way. 'Even more pleasing than that photo in *Maya* you showed us. Lucky girl.'

Reba, with her modern outlook, had not approved of Mohini marrying a young man she had never met. But now she felt Mohini herself could not have made a better choice so far as looks went.

'We'll have fun enough in the *basar* room,' cried Ela brightly. 'We'll sing and dance all night.'

Custom had it that after the bestowal rites, the bride and the groom would be led to a gaily decorated room called *basar* where only young women could assemble and till dawn there would be music and singing and a hundred merriments. There would be no privacy for the newly-weds this night, no seclusion.

'We must take care that Old Mother doesn't peer in,' warned Roma. 'She will faint if she finds us dancing before the groom.'

Roma danced well, and all day she had been rehearsing her favourite piece, *Call of the Flute,* for the occasion. Worthwhile, truly, since the groom, the centre of the interest, was so very handsome.

Jayadev, meantime, sat with the assembled guests, garlanded and besprinkled with rose water from a spray. It pleased him to find among them two senior professors he had known at the University, and he spoke to them eagerly about his work, the ideas that lay deep in his heart. But this was no hour for such learned talk. Presently, he was shown to the inner court where relatives and intimate friends of the house stood in expectation. On an altar specially erected for the ceremony the family priest had put a dainty pebble, the Holy Stone, the presiding deity on such occasions. The priest sat on Jayadev's left and the bride's father on his right, and though the priest was an old experienced man, he feared the learning of this youth and pronounced the Sanskrit *mantras,* three thousand years old, with great caution lest he make errors in syntax or diction.

The greeting ritual over, the groom was led up the two flights of stairs to the terrace, where scores of young women had assembled for a ceremony not part of the sacred texts, only of convention. The groom wore a white temple-shaped pith crown, bright with tinsel, and stood on an inch-high wooden platform with uprooted banana saplings at each corner, the symbols of fruitfulness. A young woman, the bride's first cousin, faced him and mutely welcomed him into the house with gestures as she held a trayload of other symbols; soft-flamed brass lamps, cornstalks, oil-seeds, grasses, which, since the beginning of Hindu civilisation, have stood for the warmth of life, food for the family and fodder for the cattle. Through a fanfare of conchshell noises came the shrill cry of *'Ulu-ulu-ulu-ulu-ulu!'* and the hands of the young woman, Promila, gestured semantically. Then the bride came, face veiled. She came seated with legs crossed on a plank of wood borne on the shoulders of four stalwart youths, friends of the household. Round the groom she went and round again circling seven times, rendering him the customary homage.

Mohini felt a pang for her mother. Had she lived, she would have welcomed the groom with auspicious symbols. Old Mother had not the privilege, because she was a widow. Mohini gave herself to her fancy: she saw Mother in Heavenland, pretty in white Benares silk, waving the brass lamps for her son-in-law while the nymphs who stood by cried *'Ulu-ulu-ulu-ulu-ulu!'*

And Mohini said in her heart, 'Mother, give me thy blessing. Make me the light and pride of my new household.'

She was soon awakened from her dream. It was time for the Auspicious Glance. The women drew a shawl over the heads of the bride and groom, veiling them.

'Let eye unite with eye and heart with heart. Gaze your fill,' they said in chorus.

Jayadev gazed, while Mohini's head dropped, her face flushed. Then, she lifted her eyelids a flickering instant. Long had she been preoccupied with his looks and hungry for a glimpse of his face, but in this intimate moment she was free of all vanity. His looks meant little. She prayed only for his approval, his contentment.

A hundred thousand Hindu maids each bridal day of the year give their hearts to their unknown husbands, asking nothing in return but approval.

'Do you like your bride?' her eyes asked. Under his gaze her face reddened, her heart beat fast.

He saw a graceful face, the complexion not too fair but golden. Her eyes were like black gems filled with large black pupils, slanting a little under painted brows, faintly arched. Her rosy mouth was finely curved and a dark spot, no wider than a pinhead, on her upper lip like a decoration. He was fascinated instantly.

The symbolic moment rushed by; the shawl drifted away.

Down the stairs the groom walked, the bride in tow, his flowing dhoti tied to a corner of her sari. Side by side they sat before the altar while the priest again chanted verses, and Father gave his girl to this stranger, with the Holy Stone as witness.

'Enter thy husband's home with all lucky omens. Care for his servants and his cattle. May thine eyes be ever without anger. Care for the happiness of thy husband. May thy beauty be bright, thy mind full of good cheer. Worship thy gods. O Indra, king of all the gods, let this lady be the mother of heroic sons.'

eight

'**Time flies. Hurry.** The railway train leaves at four-thirty and waits for nobody.' Father's voice was hoarse and tight. His eyebrows worked up and down.

The bride was ready to start, and so were Heeralal and the cook-woman, the two who were going with her to her new home for a month to see her take root in the new soil. A near relative and a maid must accompany the bride, the custom went.

'Behave ill when I'm gone, and I'll break your legs, both,' the cook-woman warned Bindu.

'She is a good girl,' Mohini said because Bindu looked so forlorn.

'Good, forsooth!' scoffed Bindu's mother, her plump hands on her hips.

'Didi, jewel faced one!' Bindu cried helplessly. 'Take me with you. *Didi* —'

Mohini consoled her. 'Why, Bindu, don't you know? You're soon to be wed. Your father told me yesterday. He is looking for a groom. There's a boy —'

'Now Little Mother, why must you turn her head balloon-like as it is, with this talk of marriage? There's the dowry to be found, and some silver finery for the hefty body. Who will take a dark-faced girl without these.'

'Why this fuss about marriage? You may be digging a canal from the river to your house-door, inviting the crocodile.' Bindu tossed her head, her voice was a drawl. She paused a moment as though probing her memory.

'I have vowed not to marry — ever,' she said demurely 'Why, I'm going to be a nurse at the sick hospital.'

'You hear her crooked talk?' the cook-woman shouted, and she lifted her hand to give Bindu a slap on the face. Bindu ducked quickly.

'Waist-chain?' said Bindu to her mother in a thick half-whisper.

The cook-woman stood still. 'Just like me to have forgotten. You have reminded me, girl, in the nick of time. Where should I be without my Bindu?'

The cook-woman rushed to the room downstairs where Jayadev sat talking with Old Mother. She planted her feet firmly before him, and said: 'A sliver waist-chain I ask from the Ocean of Learning. The Little Mother, our heart's delight, becomes a queen. Am I not to be rewarded, then? These two hands washed her when she came forth from the cave of darkness, and now the milk-infant's grown into a woman, she has a husband. Who more proud than I on this day of days?' Jayadev listened, amused, and murmured absently, 'Indeed! Indeed!'

His thoughts were full of the girl, his wife, his feelings heavy with her agony at separation.

'The silversmith needs an advance to buy his metal. A down payment.'

'Yes, yes,' said Jayadev with his absent air. Oh, he would love to comfort Mohini and assure her of a warm welcome in her new home, allay her fears of the unknown.

But the cook-woman was a tenacious leech. She had prickly words on her tongue.

Old Mother, watching with troubled eyes, cried: 'Have you lost your head, woman? The son is tired out and has a journey to make, and you come and shout for a waist-chain. Why, it would need lumps of metal to round all that girth of waist. And where's the hurry since you are going to Behula?'

'A thumb's width I will not budge till this just claim is settled,' the cook-woman announced. 'Let the fire-wagon go without me at four-thirty.' The thick-bodied woman jerked her ample arms heavy with massive rounds of silver, and sat down, muttering heatedly: 'Am I not to save my face before the craftsman? Is this what I get for rearing the Little Mother ever since she was a toddler with nothing but a bangle on each arm and an amulet on her neck?' Her voice broke. She rubbed her eyes and sniffed loudly.

Jayadev, now wakened, held out two ten-rupee notes and said in his low tranquil voice, 'Let the craftsman start his good work, then.'

The cook-woman wiped her eyes quickly with her hand. She smiled and cried out, for all to hear, 'Would you expect less from our Little Mother's groom? A scion of noble ancestors. Be wealthier still. Be the father of little gods.'

The farewell ritual began. Jayadev and Mohini stood in the inner courtyard on a spot painted with the symbolic conch and lotus and other floral designs, and the young woman, Promila, acting again on behalf of the house, blessed them with the speech of the hands in which were held the trayload of auspicious lamps, and grains, and grasses. While her hands spoke, Old Mother watched with the threat of rebel tears in her eyes: tears were no good omen. Misery clutched the bride's throat. Never had she been parted from Old Mother except once or twice for a few days, and the uprooting hurt, like suffocation.

At the door of the courtyard stood father, covering his emotions and crying in a hoarse tight voice. 'Time flies. Hurry.'

The formalities ended. Mohini clung to Old Mother, loth to leave her, releasing her misery in a fit of sobbing.

Old Mother struggled against her unfallen tears, caressed the girl and stroked her hair, murmuring: 'Take good care of yourself. Eat well. Be the Lakshmi of your own household.' Her voice grew solemn. 'Be fulfilled — by your husband, by the children to come.' Her heart ached that she could not accompany the girl to the railway station and so delay their parting by a precious hour, but that would be against old practice. She turned anxious eyes to Jayadev, who stood embarrassed, his face averted. 'Take good care of my golden one. She cannot bear a moment's neglect.'

'Have no worry, Grandmother,' said Jayadev with full compassion, and he bowed his head to her feet in farewell. 'She'll have all she needs. All.'

Then Old Mother turned to the girl and spoke with wisdom. 'Honour your mother-in-law as though she were your mother, and abide by her will. Answer her hot words with absolute silence. Sweeten your speech when you talk to your neighbours. Words dipped in honey cost nothing. Bend yourself to the customs and traditions of the village. And —' tenderness veiled her aged eyes — 'do not nibble off your husband's pens and pencils!'

The *shehnai* players blew into their pipes: farewell, the music moaned, farewell.

Heeralal had been hustling excitedly. He had been entrusted by Old Mother with the job of keeping persons and things of ill omen out of the bride's view: washerfolk, widows (Old Mother hid herself behind a door when the moment came), bananas and broomsticks, empty baskets and vessels. At the front door were two pitchers filled to the brim, ornamented with young mango leaves. Beside them, posted at each end of the doorsill, were Kishore, the sprightly sweeper boy, and his grimy-faced four-year-old sister, Sunni. Experience had taught Heeralal that these two were people of good omen for whenever Heeralal saw their faces in the early morning before he saw anyone else's he had a lucky day.

Father had borrowed a car from a friend for this occasion. Mohini and Heeralal sat in the rear seat, the cook-woman beside the driver. Farewell — the music lifted to high pitch before it ended with a jerk.

Familiar landmarks slipped past. Familiar ways of life, sentiments of girlhood, slipped past. Old ties slackened, and the pain of it, oh, the pain! Old Mother stood very still, on the doorstep, gazing vacant-eyed down the crowded street which, for her, was empty. And father — and beside him her husband — drove slowly in the baby car close behind, squeezing the bulb of his horn as though to hearten his daughter with. 'Coming, I'm coming.'

She felt her throat ache and her eyes mist, and she hit her lip hard lest she cry. *Pronam,* all known images, *pronam!*

The train was soon to start. father led Mohini to a ladies' second-class compartment. Jayadev had a berth in a men's carriage. Heeralal, being a mere boy, had the option of travelling with either.

'My fat penholder will miss you, girl,' said Father with a dry forced laugh, stroking her head gently, but when Mohini, sniffling, pressed her tear-streaked face to his bosom, he had to struggle hard to control himself. His hand rested on her head in benediction and he spoke tight halting words, misery straining beneath his eyelids, until he dragged himself off to the men's compartment to bid Jayadev farewell.

~

The firewagon rocked with speed. Seated in a corner, Jayadev was sunk in a book. He had no eye for the other passengers, no ear for their chatter. He was a silent, solitary man with heavy-lidded dreamy eyes in a young tranquil face. Marriage had stirred a whirlpool in the stream of his feelings, and he was anxious to smooth the disturbance and be his true self again. The ceremony had lost the solemn dignity of Vedic days of three thousand years before, and was now filled with needless rites. Three thousand years to him sounded like three hundred days. He could live for long spells among voices, not hollow echoes, of a far-off past. That way he was a projection of his scholarly ancestors, a continuation of their lives. The problem of daily living ruffled him, and he would often have stumbled except for the guiding realism of his practical and purposive mother.

It was his mother's will which had led him into marriage, even though, at this vital hour, every conscious thought and feeling was to have been dedicated, yoked, to the great task at hand. It was his dream to reorientate the values and patterns of Hindu life. India was on the verge of freedom: a new page of world history was writing itself. The political implications were visible to all but not the social problems. What was political liberty worth to the common man if it was not part of a renascence in social life? Jayadev reasoned, as all men of thought reasoned, but his reaction took an altogether individual form. While others borrowed a ready-made sword from Western ideology to cut the knots of the problem, Jayadev delved back into India's remote past for a solution.

Society, rural society (and nine-tenths of India was rural) was sick with taboos and inhibitions of its own making: the iniquities of caste and untouchability; the ritualism that passed for religion; the wide-flung cobweb of superstitious faith. It was all an outgrowth of centuries of decadence. The purity of ancient thought had been lost in misinterpretation until the dignity of man had become a mere plaything of vested interest. Jayadev would break the crust of vulgarity and reveal ancient thought in its true splendour. But the new man of his vision, growing to his full stature, was not to be a hollow reincarnation, not a spiritless copy of ancient Hindu man. That were as stupid as Hindu moulded in a Western pattern.

The freedom he envisioned must release a spiritual energy among the masses which would require every social value to be re-weighed. This was the moment to end all slavery, not least of all the slavery of the spirit. The proud nation that would soon step onto the world stage could not afford to be half-slave, half-free.

So Jayadev was possessed by his dream of true freedom. History had done this to him. The dream was a fever in his blood. Hurry, hurry, there was not a moment to be lost. Look back that you may look forward. Look to the buried material of the past to write the new social charter. And hurry! Hurry!

Heeralal crunched roasted peanuts between his teeth while he watched his *Didi's* husband with speculative eyes. Surely the great scholar so versed in ancient lore knew the mysteries of Yoga power? Yoga excited Heeralal's fancy. Perhaps he could draw out of Jayadev the secret of secrets? Even the Frozen Gleam faded before the splendour of Yoga.

Heeralal looked over to him and jerked his chin at the big volume Jayadev held. 'That book,' he said, for the sake of talk, 'that book is three hundred years old, maybe?' His eyes scanned the thick volume as though he were interested. Scholars, he knew, often read books centuries old. The older the book, the greater the scholar.

No response. Jayadev had not heard? Heeralal repeated his query, edging closer.

Jayadev looked up. 'Three hundred years?' He shook his head, and his smile showed his amusement. 'No, not, so old.'

Pause. 'Two hundred?' suggested Heeralal, persistent.

No answer.

'One hundred and fifty?' Heeralal would not give up.

'Less, less.'

Heeralal decided on a change of technique.

'*Didi* said, "Every Hindu should know the secrets of Yoga, it's his duty." And I said, "Yes, yes, but who'll teach us? How could we find the ancient books, the leaves made out of soft bark, in which the deep secrets lie locked up?" And *Didi* said, "Why not ask your brother-in-law? The great scholar. He knows all. He'll help you." And I said. "Why not?" And she said —'

Jayadev looked up then, and his voice became wistful. 'She said that? She said, "The great scholar?" '

'*Hoon.* A Yogi can do *anything.* There was Swami Premananda who died the other day, very old, two hundred years and more. One day a dozen menfolk from Calcutta city, unbelievers all, turned up at the Swami's *ashram* near the Sone River and to shame him they said: "Holy one, we are hungry. Feed us." A Hindu mustn't deny his hungry guests. The Yogi turned and spoke to an *ashram* disciple: "Son, fetch a bucketful of river mud." When the mud was brought the Swami had it served to his guests on wide banana-leaf plates. They looked at it and cried, "What's this?" The Yogi smiled and said, "My sons, eat your fill. You are hungry." One of the smart city folk grew curious and sat down and put some soft brown earth on his tongue, and — what wonder! — it was no earth but a delicious milk-and-raisin pudding.' Heeralal paused, his face intense. 'That was Yoga power.'

'Your *Didi* — she would much rather have married a smart city youth?'

'Hoon,' said Heeralal out of his absorption. 'Then, there's Yogi Krishnadev, still alive, though well past his four-hundredth birthday. He was born in Emperor Akbar's time, everyone knows that. Far up on Mount Everest, somewhere near the top he lives. One of the English folk in the expedition met him; his beard is taller than he, white as mountain snow. He lives on snow, nothing else, clean palmfuls of white snow. Yes. Yogi Krishnadev!'

'Does she not love the hundred distractions of city life?'

'Hoon,' said Heeralal. 'And then Naga Baba. Alive or dead, no one can tell. One day he comes to the river-bank and asks the ferryman to take him across but the fellow asks three pice. Naga Baba has no money, and he is in a hurry to get across. What can he do? He steps upon the river and walks over it as if it's a meadow. Yoga power! Naga Baba!'

Jayadev burst out laughing. 'Why, Heeralal, *you* don't have to cross the river on foot. You can pay the ferryman and use his boat. Why worry about Yoga power?'

Heeralal slipped a peanut into his mouth, its flavour easing his sadness and disgust. Great scholar? He knows nothing of Yoga, that's a plain fact. Why not say so? Huh!

Heeralal, his neck craned in the rushing stream of wind, looked back and saw an arm hanging out a window two coaches off, and he knew whose arm was so slender, and fair, and gleaming with gold except for the slim, iron bangle, the married woman's insignia. He stared at his sister's arm and an ache came upon him: there would be no Mohini to perch on the desk at home, to bite a pencil, to collect funny names or to put her hand up to her mouth to cover her breathless laughter. Heeralal felt his eyes moisten. Why did she have to marry? Why did she have to go away and live among strange folk?

The train shrieked past a great steel bridge. The train slowed down and presently stopped with a jerk. Heeralal jumped to the station platform. Mohini saw him from the window and rushed to the door.

'Step in here, quick. The train will move in no time.'

'Women's compartment!' scoffed Heeralal.

'Then go back to your own. Run. I knew you'd be a handful of trouble.'

'Fifteen minutes' halt,' said the boy calmly. A fellow passenger had told him. And he added: 'You have good company, *Didi?'*

Her brows came together, and she lowered her voice.

'If only they would leave me alone! Such curiosity about my personal affairs! Caste? Home town? Father's profession? A new bride, they knew, because of my armful of gold. Bridegroom's residence, his income? So it went on. And they fondled my pearl neckstring with its ruby-set locket. What could this be worth — *if* real?' Her frown relaxed, her voice eased into an undertone full of laughter. 'One young woman knows all about precious stones — a near relation, the second nephew of the third cousin of her uncle's brother-in-law, owns a sixteenth share in some jewellery shop!'

'Mere rustics!' observed Heeralal. 'The tail of a cow and the tongue of a rustic never cease wagging.'

'You know what I told them?' She spoke breathlessly because she was excited by this journey to an unknown life, curious but somewhat alarmed. 'I said I'd met the groom at a picnic party in a Maharaja's palace and when he saw me, he recalled at once, miraculously, that in a pre-birth we were man and wife. It was a wonder how the understream of his memory gushed up! He is the master of Behula, and he keeps three elephants at his palace gates, two females and a tusker — they've been in the family a hundred years. Even the maid-servants in his house use toothpicks of guinea *gold,* and these must be thrown away after each meal. Oh, *Bhai,* you should have seen them — goggling eyes and gaping mouths!' Her eyes and mouth mimicked them.

At that instant she heard an amused laugh and quickly turned her eyes. There stood her husband barely twenty strides off, gazing at her merrily. Her heart jumped. He had seen her making mouths. Shame! Her face reddened. Their eyes met and did not look away.

This last half-hour Jayadev had been in an alien mood. His mind had strayed from social philosophy and was occupied, strangely, with facts about ancient Vedic women. The Vedic woman lived a thousand years before the start of the Christian era. She was no household drudge, no decorative being, but an intellectual, striding beside man in a tireless quest for knowledge. Her contribution to Aryan, though, lived still, shining as ever. There was Gargi. There was Maitreyi. Jayadev had evoked them before as bodiless thinkers, never as women. Suddenly, today, he saw them as women who had married, performed trivial household duties, borne children. And his vision of the Vedic woman, drawn out of the mist of ancient ages, had a curious likeness to a living vision he had seen for fleeting seconds at his Ceremony of the Auspicious Glance.

Then Jayadev, eyes still on his book, had longed for another glimpse of Mohini who had some mystic resemblance — the idea came upon him in a flash — to Maitreyi. That semblance enchanted him. He was impatient for the train to come to a halt. He had been somewhat unhappy about this marriage. What would he do with a stranger who might never share his ideas? Now, those fears were rootless.

The train stopped. Jayadev walked out on the platform, and while his bride spoke to Heeralal in a jovial way, he stood at a distance, wistful but shy.

That wonderous girl! Vivacity suited her well. Vivacity streamed through her gestures, her smile, her joyous look. She made a face and Jayadev had to laugh. How could he help it?

Then he walked up and spoke to her, his voice clear and pleasing: 'May I not hear the story, too?'

A group of women rushed to the window, peering out.

'Two female elephants and a tusker!' cried one woman, measuring the bridegroom with her glance, appraising his status.

'Toothpicks of guinea gold!' said another, torn between belief and unbelief.

'Handsome!' breathed an admiring one.

Jayadev, embarrassed, looked at his wife, as though seeking help, but she shook her head and let her hand fly to her mouth lest she laugh. She turned quickly and moved away. Let those women have their fill of him. Let him pay for his handsomeness. But he, too, turned and walked back to his compartment.

'My husband!' Mohini's heart was thrilled as she sat pretending to read a book. All her being clung to him, content. The Auspicious Glance, a passing moment, had given her a vague image, filled out later by secret sideways looks in the crowded basar chamber. Now, at last, she had seen him.

He was truly handsome: lean and tall, the face clearcut, sculptured, his eyes had the far-away look of a dreamer, but his mouth and chin were firm and well-shaped. His thick, lovely hair, had a secret suggestion of brown, though it couldn't really be brown.

This was her *swayamvara,* for she had chosen her husband! And — oh joy! — he liked her. She could see that in his face and his voice and his glance. A woman always knew — in an instant.

My husband! What magic was there in those two words? There he had stood, remote, a complete stranger, but why had she felt as though no one on earth was nearer to her? How had he come, as it were, into her pulse? Stranger? He was not a stranger. She had created him, in the secret self. He was her idealised image, her dream husband.

The emotions that came upon her in a mounting tide were the tenderness that was an ache, the expectations that were festive bells, and, beneath all, a clutching sense of love's utter lonesomeness.

~

Astride the sweep of plains green with corn, the day grew old and slid down the gold dust of the sky's slope. Night fell, black as melon seeds, and the patches of trees which flew by were so lit with fireflies that they were like strips of the Milky Way, tossed around on earth. Heeralal put out a hand to touch the black beauty of the night, and he was filled with a strange ecstasy. He grinned to himself, fancying that this rush through the night would lead him to Eyeless Wild. Climb a treetop and watch the sun for your bearings. At night, watch the stars. S-sh *Didi!* Do not speak. Do not be afraid. Hold this torch: keep your thumb on the press-button. He, a gliding palm tree, is less than a lizard under the power of a gun. You'll see.

'Where will you sleep, Heeralal?' Jayadev broke into Heeralal's dream.

It was a long moment before Heeralal could waken himself and answer: 'In the ladies' cabin.'

The thrill of adventure had concealed the heavy pain of *Didi's* going. Now, he needed ease for the pain.

His sister, too, was wrapped in dream, a deeper dream of love, of her husband. She wanted intensely to light for him all the lamps of her body and soul, to show him all her gifts. What richer gift had she than her voice making song? He, surely, loved music. It would be joy to please him. If he, too, played and sang, she would be his proud pupil.

What an enigma was marriage! Before yesterday your husband did not exist in your life. The simple fact that you were married to him acted upon you as a living force, so that you were hungry for his physical presence, your limbs warmed with a new yearning, and you felt a tremulous need for his eager response.

His response — the very thought brought an exciting rush of curiosity. Scraps of knowledge collected at school grew vivid, vital. Colour crept to her cheeks. She closed her eyes in shame — and pleasure.

Heeralal tapped at the marriage door. '*Didi,* let me in.'

The train had stopped.

'Lie down, *Bhai,* for a few hours' sleep. We have to leave the train in the night.'

Mohini moved about languid with feeling, spread a bedsheet on her berth and made her brother lie down. She stretched herself at his feet, her long legs curled up for want of space.

Heeralal twisted, and then turned over on his side. The whole train slept. Mohini alone lay awake.

nine

The cartman prodded the ribs of his oxen with a short thick rod, pulled them by the tail and cried: *'Tchuk! Tchuk!* Run, good folk. Do not sleep.'

'Why pull the tails of dumb animals, cartman?' Heeralal charged. 'It hurts them sorely — you should know. Oxen can't run like horses. Look at their short stubby legs. And where's the hurry? We are not dying to see your rat-hole of a village!'

The cartman looked back over his shoulder with a bland expression.

'Our Elder Brother is well-versed in oxen, and I bow low at his feet. What can I tell him? Wilful thy be, oxen, like children. Beat them not, and see how they start their fun. Why, fast as horses my Bishu, my Subal can run if they so fancy. Come, Bishu, wake up Subal. Let Elder Brother know your speed.'

'Speed!' Heeralal sighed with distaste. He had had enough of it in a half-day and a night. When, towards the night's end, he lay stretched beside his sister on the straw-padded floor of the cart, under a barrel-shaped thatch, he was still rocked by the whistling, screaming fire wagon as it rolled thunder-fast and swallowed the miles like the dark of a lizard. Now, the heavy-limbed oxen had broken into a crazy trot, flanks quaking, collar bells jingling. Still the cartman prodded their ribs and *tchuk-tchuked!*

'Why, is this not speed?' he called to Heeralal.

The cartman had laughed at him and it had stung. It was pitch dark, then. The winding road, scarred with mudholes and ruts, showed dimly in the moving light of the lantern which swung from the cart's yoke. Heeralal could not sleep. He gripped his electric torch which he had wisely brought with him, and flashed a long white beam, down which his eyes ran, straight ahead. Suddenly, he saw two tiny gleams picked out by the light. He held his breath, watching, and touched the cartman's arm.

'Stop! We're lost, for we have no guns,' he whispered tensely. 'A tiger ahead.'

'A tiger?' The cartman was astounded.

'You see nothing? Not two eyes like two little fires?'

The cartman looked and shivered with laughter. He shook his small coconut head with its close-cropped hair as he said: 'Our Elder Brother's all full of scares. The eyes of an ox! A cart coming our way!'

Heeralal was doubtful. He shifted his torch beam which showed two pairs of glowing eyes moving nearer. Deeptoned bells could be heard. A cart truly. A voice met them out of the night.

'Hark, our lamp is dead for wan of oil. Will you pour out a few drops from yours?'

The cart drew up abreast.

'Six pice,' said Ganesh, the carter from Behula.

'Three,' said the other. 'Will you cheat us in this sacred hour of dawn when the gods are about?'

'It is not dawn yet,' said Ganesh promptly. 'Five pice. Pay, or you'll get lost on the dark road. Your oxen's feet will slip in potholes.

'The stars are watching,' warned the other. 'Must you ruin a fellow cartman and his oxen? Are you a thug, then? Keep your oil. We can go without oil. We know the road as we know the lines on our palm. Four pice.'

Ganesh prodded his oxen. *'Tchuk! Tchuk!* Run. We are no thugs, nor hagglers. Four pice and a half.'

'Stop, brother. Take your copper. We do not grudge you the profit. We'll get it back one night when we meet again and your cartlight is dead and we have oil.'

The axle creaked, the cartman dozed and muttered, *'Tchuk! Tchuk!* Do not sleep, good folk!' and the oxen plodded on, unguided, in the chill remnants of night.

Heeralal slid back into the barrel-shaped awning and curled up beside his sister, sharing her pillow. On the edge of sleep he mused that oxen, so dumb and helpless, at night had the fiery eyes of tigers.

Mohini shook him by the shoulders till he cried 'Shoot! Bandits!'

When at last he woke up, she said, *'Bhai,* must you sleep till noontime? You missed a grand sight. I saw a goat riding on a pony — their master trudging after them. And that's as it should be, the cartman tells me. Goats get footsore if they have to walk a long way.'

'I saw cart-oxen with eyes like fireballs,' said Heeralal, 'the eyes of tigers.'

'Why not?' Mohini was unimpressed. 'The eyeballs of all animals shine in the dark. Didn't you know?'

He didn't. Shamed, he slid out of the thatch. 'What strange flowering grass!' He stared at fields lit with June sunshine. 'Tiny yellow blooms like your gold eardrops, Mohini, only much smaller. What wild grass is this, cartman?'

'No wild grass, no grass at all, only a patch of mustard,' said the carter, amazed at this ignorance. 'Do they not have mustard in the city, then? Do they eat their potato, and pumpkin, and fish without mustard?' And he shook his head to himself: 'Lo! City folk! In the meek *hummbaa* of cattle they hear the great growl of tigers!'

Heeralal grinned uneasily. How explain that it was one thing to eat mustard seeds in a curry and quite another to recognise on sight the plant that bore them? Village folk were prideful because of their special knowledge. Could they ever fancy that in a big city one never saw cornstalk, green and lush with the fat they drew from the soil? It was a pity, though, that cities were so bleak and barren.

'Let me get some mustard blooms, *Didi;* they'll look nice on your hair.' Heeralal affected a crisp tone to hide his fluster: 'Pull up your oxen, cartman. I must wait for my brother-in-law. His animals are laggards, or, maybe, his cartman doesn't goad them into a trot by twisting their tails. Some men are born kind; others are monsters.'

'Faults I have galore,' the cartman conceded as he drew up slowly, 'but no tongue has ever said, "Ganesh is cruel. Ganesh is a butcher. Ganesh will not treat his oxen as brothers and friends." '

Heeralal dashed into the gay golden fields, sparkling from the recent rain, and standing on a narrow ridge, feasted his eyes on the colour and light. As he sniffed the good scent of the dark churned-up earth, his small nose twitched rapturously. What fun, he thought, to see these plants break from tiny seed-cases and grow a thumbnail's length each week until they bear frail and fiery blooms at last. The brilliant blooms would be replaced by new clusters of seeds which would become a sharp and pungent seasoning for curried greens, fish, meats. The village had sights and smells and a silence denied to hustling cities. In his own town they made things out of jute fibre in enormous ugly factories where crowds of men slaved like swarms of ants. But the raw jute came from the fat country fields where, under the wide bending blue of the sky, ploughmen, true children of the soil, worked. Feeling and holding Mother Earth with their hands gave them strength and pleasure. The simple countryfolk had not heard of modern city toys — tram car, telephone, radio, but their luxuries satisfied all the senses.

Heeralal started to run along the narrow grass ridges between cultivated strips of land. He balanced himself by swiftly bending his slight figure, his hands stretched in the sun above the mustard blossoms.

Jayadev stood at the back of his wife's cart, and spoke to her: 'Not tired Mohini? This cart ride is painful for you, isn't it?' His voice was anxious and tender. 'You didn't expect —'

No, she hadn't expected a cart ride, but she wouldn't let him know.

Instead, she answered quickly, smiling up at him, 'Why, it's fun!' She faced round to the fields. 'What lovely countryside! Look at Heeralal down there. He's discovered a new flowering-grass — mustard!'

Jayadev laughed, sharing her merriment. 'He has never been out of the city?'

She shook her head. 'Heeralal has seen only cities.'

'And you, Mohini?'

She evaded the question: she too had seen little of the countryside. 'The golden earth of Bengal,' her voice was solemn, 'so they say — and how true!'

His glance swept to the horizon, 'The golden earth of Bengal,' and he added with sudden sharpness, 'and the blue sky hung with vultures —' He cut himself short.

'Vultures?'

He would not explain his sudden change of feeling. He waved it away with a smile, speaking lightly. This was no moment to delve into economic problems.

'There's another conveyance we'll use, Mohini, even more primitive. It's without wheels. This time the city girl will be really shocked.'

She cried quickly, still gazing at his face: 'I know. Palanquin! One painted indigo blue. And the bearers in blue, too. What fun!'

He burst into laughter, boyish in his mirth. 'A city girl used to motor-cars dreams of a blue palanquin! It is a strange coincidence, because ours is blue. But the bearers have no special dress. Mother has no liking for show. Austere.' He paused a bit before he went on: 'She acquired this virtue, so they say, from my father whom I was destined never to see. My grandfather was of an altogether different mould. His smart carriage and pair with his retinue were the talk of the countryside.'

His mother. How would she, stern and exacting, react to his girl's vivacity, her radiance? What if Mother disliked her as too high-spirited? Jayadev answered the question: mother must yield to so much fascination. Mother must love this girl and fill an emptiness in her heart. How she had longed, these past years, for her son to be married. And he, resisting her will had yielded at last.

What was his mother like? Mohini tried to see her. So austere. She would keep a cart and palanquin but not a carriage. Very orthodox? Much more than Old Mother? It would seem so from her insistence on all the luck signs on the person of her son's bride. Odd! Mohini smiled to herself. It was odd that she, a skeptic because of father's teaching, should have those rare emblems on her person.

'A city girl you call me, but you'll see how soon and easily I become Behula's own,' she said with cool assurance.

His heart warmed to Mohini as his fears and doubts grew unreal. Out of the mist of the past the Vedic woman took form, the woman who had been the spiritual font of the greatest thinker of his age. It came on him, then, that this fusion of personalities was symbolic of the deeper fusion of which he dreamed, a profound union of today with yesterday.

'The Big House will make heavy demands on its young mistress,' he warned her tenderly. 'Demands that you'll find unreasonable. Some of them will have to be met with patience and a spirit of give-and-take. Other foolish demands must be resisted.'

The Big House was her husband's family residence, she knew. It was good to be called mistress of the Big House. Must she be very dignified and stiff, never laugh, lest she be called frivolous? What more demands would be made? Mohini looked at her husband with alarm.

The Big House was much more than a residence, he wanted to tell her: it was a way of living, a stern discipline and iron tradition. But this was not the time. There was time enough later for her to learn.

The third cart, bearing the cook-woman, came up at this moment. Heeralal gave a joyous yell from the edge of the field. 'Food bowls! Now we must eat.'

He had a vision of his favourite treacle in fat earthen jars — the cook-woman had charge of them all — and what a generous portion he had eaten last night in the train!

But Jayadev would not eat. He would wait till he reached home and had a bath.

'Lay the food for yourselves,' he said.

He was impatient to start, for there was still half an hour's travel by cart and an hour by palanquin.

The party set out again. Mohini arranged fried bread and sweets on broad sal leaves stitched together with hard twigs to make platters. She gave one to the cart man, the other to her brother.

'What joy!' the cartman gratefully cried. 'The firs in Behula village to eat from the hands of the mistress. What bliss!'

It was good to be called the mistress, she, a school-girl till yesterday. How strange marriage was! How fast you had to grow up! Yes, more inches were added to your height by feelings, by the heart's experience than by the passage of time.

'Your leaf-plate?' Heeralal asked his sister.

He watched her anxiously, for even in the train she had hardly eaten. She had felt too sick for a hearty meal, she had said. Jayadev *Dada* had come to her compartment door, pleading, 'Mohini, have something please.' 'I will,' she had said, yielding, but the some thing she ate later was so little!

Mohini shook her head. 'He has not eaten.'

'What, then? Don't make a fuss, *Didi,*' Heeralal spoke firmly. 'When you travel in a cart and get jolted, your stomach needs strengthening lest you sicken. You know.'

Mohini smiled at this theory. 'Indeed?' But she stuck to her point. 'Even if the sun-god rises in the western sky,' she said finally, 'a Hindu wife won't eat before her husband.' It was Old Mother speaking through her lips!

It was a question of feeling and formality, a restraint rooted in spirit and in seemliness. Shame enough that she had given way to temptation on her marriage night and eaten curried lobster. And he fasting. What would he think of her if he knew? Old Mother, again!

The cartman, having eaten, leaned back content, and sang a folk song in his low-pitched devotee's voice:

Who shall take this self across the stream, bhai,
    Who shall?
On the bank of Life's rough stream I stand, I wait.
    The ferry is here, not the ferryman!
I cry the name of the ferryman!
    Hei-ee-o! Hei-ee-oh!
There is no other name on my tongue.
    He hears not,
He hears naught but the voice of the devout who has merit.

Lovely melody. When the cartman paused, Mohini picked his song:

Who shall take this self across the stream, bhai,
    Who shall?

'The words, cartman?' she asked.

Eyes closed, the cartman was wagging his head with keen pleasure.

'What voice! Heavenly! The ears are soothed; the soul is rested.' And he recited the words.

'She is a radio artist, didn't you know?' Heeralal proudly informed the cartman, forgetting that radio was yet almost unknown in the countryside.

When Mohini had sung, the cartman lifted his voice again.

You say the name of Hari on the hundred beads of rosary
    And hope to attain Him,
Oh, delusion!
    The barren woman cries for a child,
The lone spouse cries for a mate,
    The hungry cry for a morsel;
All those cryings, full-throated, passionate,
    Mixed together —
Not enough for Attainment!'

Heeralal now crawled out to the cartman and took charge of the oxen. *'Tchuk, tchuk,* good folk,' he cried.

Mohini was bemused over her life to come. To love and to be loved, and a bit admired, those were her needs simple human needs. In spite of the Big House and whatever stern demands it made, she would be unafraid. Her husband would never have to be ashamed of her. She would remake her ideas and her outlook and all would be well.

Yes, Mohini assured herself with a firm nod, all would be well.

The cart stopped before a group of village folk who had come miles up the road to see the bride of the Big House. The sprawling two-storey mansion towering over the peasant's mud-huts had been known by that name for three hundred years and more.

Heeralal jumped out, watching interestedly while Jayadev stood at the roadside to accept the *pronam* of his people who stretched themselves on the dust, one by one, and touched his feet with deference. The cook-woman, Bindu's mother, jumped out of her cart and stepped up, shiny in the splendour of her massive silver collar, armlets and curious toe ornaments.

'What a road, Mother Ganga! What a country! The eighteen easeful bones have cracked up piecemeal with the jostling. Clean as a bald pate are the roads of our town.' A scornful sniff. 'And the worst not over yet. Now comes the long wooden box, painted blue, with handlebars sticking out at each end to be lifted to the shoulders of scraggy peasants! You smell the oil of their labour. What if they drop the *palki?* Will there be a bone left whole in our tender person?' She fanned herself vigorously with a palm-leaf fan and moved off to the palanquins resting on the ground.

Jayadev spoke. 'A bride of the Big House enters her village in a *palki,* that is our practice. It will be well if we start at once, before the sun has become pitiless.'

The party set out. Eight bearers were yoked to each palanquin, four at the front end of the bar and four at the rear. They sang a chorus of strange cries in the rhythm of their footfalls. The bride's palanquin led the procession. She sat facing her brother, her legs under her, her back against a fat silken cushion. Together they looked out through the sliding doors on both sides and fed their eyes on the young, green paddy covering the ploughed earth, furlong on furlong. But its beauty made Mohini homesick. She saw Old Mother's face, pale with repressed weeping, and she heard father's voice, pitched high to conceal its tremble: 'Time flies. The railway train waits for nobody.'

The syncopated chant of the palanquin-bearers as they hastened their pace broke in on Mohini's reverie:

> Weigh one feather.
>   Bone and leather!

'*Didi* —' said Heeralal.

'What?'

'*Didi,* you'll be so rich, won't you make me a loan?' Her wide eyes misted with love but she smiled.

'What is it?'

'I need a bicycle. A cheap one —' Heeralal was breathless with suspense.

'I'll buy you the best of cycles,' she promised. 'And an electric cycle lamp.'

Was she not the mistress of the Big House?

Heeralal grinned with delight and pulled his fingers till his knuckles cracked.

The bearers slackened their pace; their legs and backs were shining with sweat. They panted as they took up a new cry in chorus:

> Heavy as a hill our newborn lord,
>   Give us grit, Monkey-god!

'Look, *Didi,* what a land, what greenness! What joy to lie down on the green carpet and do nothing day and night, except to eat and sleep, eat and sleep. Huh!'

But Mohini hung her head and moaned through pinched lips, 'I am so hungry.'

Heeralal pitied her. Hunger was a form of suffering he could understand. The food bowls were with the cook-woman whose *palki* lagged way behind, out of sight. Heeralal could do nothing for *Didi* unless he stopped their *palki,* got down and picked bunches of wild blackberries which grew wild on the roadside.

Heeralal looked at Mohini and then looked away. Big tears stood in her eyes. Poor *Didi.* Homesick. Helpless. How could she live away from Old Mother? With strangers? He felt her arms about him. She drew him close, holding him forlornly. Heeralal could not bear it, he burst into unmanly tears.

'*Didi,* why did you have to marry?' he cried.

Across the furlongs of green the palanquin swept on a rush of feet, the tired coolies singing a plaintive chant:

Shoulders gall,
    Let fall!
Let fall!!

They were panting rapidly now:

How far, how far, Be-hu-la? Heigh-ho!
    Ankles ache, knee-bones shake,
How far, how far, Be-hu-la? Heigh-ho!

ten

SHE STOOD BAREFOOT in a large, shallow claystone bowl of milk, red with lac dye, the target of a hundred stares. She bowed her head as a bride will, but not before she had looked around. Her thoughts were of her new mother, who was not at this ritual of welcome because she was a widow and, therefore, an inauspicious presence. How Jayadev would feel the sting! There was his city sister, the sister who had engaged the bangle-seller to seek a match, proud with the symbols of wifehood, offering the bride the greeting of the house, mutely, with fluent hands. She touched the bride's head with a trayload of the five grains, the many oilseeds and fruits of the soil, a gesture which said, 'Let Mother Lakshmi fill the store.' She touched the bride's right hand with a pot of freshly cooked rice, meaning. 'Let the hungry ever receive out of thy mercy.' She touched the bride's ears with honey. 'Let all thou hearest be sweet.' She touched the bride's stomach with a little Ganga earth: 'Like the jewel-wombed Earth be thou fulfilled.' Milk was heating in iron pan on a two-brick range which had been set up in the courtyard. Frothily, it boiled over, and all eyes turned to look at it for an instant — prosperity of the house shall be so great as to spill over.

But of all this the bride saw and heard little. Her head was bent and she thought of her mother-in-law, the only member of the house left out of the ritual of reception. The bride's heart felt for her new mother who would have fasted the day before, for it was *Ekadashi,* the fortnightly fast day for all Hindu widows, and though she could have eaten at sunset she would wait for her son to come and sit by her at the meal. How would an alien fit into this intimate picture? Would she be asked to the fast-breaking meal? Would these *baran* rites never end?

After another long half-hour, to a jubilant chorus of *Ulu-ulu-ulu-ulu-ulu!* the bride was led into the house across the inner court, with village girls at her heels, laughing and blowing conches.

On the threshold to the kitchen, the bride saw the white-clad figure of the mother. Lean and tall like her son, she had his thin sharp Aryan nose, his conch-white complexion, but neither his dreamy eyes, nor his intent air. Her face had a lustre which denied her age and was enhanced by her homespun cotton cloth, a borderless austere sheet, which was wrapped around her in graceful folds. The bride bent her knees and, bowing low, took the dust from the feet of the mother.

'Daughter mine, be thrice blessed.'

The mother tilted the bride's face upward by the chin with her finger tips and gazed eagerly at the bashful face.

Her voice was clear and bright as she said, 'Let the *sindur* mark ever trace the parting in your hair. Long has this house awaited the Daughter of Fortune, its new mistress.'

And as she gazed, the lucent calm of her eyes deepened with happiness. She had chosen well. Here was a fitting bride for her son. The luck signs were not all: this girl, with grace and poise, had a beauty beyond mere prettiness. The mother's heart throbbed with love. This girl, her Jayadev's bride. A duty was done. He, looking down from *swarga,* would approve and rejoice. Daughter mine, be thrice blessed.

Heeralal had slipped out during the *baran* rites and had passed a busy hour surveying the Big House on which time had left a smudged finger-mark. The facade with its many arches and columns could not have been washed with lime for half a century or more. It was mildewed in spots, overgrown with weeds, and trees growing aslant out of its gaping cracks, sturdy *asvatha* trees which had to be cut from time to time lest they damaged the structure. Swarms of blue and white pigeons nested on the projecting cornices. The acres around the house were enclosed by a tall compound wall with massive iron gates guarded by two huge couchant stone lions, thrice lifesize, with ascetic faces and dusty manes. Fruit trees abounded — mangoes, guavas, plums, berries, along with giant banyans and bushy-topped palms and *kadambas* whose glossy sweet-smelling flowers were shaped like yellow balls of wool. Heeralal, after this survey sauntered back to the inner court, where he met his sister's meaningful glance which seemed to say: 'Bow to mother.'

The mother blessed him as he touched her feet.

'Where have you been, my child?' she asked. 'You must be hungry.' She addressed the bride too: 'You too, daughter. Such a tiring journey. Wash your face and hands, and have your noon meal.'

That is good talk, thought Heeralal, with a swift glance at his sister. Poor Mohini, to torture a hungry girl by waving lamps and trays in her face!

~

Little squares of carpet to sit on were laid in two rows on the wide verandah of the kitchen; a spacious courtyard separated a thatched brick house for cooking and storage from the main building. Rooplekha, the married city daughter, had arranged that the household would sit and eat together, yes, even the newly-weds, though it be indecorous by country convention. The three women would sit side by side facing Jayadev, and Heeralal, and Rooplekha's husband.

'We'll fetch the rice,' said the young village girls who had come to greet the bride in a gay chorus. They lifted their conches to their mouths and each girl gave a long, loud blast.

Food was served on wide, shining silver plates: rich steamed rice with raisins and almonds, fried vegetable and rissoles, six kinds of curry, each in a small silver bowl at each plate, thickened milk with spices and curds, and four varieties of sweets and relishes. It was a good feast, the food wholesome, not showy.

'No serving on marble or brass plates on this day of joy,' said the mother, hurrying about before she sat down to the meal. Her sari had slipped off her head, revealing her black hair, cropped shoulder-length. 'Meera,' she urged, 'run to the kitchen, girl, and fill the silver glasses with cool water from the earthen pitcher. Renu, fetch a palm-leaf fan and wave off the flies. Maloti, bring the pickle pot, the lemon one, and serve out some pieces.'

And before she sat down to her meal she poured out melted butter on the hot white rice heaped on each plate.

'A queen has come to us,' said the daughter of the house with a gracious smile, 'and we eat out of silver plates in her honour.'

The face of the bride was brimming with happiness. These were good people: kind, considerate. She kept an anxious eye on Heeralal lest he be disrespectful, and presently she saw him stare at the mother in amazement. The mother had put her right hand in her lap and was eating with her left. Strange! Mohini threw a swift glance at her brother and saw him open his mouth. In a rush to forestall him, she forfeited a bride's decorum and cried:

'Have you hurt the right hand, Mother, that you keep it idle?'

There was a moment of stunned silence, as the mother looked up calmly, until a dour-faced woman of middle years answered irately, over the mangoes she was peeling and slicing with a large knife:

'The mother dedicated her right hand to Siva at the Holy City past twice ten years, for the health of her son who was then a little sickly, all skin and bone because of spleen and fever. She may not use the right hand at meals, since it was given to the deity and would be defiled by the touch of the mouth. These twice ten years she's eaten with the fingers of the left hand only. A Hindu mother's true sacrifice for her son. Maybe such an act of faith is mocked in the cities where women are insincere and tough.'

Mohini winced at the undeserved reproach and her eyes dropped in shame. Why had she spoken? Her anxious glance flew to her husband, who looked up and gave her a reassuring smile, as though he understood. Her heart leaped with intense joy, for nothing else could matter. Nothing.

Rooplekha watched this wordless communion between her brother and the bride with pleasure, and lest the others also watch and disapprove, she hurried to distract them and turn their attention to herself.

'Why, my Second Aunt, some village women are insincere enough,' she said in a clear tone. 'I know one who vowed no common fruit or vegetable to Siva — not mango, melon, potato, pumpkin, but a rarity like grapes! What kind of sacrifice are grapes? The city, too, has its sincere women who are not afraid to make hard dedications. I know a rich widow in Calcutta City who gave up her evening meal to the goddess Kali, so that all her life she would eat nothing after sunset.'

The Second Aunt was silent awhile, for the insincere woman who had vowed never to eat grapes was none other than her own sister. When she spoke, it was with condescension:

'*Han, han,* it is not all evil with city folk, who are redeemed by such as you, reared in village, wed in town. Do you not carry our ways and practice?' And her voice dropped suddenly. 'Have you not heard? Our Durga's grandfather is back from his pilgrimage to the temple of the four-faced god. He went crawling the whole way, as a penance, crawling on hands and knees across meadow and rock and riverbed and up steep heights, until he reached the white shrine on a hill crest.'

The bride had no ear for this talk. Her eyes flew again and again to her husband, and her face warmed as she met his glance. For all her hunger, she ate slowly, absently.

It was not seemly for the caste highborn in a village to chatter at meals, but Jayadev turned toward his sister with a sudden thought: 'Sudha?'

'Sudha? I sent for her. She has a headache. She won't come.'

Mohini looked up from her plate. Sudha! Why was he worrying about her? Who was Sudha? That question fretted her a long time, until she knew.

The meal over, Jayadev took Heeralal's arm.

'Come see our village, Heeralal,' he said. 'We have no city sights, no museum, zoo, palaces, towers, but you'll see trees heavy with fruit, ponds full of fish. We must find you some playmates.'

'Give him no chance to slander us when he gets back home,' a plump, round-faced girl said jestingly.

'We're dying to see the bride's clothes,' cried another. Eagerly, she turned to the bride. 'No rest for you, sister, till you've shown us your saris and jewels.'

So the young married girls of good caste and status bustled the bride up the stairs. Mohini, out of breath, mused: one can see how the son came by his looks. He has his mother's grace. This mother is like Old Mother in her ideas but different from her in feeling. This mother is aloof, alone, clothed in her own uncommon atmosphere.

The mother was at the door of the prayer room. She glanced back at the bride as she came:

'Daughter, prostrate yourself to your father-in-law and ask his blessing from Heavenland. Those sandals of his — he wore them in his last days. I have no other god but him.'

A pair of wooden sandals, drab with age, sat flower-strewn on a throne of gold. The bride kneeled and gave herself for a minute to the ritual of silence due to this symbol of the father-in-law she was worshipping. When she looked up she saw the mother deep in meditation. Quietly, not to disturb her, Mohini slipped out to the village girls who rushed her along the corridor to a room where her boxes lay arranged. A fever of action seized the girls, now released from the mother's restraining presence, and they clamoured all together until Meera, wife of a revenue inspector, raised her voice and cried:

'Will the city fairy tell us what wonders are to be seen in her town?'

And Maloti, married to a forest ranger, said: 'Her father, maybe, owns a wind-car.'

And Renu, daughter-in-law of the temple priest, asked: 'Will the city fairy now open her clothes trunk?'

'Yes, yes, the saris first,' a chorus of voices cried. 'Time aplenty for talk.'

The bride unlocked a steel trunk as the girls, looking down, held their breath.

The saris had the gleaming colour of a rainbow, some were plain; others were patterned and shot with silver and gold — linen and silk and muslin and brocade from Benares and georgette from Mysore. Each had a blouse to match, neatly pinned into the folds.

'Beauties!' gasped the village belles.

'Gold galore!' cried Maloti, picking up a crimson silk sari shot with threads of gold. 'My great-aunt had one of that pattern. Same texture, same glitter. It was in the family a half-hundred years. When it thinned out and was useless, my aunt head it to a flame and lo! A guinea-weight of gold was collected from the melted thread.'

'They care only for value,' Mohini thought. No eye for artistry. And she recalled a saying she had heard from her Old Mother: 'To a lotus pool the wary jeweller goes, and values the white blooms with his teststone.'

Meera was rummaging through the trunk — shawls, chemises of many colours, toilet things. She found the bottle of Himani cream and dabbed a lot of it on her face, watching the effect in the silver-framed mirror.

'What are these pants for?' she asked, lifting a pair of knickers. 'Baby wear, made with an eye to the near future? Much too big! What lovely silk, you could hide the stuff in your fist.'

'Why, they're my underclothes,' the bride answered feebly.

Eyebrows went up. There was a moment's silence, shattered by breathless laughter.

'Is this the time to rest your ankles, girls?' the daughter of the house bustled in at this moment. 'Am I to do all the work for the banquet and the flowerbed, all by myself?' She noticed the piles of clothes and the bride's flushed face, and she, too, flushed a little. 'They're prying into your things, Mohini? The bride's expected to show her saris and her marriage jewels to her husband's people — absurd old practice. Do not mind girl. I must run off. Three hundred guests have been asked this evening, not counting the children.'

'Sweet person!' the bride said gratefully as Rooplekha hustled away.

Renu stuck out her tongue and said: 'Look at the city doctor's wife. From head to foot a townswoman!'

'Why should a woman wear pants under her sari?' Meera resumed while she dangled the knickers in her hands. All eyes watched. 'She might as well put on long English trousers and a hat!'

'Don't let your husband see you with pants on,' Maloti said with a twinkling laugh. 'He won't know what to do with them!'

Mohini was a little shocked but amused. To think that there were girls who had never seen knickers! What would they say when they found the brassieres? Fun, anyhow!

'Jayadev *Dada* has done well to marry a city girl. City girls know the hundred-and-one facts of life — no over-much shyness in their making. You must show him the way and lead him on, sister. A shy, simple ascetic. It will be fun for you to waken him! Truly the stars have bespoken a royal union.'

'A shy, simple ascetic.' Mohini's heart missed a beat. A sharp longing to see his calm face came over her. She could not sit still. She walked to the window and let her eyes follow the narrow earth road running into the village — down that road he had gone with Heeralal. And she barely listened as Meera, so free with her tongue, went on:

'You have married a bookworm, city fairy. He seems to have no use for our kind. I'd give anything to see how you pass the night with him in the Flower-bed!'

Bimola, the youngest of the girls and the last to be married, broke into a giggle.

'Let her see the bed,' said Renu as she rose and flung open an inner door. 'The flowers will come later, in the evening, a cartload. We'll make the marriage bed then.'

The bride turned her head and saw, in a flying glance, an antique brass-railed four-poster, so high that you mounted it up four wooden steps. Never before had she seen its like. Her face darkened with a flush, as though the enormous bed invaded her privacy, violated some inner sanctity. If only she could be alone, alone with herself for a bit, to ease her confusion.

'Four steps to heaven itself!' Meera roguishly explained.

'What good are you, Meera?' said a teasing voice. 'You took six months to get pregnant. Six months!'

Meera scowled, her feelings hurt. 'Is that any of your business, Maloti?'

'I was pregnant within a month of my Flower-bed. Same with these girls here. Same with everyone on earth. You know that well enough, Meera, sister.'

'True,' exploded Meera, 'but is there a need to publish the fact to a beat of drums, Maloti?'

The other girls exchanged swift glances. Fun!

'Oh, Meera, six months!' their voices, full of mischief, were shrill. 'Oh, six months!'

And their lips, scarlet with betel juice, opened in gay laughter.

One by one the girls recalled their bridal night — the chord of reminiscence had been touched in all. They sighed for the thrill of those moments, now a memory. And to tease the bride they said again:

'Just as well Jayadev has found a city girl. Just as well he hasn't married a bashful village maid, like us.'

'Bashful village maid,' repeated Mohini, her eyed bright with fun.

'We, too, have a fairy in Behula,' said Veena proudly. 'Our Sudha — Saturn's Eyesore. Fair and shapely. Looking at her, the eyes get dazed by her beauty.'

The bride listened interestedly to the talk of Sudha whose absence from the meal had worried her husband.

'Winsome!' said Renu grandly. 'Made out of the white flowers of jasmine.'

'Monsoon cloud, a skyful, is her rich-black hair. It reaches her kneepits.'

Mohini asked in wonder, 'Why call so fair a maid Saturn's Eyesore? You couldn't give her a more fitting name?'

The girls were silenced. Their faces fell.

'There is a story,' Meera answered Mohini at last.

'Tell me,' said Mohini, tensely. She had a premonition.

'Truly, Sudha is Saturn's Eyesore. You will meet her soon. You can see her house from this window, that white-washed building behind the tall coco-palms.'

'The story?' Mohini's voice was strained.

But the story had to wait. Mother stood in the door frame.

'Is this the hour for gossip, Meera, Beena, Renu?' she asked. 'Ten big pumpkins to be sliced, a thousand leaf plates to be washed and dried, a pile of almonds to be cracked for the sweet rice. Let my new daughter sleep a little in her room. She must look fresh for the banquet when, with her own hand, she must serve the caste elders. Come away, daughters.'

~

She wore neither gold nor stones on her person, only flowers — some in bud, some full-blown — sweet-breathing flowers as bangles, and armlets, and neckchains, as hair ornaments and a proud crown on her forehead.

Kunda blossoms, shell-white, lay strewn on the bed, *Mallika* garlands hung thick from its railings and posts. Lotuses lay by the groom's pillow, and *champa* for the bride, fair scented *champa,* with a bright bosom of gold. Down the middle of the bed ran a wall of flowers on and over which the groom and his bride would edge nearer each other, if they would. They could lie close over the crushed glory of lotus and *champa.*

'The flowers will tell us a story,' the village girls warned the bride laughingly as Rooplekha, a little before midnight, pushed them out of the room and closed the inner windows against inquisitive eyes. Then she blew out half the candles on the great chandelier of silver and cut-glass. And Meera, before she went, pinched the bride's arm with a knowing glance.

'Do not be too bashful,' she whispered. 'The Flower-bed does not come twice in a woman's life.'

Mohini stood by the tall bed, the antique brass rail cold against her face, her head bowed. She felt rather than saw him step in and close the door, shutting out whispers and giggles. There, alone with him, she was tight with excitement, curiosity. And his low voice, a bit husky as though he, too, shared her feelings, startled her slightly.

'How graceful!' he exclaimed, lost in her loveliness.

His heart was full, but his gaze did not falter. Never before had he been overwhelmed by a woman, as a woman.

The delicacy of her features, a clear purity of line, the wonder of her eyes, wide and expressive, from which flared a bright blackness, these details and the dark spot on the upper lip set off tender beauty in all its fullness. The poise of her figure, her jasmine grace quickened the beat of his heart, the flood of his feelings!

Sternly, he caught himself. This, their first hour together, an hour of rich realisation, was not to be frittered away in sentiment. Did she know the true value of marriage? The deeper meaning of their new relationship? Did she know herself, know the Maitreyi in her? It was his foremost duty to make her aware of herself, he had been telling himself for several hours, and, now that the time had come, he started to speak his rehearsed piece, flustered yet determined.

'Bonds interminable hold us in sacred relation, more sacred than any on earth,' he began and then paused, for he felt his words sounded hollow.

Again he yielded to her witchery but only for a few moments.

Then with an effort, he went on, 'A common synonym for the wife is partner in faith: she shares her husband's thoughts and ideals just as he shares hers. They have one spiritual income between them.'

She lifted her eyes for a flash in astonishment. His voice was intense, his face so solemn. Was this the moment for such stiff talk? If only he would smile as she had twice seen him smile. If only he would be himself. A shy, simple ascetic as the glib-tongued girl had said of him, the one who had laughed at her knickers. A strange new warmth filled her being, overflowing into her limbs. Her head drooped under its white crown of flowers as she stood tense, one red toenail scratching the floor. Finally, she took the jasmine chain which hung on her bosom and lifted it to her mouth. She tore it with a quiet intensity, petal by petal.

The sight of her bright teeth tearing at the flower chain stopped him in mid-sentence. His words rang hollow and unreal. Her face showed the power of her passion. Something vital but sublimated was struggling in him for expression.

'No need for candles?' His hand rose abruptly to her arm as he looked up at the chandelier with its thirty points of light.

She looked up, too, her eyes meeting his again for a second. The torn flower petals were acrid on her tongue. As the lights went out one by one and the room darkened, she turned. She moved two steps to the window, fleeing, fleeing into the security of night. There was no moon, but the sky glittered, hung with all its stars. The couchant lions guarding the dim hulk of the half-closed iron gate seemed strangely alive. Far beyond the meadow a phantom light glimmered, and died and glimmered.

'Mohini —'

The voice of the stranger who was no stranger touched her with enchantment. She held her breath and trembled.

eleven

Mother, son and daughter had the same clearcut, sculptured features, the same serene faces. But Rooplekha, Mohini felt in her heart, was not so cold, so self-contained as her mother, not so meditative, so remote as her brother. Her quick, friendly smile, like his, lit her grave face and made her lovable. Roop-lekha. Beauty's Writing, was a fit name for her.

'If only I could stay on for a bit and help you get into the life here,' said Rooplekha with true regret. 'But my husband must be back at his work. He could manage just three days' leave.' She paused, hesitant. 'The village washes and bathes in the open, Mohini,' she went on. 'There are so many ponds about, and we have our own, Rook's Eye, at the back of the garden. Won't you come for a swim? This afternoon I'll be gone and who knows when we'll meet again?'

'You're coming again soon?' asked Mohini pleading.

Rooplekha smiled and took Mohini's hand.

'Holidays are all too rare for my husband. Take a change of clothes, and let's start now.'

'As if I could swim!'

'I can't either, with all this bulk. I just keep afloat.'

'Keep afloat? I'll go down like a rock!'

They walked to the pond. Rooplekha was amused as Mohini told of the trouble she had had with the girls about her knickers.

'But they mean well, those girls, I know that,' she conceded.

Rooplekha nodded. 'They mean well,' she said.

Her waist was trim with the sari twisted around it like a sash.

'Hurry, rush in.' Rooplekha dragged Mohini down the pond steps till they stood submerged to the breast. Suddenly, as though they had one mind, they cupped their hands full of sunlit water and splashed each other.

They became friends. Rooplekha stretched herself on the sky-cool Rook's Eye and floated gracefully with the swans. Then she swam farther and farther away from Mohini, who sat on a mossy step, the pond up to her knees.

'Come back, *Didi*. You'll breathe, you'll be drowned,' Mohini called in fright.

Rooplekha returned, panting, and stood waist-deep in the water. Her wet hair glistened in the sun. When she had caught her breath, she sat next to Mohini on the steps and rubbed perforated pumice stone, the village substitute for a sponge, on her ankles and feet.

'I must tell you my story, sister, that you may learn from my experience. You are city-bred, village-wed. I am village-bred, city-wed. We share one common lot: we've been pulled up by the roots. A city has as little mercy for an alien as the country, no more, no less. Years it was before I could fit in, Mohini, hard years.'

Mohini protested. 'A city, cruel? A city like Calcutta? It is so knowing, so reasonable.'

Roopleakha laughed. Her voice was quiet but earnest.

'Listen. A maid of the Big House has to be married to a youth of equal status. No one suitable was found in the Bengal village, so Mother gave me, against her will, to a city youth, a surgeon in the Medical College in Calcutta. I was just sixteen. My husband's relatives came to see me when I arrived at my new home, smart women with enamelled faces, and they gave me a look and cried, gushing, "Oh, how sweet she is!" But I saw my husband's face darken. The women were laughing at his bride. Later, I, too, knew what had amused them: my sari and blouse were all wrong, old-fashioned, and the colours didn't match. I wore no make-up, and my hair was done the wrong way. When I spoke with my country inflection, the women cried again, "Oh, how sweet she is!" They turned to my husband with laughter: "Lucky as ever. Where did you find a bride so exquisite?" And they all stared at my nose. "What a pretty stone, oh, how sweet!" Horrid — that was what they meant, for my left nostril had been bored; it held a gleaming diamond. No city girl would wear such a decoration. In a word, I was a savage. As the days passed I saw more and more what a misfit I was. All my life I had lived on vegetarian fare, and here I was expected to eat eggs, fish, meat — food I loathed. My husband wanted me to go out on the street with my face bare and to mix freely with his friends, men of his own age, at the sight of whom I became tongue-tied with modesty. What could I say to them? Yes, it was very hard.'

'And then?' cried Mohini, listening, intent.

'Then, I made up my mind and began my struggle. It was a strain to give up my ideas, my customs and manners and adopt theirs. It would be easier to grow a new skin! I had plenty of patience. I gave up my old modesty. I ate fish and meat — though at first the smell and taste sickened me. But it was all worthwhile for my husband's sake. I couldn't let him down. I had to make him happy.'

'I understand,' said Mohini with a slight nod.

'You have to adjust yourself the other way about. You have to rid your mind of its cosy city furniture, as it were, or else, Mohini, there will be much ugly talk and scornful behaviour.'

The Rook's Eye was alive with large darting carp. Mohini threw pebbles at them.

'Why all this bother?' she spoke with sudden sharpness. 'City and village are apart. Perhaps they should stay apart; perhaps this inter-marriage is wrong. We girls suffer, not the men.'

Rooplekha held Mohini in the warmth of her smile.

'Shall I answer you? We who're so wed, serve some real purpose. It's as though we make a bridge between two banks of a river. We connect culture with culture, Mohini, our old Eastern view of life with the new semi-Western outlook. The city absorbs a little of the "barbaric" village, the village absorbs a little of the "West-polluted" city. Both change, unaware. They are less angry with each other. This is more urgent today than ever before. Our new India must rest on this foundation.

Mohini was staring at her, surprised, visibly impressed.

'Where did you get such learned talk, *Didi?* My brother-in-law must have taught you.'

Rooplekha went on with a smile:

'Mohini, look. To start with, you have to understand the Big House. My mother is the usual orthodox Hindu woman, only she is more intense than others, and all her faith is pinned to family tradition. No deviation for her, not one inch. Stern-willed, though tender at heart, she is a simple soul, with singleness of purpose, a one-eyed mind. She exists for the Big House; she wouldn't have it changed the least way. Even the age-grey walls are not to be lime-washed because Mother loves to see them absorb time. Father's wooden sandals are an object of worship, you've seen that. And Jayadev? He had no heart for such worship; he has no liking for ritual of any kind, but, out of his love for Mother, he bends to her eccentric will.

A strange mixture of the old and new is he, my brother. Self-divided, as it were, if you get me. We've known him as a scholar in the philosophies of East and West, but of late he seems to have become more, much more. One day he will surely tell you about his work. You see him against his true background? This scholarship is an inherited gift. For generations past it's run in the family. Father died when I was three years old and Jayadev about to be born. Mother was in her sixth month. Jayadev grew up, went to a city school and college. Gifted, all through. He could have had a career in the University but he preferred to return to the Big House. That is only half the story, though. You see, the New Learning holds him as much as the old, so that his heart is set on a synthesis, as he calls it. He would have a harmony of cultures for India. He reads ancient thought in today's light. He seeks in ancient thought sanction for the West-influenced ideals of our time. And he finds it. He is a man with a message for his country. He may be a genius or a freak — who can tell?'

Mohini, listening in rapt silence, suddenly felt very small. Synthesis, harmony of cultures — she could make nothing of such terms. She had not learnt much at school and her liking for books had centred on light fiction. To have such a great scholar as her husband! What if — her heart missed a beat — what if he was disappointed in her?

'One day he will be famous, won't he?' she asked with bated breath. The portrait in *Maya* stood before her eyes.

'Perhaps. But it isn't fame he cares for. He thinks the people of India need the fruit of his labour at his turning-point in their history. He is an idealist.'

'Oh!' said Mohini, her eyes wider.

'Mother is afraid of her son's heresy,' resumed Rooplekha. 'Mother thinks city education has spoiled him and he'll destroy tradition, ruin the Big House.' She paused, holding her eyes on Mohini. 'And here you come in, my sister.'

'I?'

'You, Mohini. You'll have to be patient with the Big House. Mother is old-world, exacting, but do not fail to see her point of view — and her heart. Jayadev is unutterably lonely, idealists always are. He will need all your compassion. And you, Mohini, you'll be lonely too. A house with some twenty rooms, a dozen servants. But I don't mean *that.* Lonely *within.*' Rooplekha stressed her meaning with her voice and a pause. 'Heart-breaking business, to be the wife of a philosopher and writer! I see all that, being a woman. You know —' She stopped, uncertain, as though with some cloud in her mind, then she continued: 'Yes, except for Mother's persistence, which grew fiercer as the days passed, Jayadev wouldn't have married.'

Mohini smiled a bit. Lingering in her was the richness of the night past. Lonely? With him, lonely?

'Do not worry. *Didi,*' answered Mohini, wistful. 'The Big House will be happy.'

Then a name flashed through her mind, an unknown shadow, Sudha. Sudha who had kept away from the house, though expected. Sudha who was called Saturn's Eyesore. Who was Sudha? Rooplekha *Didi* might tell her.

Rooplekha caressed Mohini's cheeks. 'Truly you are a priceless jewel. You will work wonders, I know.'

The eager girl had no intuition that often, in her impatient moods, as time went by, she would have to look back for strength to this revealing talk.

~

Yes there was Sudha whom the village cruelly called Saturn's Eyesore. Eventually, Mohini pieced together Sudha's curious story.

It was Sudha's old great-uncle who first earned the nickname, a simple, honest, pious man, free from self seeking, the very soul of gentleness. Whenever a house was festive, he would be out in the fields gathering the auspicious *kusa* grass. When there was a death, he was among the stretcher bearers. When a man fell ill, he sat by the sickbed, night and day. Strange that he, of all men, should have the clean stretch of his days marred by the wrath of Saturn!

Yet he would never have known the wrath of this baleful planet save for his chance decision years ago to learn the ways of the stars. Fate took him to the great fair at Haripura, made him pause at a bookstall and guided his eyes to a pamphlet called *Smile of the Cosmos.* He learned how to cast a horoscope, how to find an auspicious hour, a hundred other things. He learned how the planets affect and shape the lives of men, how they work out good and evil, and then, with a shock of horror, he saw the vile shadow of Saturn approaching the stellar line of his own being, approaching slowly, inexorably. No power could save him. He was doomed.

What wonder that, soon after, his best milch cow should die of snakebite? That an insect pest should appear in his potato patch and eat up the young roots? That, one dark night, he should trip against a bulging root and sprain his ankle?

'There! There! Does not my reading say the wrath of Saturn will blaze upon me this year and the years to come?'

He ceased to expect any good from life. What chance had he against the heavy malice of so mighty a planet? When friends approached him with business proposals, he gave a sad smile and shook his head. 'No use. Just look at my horoscope.' He sat often with a piece of chalk, stretching diagrams on the floor, locating the position of Saturn at the moment. The shadow was right astride his life. No escape! A fly in a spider-web would not be more helpless. While it saddened him, it flattered him perversely that so great a planet had fixed its evil eye on a poor country man. What could have caused this selection? He spoke his thoughts to everyone, and people, laughing, nick-named him Saturn's Eyesore.

Then, one day, news came that his only nephew, a young lawyer in the nearest town, had died of a sudden attack of malignant malaria. Within the next three days the young man's wife followed him. A child of six or seven was left. 'There! There!' said the old man. He was not shocked, even if his heart was broken. He was indeed expecting some disaster or other. He went downtown and fetched the orphan girl, Sudha, to his lone house; he had long been a widower, and his life became centred on her. His old weary bones became her shield of protection. The years passed and Sudha grew up, a comely maiden.

Never had the old man wronged anybody, so Saturn, the dour spinner of the evil web, decided that his wretched victim should do harm to the one person who was the honey of his soul. Sudha, at fifteen, was about to be given to a young handsome groom in the jute-business. On the day of *asirvad* the old man said to himself, 'Why don't I find out how the planets stand in relation to my Sudha's life-thread? Why not make sure that the professional horoscope-caster, with one eye on his work and the other on his fee, has not missed something?' So he, amateur astrologer, put on his steel spectacles and squatted on the floor, casting up figures, making diagrams. Suddenly, he started to tremble as if he had caught malaria. 'There's no mistaking the dread shadow. Poor Sudha! Luckily, it is receding. Saturn is about to whirl away from her life.'

The old man held his head between his hands and finally made up his mind. The marriage must not take place now. Better wait a few months. So, out of love, he acted boldly. The bridegroom's party had arrived for the *asirvad* ceremony.

The old man spoke to the good people: 'Brothers, my Sudha is unfit to wed at present. She is under the watch of Saturn's evil eye. Wait a while. Wait till Saturn goes his way.'

There was an uproar and the party left in haste. The invited village elders were in a rage. Sudha was in tears. But the old man was happy. He had saved her.

That was how it happened that Sudha also earned the nickname of Saturn's Eyesore. Sudha, too, became a creature of the darkest ill omen. No one would marry her. The years passed. Sudha came into full bloom. Saturn had long moved away, and this the good man proclaimed every day, everywhere, but Sudha remained Saturn's Eyesore, doomed to heartbreak for no fault of her own. The old man now did his best to teach her patient submission to her evil fate, as he himself had learned to accept his, but sometimes, so it was said, the wind, blowing across the house at dead of night, carried with it a curious sound as of bitter sobbing.

The story had a sequel, but Mohini could never get the details. The girls, Meera, Veena, Maloti, none would tell her. Perhaps they, too, did not know.

Sudha, alone and neglected, slipped into a chance friendship with a youth from the neighbouring village, Sonarpur, a mere blacksmith. In the dark hours they were seen together in the cool shadows of mango groves or the quiet seclusion of bamboo-screened pools. Tongues wagged. The lynx-eyed village elders watched. She, a Brahmin maid! Nothing like this had happened in Behula, ever — the elders stretched back their memories — the village had been stainless. True, there had been a case of abortion, but the woman was a peasant. But this Sudha, a high-caste girl! A curse lay on her head; must she smear society with its blackness? And a deputation of the wrathful elders stepped to the Big House and saw the mother.

The mother gave her decision and it was a command. No slander was to be cast upon the girl, not one scornful word. And the mother herself would take charge of her. She would lift Sudha to higher ideals and help her out of the mud of futility which had been her doom. This was the only way. The mother, no mean scholar herself, having been taught by her husband, would make the luckless girl strive after knowledge, and knowledge would be like a sponge: it would absorb the smothered feelings, the wakened unfulfilled passions of her womanhood.

Strangely, it seemed to work. Sudha became a constant visitor at the Big House, almost a part of it. No one heard any more of her blacksmith friend. But the real wonder was the sharpness of her mind and her rapid progress. Yes, the mother had rescued a soul from deathlike defilement and given it a splendour of its own.

~

Countryfolk were no fools, decided Heeralal. They were eager about city wonders. Radio, airplane, elevators, ships on the river — Heeralal described them all with dramatic colour. He told, too, of a mansion where dead beasts of queer shapes lay stuffed, looking as though fierce with life, of miles of park in which living animals, some of them very strange, were housed in comfort. Heeralal spoke of tiger and lion as of ship and airplane with a proud proprietary air.

The fellows were humbled, goggling with open mouths. Heeralal rose to heroic heights.

But the village, too, had its glories. The smithy was one. Heeralal was thrilled by the heavy-browed man lathered with sweat, handling lumps of flaming metal with ease. And Heeralal held his breath as a peasant lad climbed to the bushy top of a palm tree, a tall finger of a tree smooth as an egg, and lo! The fearless lad slid down the great height with a pitcher of palm juice slung to his back. He watched the country fellows, his new friends, trick crows into snares, fasten a loop of red thread to their necks and set them free. The boys had sworn to give every crow in the village Behula a red neck-string!

Then Heeralal, humbled in his turn, spoke of fifty-storied skyscrapers, underground railway, submarine, X-ray, television — all the wonders of which he had heard or read, and was cheered by the dazed look of his listeners. His excited talk flowed on to the famous scientist who was darting moonward at this very moment (Heeralal almost believed he was telling the truth) in a sealed rocket fired from the throat of an enormous gun — on a mission of discovery, like Columbus.

The village tour was nearly over when one of Heeralal's companions rushed away and seized a goat nibbling succulent green bits from a cactus hedge. A white mother goat with milk-heavy udders. Heeralal, amazed, saw the fellow crouch and set his mouth to the teat and suck like an animal!

'Come, hurry!' he invited Heeralal.

'Goat's milk!' Heeralal was scornful. But he, too, crouched and was delighted with the feel of warm, sweet milk in his tongue. There was no such fun in the city. He must tell *Didi. Didi* would have enjoyed the sight. How she would have laughed.

'Go for a swim?' a boy suggested. There was a pond close by, cool, green with mirrored thickets.

The boys slid into the water. Heeralal stood on the steps, watching. Countryfolk swam like fish. In a while the boys came sweeping back.

'Throw yourself in,' they urged.

Heeralal took off his shoes, dipped his toes in the pond, and his heart sank. He went one step down and stood scratching his neck with a pebble.

'Hop in,' yelled the boys, legs and arms threshing with impatience. 'Race us. Can you cross the whole length and back?'

'Can you touch the bottom where it's deepest, five man height?'

'Can you hold your breath underwater a good long while?'

'I... I...' stammered Heeralal. His eyes, polished pebbles, stared, at the shimmering pool.

'I... I... can't swim,' Heeralal stuttered at last.

There was a dazed silence. Heeralal fidgeted from one foot to the other, awaiting a cruel burst of laughter.

'What's there to swimming?' said a placid voice. 'So easy. You pick it up in no time.'

'We'll teach you,' others cried. 'In an hour you'll move around like fish.'

Heeralal felt a choke in his throat. City boys would have laughed at him; country fellows — so good, so friendly.

Later, as he splashed around, eager hands propping him up, he was cheered by the thought: '*Didi* will have great fun in Behula village.'

twelve

'THIS BEDSTEAD,' said the Mother, 'has known honey and bitter: birth, growth, married life, age, disease, death, festive gayness, tears. My son's grandmother brought this bedstead as part of her marriage portion. On this her Flower-bed, her seven children were born. Here died my son's grandfather. Grandmother, too. This was my Flower-bed and here I had my four children, the first-born son and the next girl who died as babes. This bed is now yours, daughter. When you lie in it, do not forget its history, its sanctity.'

Mohini listened and was a little chilled. So many had died on the bed! What need had the mother to tell her? It was enormous, shoulder-high, its mattresses a cubit deep, brass rails on three sides and engravings all over, supported by elephantine legs adorned by mosquito poles thick as an arm. The bed could not have been repainted and polished this last half-hundred years. Like the Big House, it was absorbing time. Why make it morbid with a black coverlet of history?

Yet this room which she shared with her husband, had beauty and splendour: large and high-ceilinged; the floor was mosaic, a pattern of great blossoming lotuses, some white, some blue, with green moons of leaves afloat in a clear sun-bright pool somewhat muddied by time. The tall lime-coloured walls were smooth as satin, painted at intervals with murals, scenes from the Hindi epics. The enormous, faintly curved ceiling was light blue with decorations in pale gold. A rich and lovely room, but you could not be intimate with it, for you felt strangely as though it did not belong to you. *You* belonged to the room!

'Hindu children are not usually born on a bedstead,' the mother went on. 'Custom — in this village anyhow — forbids it. Our people in Behula may think I am oddly modern! Yet who was I to depart from the tradition of our own house, even if it is different from general practice? No woman under this roof has lain in labour on a floormat. A golden bed, if we had one, would not be worthy of the coming gift of the gods.'

Mohini caught her meaning, reddened and hung her head. The mother, her face softened with a tender light, smiled and turned. She went to an old-fashioned iron safe recessed in the wall under a pretty painted image of the Lakshmi goddess. She fitted in the keys and pulled the door open, saying, 'My trusteeship is ended. From today you, daughter mine, shall take care of this age-old smile of the goddess of fortune. Keep it sacred and secret.' Her clear ringing voice held a deep caress.

Mohini stared, her eyes filled with wonder. A mass of jewellery in strange antique designs. What an impression they'd make in the city where old patterns were the newest mode! Large gold sovereigns with curious markings. Columns of silver rupees. Seldom had Mohini seen more than five rupees at a time, her monthly allowance from father, and here was a big pile, hundreds, thousands. All this was hers, all!

The mother, perhaps, read her thoughts.

'These are remnants of what the safe held five or six years back, before the famine swept over Bengal. We had to sell off many precious jewels and some two hundred sovereigns dating back to the Mughal days, so that we could feed the starving people.

Mohini looked at the mother with surprise. The famine was still real in her memory. She had been twelve then and the horrid scenes of misery and death, the hunger cry of the destitute people who came flocking into the city, would live in her mind, forever. What joy to know that the master of Behula was apart altogether from many others of his class who, it was no secret, had reaped a rich harvest out of mass misery by selling hoarded grain at fancy rates. Her husband, with the full support of his mother, had depleted even his ancestral treasures and heirlooms to feed the hungry. Mohini gave the mother a deep look of tenderness and respect.

The mother was unrolling a thick roll of greyish white parchment made from the smooth bark of the *bhurja* tree, which in the old days had served as paper.

'My son's genealogy,' she explained solemnly. 'The last seventeen generations. The record of a thousand years.'

Mohini, with bated breath, watched the yards of family tree unroll; the long narrow strips fastened together — the crumbled parts had been renewed with fresh parchment — could stretch across half the room's length. Mohini remembered that she had no family tree of her own, she could not trace back her lineage beyond her great-grandfather. She felt humbled, yet exalted — were not her husband's people truly her own? Was not the family name hers as much as his? Since her marriage she, too, had for her background vivid centuries of history.

It was essentially the history of the inward life. Thunderous invasions had shaken Bengal — Pathan, Mughal, Mahratta, British — and even though the thousand echoes of struggle and change had washed on to this remote village, its ancient Aryan culture safe in the trust of stern-living Brahmins had remained basically unaffected. Unstained as ever were the old values of meditation, self-discipline, faith, charity, renunciation, truthfulness — not as lip ideals but as essential aids to life, in an unshakable pattern of conduct.

Mohini worried for hours where to keep the three long keys of the safe. She walked loaded with responsibility, as though bearing the secret of hundreds of years. The three keys, too, as she fumbled with them, opened the locks to the mother's mind, and she could peer into its depths. She saw why the mother was apparently so hard to please, so stern and exacting. That was her way to make her son's bride grow into duty, discipline, grow into the structure of family tradition. With this one gesture she had taken the city stranger into her trust, given her all the responsibility, made her the real mistress of the Big House.

She had stripped the city stranger of her strangeness and filled her with a proud, passionate faith. Mohini understood. For all time to come she was pledged to a trusteeship of that formula of faith: the family tradition.

After sundown, she carried three little earthen saucer lamps to the holy plant, *tulsi,* in the inner courtyard, the way the mother had taught her, and lit the wicks devoutly, as though she had worshipped in this way all her life. She knelt and spoke a prayer, palms joined at her breast:

'Give us thy blessing, mother of the gods, let all be well.'

The frail plant with its brown, sweet-scented leaves was a mere emblem, she knew, vested with a mystic value, as a picture was or a pebble, moving the mind toward self-suggestion, so that the inner eye should strip the veil of appearances and look beyond.

Soon, the village was blowing conches to the goddess of dusk. This village or some other, more ancient, had greeted the goddess at this same hour perhaps the past two hundred years. Mohini hurried to blow her conch three long blasts. She picked up an earthen lamp, reentered the house and swung the light round to startle out the first darkness.

A round of evening duty was done. Now she could sit awhile in the twilight on the balcony and play the soft-stringed *dilruba* she had brought with her and sing in a hushed tone — a newely-wed girl, so she had learnt, must not lift her voice — until the going in the *puja* room sounded.

'Servants galore in the house of wealth, yet the Little Mother has to stir the cooking-pans,' Bindu's mother complained to Mohini, 'and she hates the sight and smell of a kitchen.'

Mohini gave her a long look and with a mocking joy said:

'You don't understand. The mistress of the kitchen is the mistress of the whole household. And how eagerly mother teaches me. How I love to learn from her — haven't you noticed?'

She remembered, without guilt, Old Mother's wasted efforts to give her lessons in cookery. Here, in the Big House, she had quickly outgrown her aversion to it.

'No fish for the Little Mother in this land of fish! And this the season for roes, the bellies of fish thick and white with roes!'

The cook-woman paused and slapped at a mosquito feeding on her neck.

'Eggs — even eggs must not come to this house. What need had the elders to banish their heart's treasure to this jungle? One bright half of a single moon I am here, and I pant to be gone. So tiresome!'

'Tiresome!' Mohini almost echoed the cry out of her desolation, but she caught herself in time and was up in arms against the woman.

'Have you talked your fill? A kettle-drum sounds best when it's hushed! Back home, if you scatter your pearls of speech....' There was no need to continue; a sharp glance was enough.

Bindu's mother held her sari to her eyes, and Mohini stiffened instantly. Why blame her for telling the truth? She knew Mohini's tastes! But then, happiness surely was not a matter of food! A proud smile crossed her lips. As though she couldn't give up fish, and meat, and eggs for her husband! Let Rooplekha come and see her.

'The Big House had been vegetarian for centuries,' she spoke gently, laughingly. 'You can't break an old tradition as if it were an egg shell!'

The gong. Prayer time, Mohini jumped to her feet. Her husband would sit by the holy sandals in the *puja* room, legs crossed in the lotus posture, hymning in his calm, deep voice, swinging a five-faced gold candelabrum with five pointed flames, while the mother beat rhythmically on a small gong. Mohini must step in, seat herself on the marble floor — the smell of incense would fill her nostrils — and wave a gold-mounted yak's tail fan in reverence. The worship over, her husband would hold out the five-faced lamp for them, so that they might feel the warmth of the consecrated flames. He would sprinkle them with sacred Ganga water and murmur:

'Om shanti, om shanti, om shanti!' (Let peace, and peace, and peace be everywhere.)

'Another trouble!' Bindu's mother whined again. 'Is this the time of life to ring the bells of worship, Little Mother? You are young. You should eat, and sing, and laugh. The *puja* is for the old ones who must earn merit enough to pay their passage to Heavenland. Time enough for you ahead.'

Mohini, forgetting her new dignity, stuck out her tongue at the woman.

'You never speak the name of a god or goddess; you've no rosary to tell the beads; merrily will you go to the crocodile pit in hell. Do not expect me to keep you company in that lovely place!'

But the woman was unquenched, not because she was an unbeliever, but because a picture came to her mind. Far away on the seashore, in the great white temple of Jagannath, endless flagged steps and courtyards had insets of marble. Each inset was engraved with name, which was blessed by the dust of the bare feet of the hordes of devotees who walked over them day and night. On one inset slab was the name of Bindu's mother. A year's wages had gone into erecting this monument, but the money was invested well. Some day, sooner or later, a great yogi who had reached the Nirvana state would tread upon her name and out of the momentary contact her soul would be saved forever.

'Eat and sing and laugh,' crowed the irrepressible woman, a twist of self-satisfaction on the plump face. 'No need, until you become a grandmother, to worry the kind gods with beads and bells.'

~

Jayadev called her Maitreyi. Maitreyi, who lived three thousand years ago, Maitreyi the wife and inspiration of Yagnavalkya, the greatest thinker of his age, who had strained for immortality.

Mohini was perplexed. Mohini was worried. She, ignorant one, with a mere smatter of knowledge, was unpretentious. She had no ambitions to be Maitreyi. She hated serious study for which she had no patience. She needed life, feeling. She was not curious about East-West culture patterns. No one, by temperament, could be less like Maitreyi.

But Jayadev, who had no knowledge of the soul of a woman, nourished his odd illusion, and sought in his wife a source of inspiration. Maitreyi must have helped her husband more with her intuitive realisation than with her knowledge. So could his Maitreyi.

Modern-minded, she would nevertheless grasp the essence of ancient thought and attune herself to its rhythm. Then, she would illumine her husband's way towards his goal.

True, her ignorance had at first startled him. He had felt depressed. Then he had reflected that Maitreyi herself was in no small measure Yagnavalkya's own creation. And he decided eagerly to teach Mohini. What if she must begin at the beginning? He began by giving her lessons in Sanskrit.

But to Mohini they were tiresome! She closed the book with a snap. How dark was night in the village! The blackness had substance and shape and the throb of life — it touched you, seeped into your body and your spirit. Jackals hooted near the outer wall of the house. (Fear chilled her, she could hardly breathe when she first heard their weird cry.) Sooty trees sighed in the wind, lone melancholy ghosts. There had been rain in the daytime, so the bull-frogs now crept out of their holes, croaking throatily. Mohini tossed her book to the floor — if only she'd never have to touch it again! She amused herself for a time mimicking the frogs, grrrr!

Heeralal would soon be back — he was having a great time with the village boys — and it would be good to hear his excited talk. Tomorrow he, too, would be gone with Bindu's mother. Then the frog-haunted evenings would drag more heavily still.

She picked up her *dilruba,* playing, singing in a low voice, but her loneliness was hard to bear (Rooplekha was right!). She longed for her husband who was in an outer room called the pavilion of study. Once or twice she had stepped into that large circular room walled with books, a many-pillared verandah around it, hidden among flowering shrubs. She longed, too, for father and for Old Mother. Tears started up, moistening her eyelashes.

And so she sat with her *dilruba,* waiting, feeling imprisoned. This life was too different from her mind-picture of it, and so it was even harder to bear.

But she had her husband. For his sake she would absorb new ways of thought and habit, cultivate new interests. She set her mouth: life was a serious business, and she was no doll in silk and satin. She was the mistress of the Big House, a position higher than any other woman's in Behula village. She had duties to discharge, responsibilities. How could she let herself be defeated by discomfort and desolation?

It was supper time at last. She would serve her husband under the mother's guidance. Later, the two women would eat together, eat vegetable fare. Jayadev, to whom eating was only a necessity, not a pleasure, would never see her distaste for such fare, never know the measure of her denial. His imagination would not work that way. Did he see any of her denials? Or did he simply take them for granted?

Supper over, Jayadev would step into the room of the four-poster, sit at a desk in the corner, and read again. For years past he had read till late at night. Reading? He was waiting, longing, watching the door, listening for a familiar step. It was so unlike himself! Yes, Jayadev had lost that centred, rapt, disciplined way of life. Even in the *puja* room, while his lips spoke the holy words and his hand made circular sweeps with the lamp, his thoughts were too often on her as she sat waving a fan made of bushy yak's tail. He saw the slim daintiness of a bangled wrist, the shape, the delicacy of tight-closed fingers. The grace of her as she bowed her head to the floor, the rhythm of her. Jayadev would have loved to sit still, to watch her in the attitude of worship. His heart warmed to the image of his Maitreyi as she worshipped his gods. It was, he thought, a measure of their spiritual union.

Tonight, however, he went out after supper though his marriage was only a week old. He returned home late walked into his room on silent feet lest Mohini be awakened from sleep, and then stood still. Mohini was not in bed. She was by the window, leaning over the sill, her unbound hair down to her hips, her bare shoulder and neck caught in the strong moonlight. She was singing quietly:

What my heart longs for, and longs for,
    Thou are that! Friend, thou are that!
Naught else have I in this world. Naught.
    If thou hast no happiness in me,
Go, seek it, seek.
    I have thee within my heart, true, unfading,
Naught else I need.

In thine image I shall ever live,
Days... nights... months... years...
Lost in memory of thee,
If thou lovest another, if thou returnest never,
Find, find, what thing heart seeks.
Let all misery be mine.*

Jayadev, deeply moved, tiptoed close, listening intently. The soft melancholy of the words filled him with a troubled tenderness. He edged closer until he could stoop, press his lips to her hair and to the nape of her neck, and her shoulder. He drank in the fragrance of her, the warmth, the sweet youthfulness.

She gave a startled gasp. When he lifted his face, she looked at him with bright eyes and, in a strange way, laughed.

'You frightened me!'

'The beauty in your voice! The wonderous gift you have!' He was gazing at her in fascinated pleasure. 'Mohini, you never told me.'

She was pleased by his eager compliment, but her heart saddened. She could not sing freely, at her best, her voice lifted to the right pitch, because it would be unbecoming, she had learned. A lovely night, so cool, so tranquil, enfolded Behula village, and it lured them to wander in its eyeless dark together, to sit on the steps of Rook's Eye, ankles dipped in the water and sing, sing till the cricket with its dull *jhinns* was shamed into silence. Decorum — odd and rocklike — false decorum blocked their road to fulfilment.

'A bride like you has never come to this house, we have so little to offer,' he said and his voice shook a little. Even he, unobservant as he was, sensed her secret pain. 'I am worried lest you be impatient with our faults, lest you be unhappy.'

'Oh, no!' Mohini murmured, grateful for his concern. 'The mother has put everything in my trust. How proud I feel! What more could I ask?'

'Not lonely, Mohini?' He took her hands. He read her face.

* Translated from Rabindranath Tagore.

'Lonely!' Her lips curled, and she scoffed at the idea. 'I've become an important person! So much to do, so many responsibilities. Only idle minds have time to feel lonely. Too much of a luxury.'

So she deceived him with her wishful thinking. And he naively believed her and was soothed. The true happiness of a woman, he told himself with a smile, was to be mistress of her own household. Give a woman bright playthings — the money to spend, the kitchen to run, the power and prestige. There lay the material to make her content. Yes, men and women were altogether different.

This marriage had been a gamble, the odds heavy against him — the city girl might pine for the accustomed pleasures her new life denied her. But Mohini was not made that way. She was adaptable. She had depth. Oh, the relief. His heart went to her, eager, in tenderness and pride, and praise.

A jackal barked at the gates of the house. Mohini shivered and clutched her husband's arm. He held her close, and under the hard pressure of his lips, her lips opened to him and her head bent back.

'The wonder of you!' he whispered, his face rapt, as hand-in-hand they walked to the four-poster bed. 'What have I done to deserve this bliss?' He paused, and added with a faraway look, 'The ancestors whose names make our great family tree will all give the new mistress of the Big House their benediction.'

The family tree. The Big House. Even in their intimate moments he thought of them, which oppressed her and hindered her pleasure in him.

Presently Jayadev slept. Mohini lay thinking.

This house lived always in the shadow of the family tree; nothing mattered so much as the family tree. The tall, gilt-framed portraits of ancestors that seemed to hang on every wall had a rich vivid life beyond canvas and paint. An old, proud house of an old, proud family. A tradition within a tradition. And here she was sprung out of shallow soil, forced by circumstance to be mistress of the ancient house and trustee of an alien tradition. The struggle to retouch her mental values, readjust her expectations, hurt fiercely.

And why must she surrender completely? Why must she bury her dreams? Love alone could make her pain worthwhile. Did he, her husband, love her truly? And she touched his arm and lay listening to his low, even breathing as though awaiting an answer.

Later, as she slept, she saw the spirit of her husband's ancestors come crowding to the four-poster — men and women of all centuries, their faces ageless, their costumes varying and strange. When she sat up in chill terror they, one by one, touched her head with a trayload of grains, her hands with a pot of fresh-cooked rice and her ears with honey. They swung before her lighted lamps of clay and cried in one voice: 'Receive us, daughter, in thine head, and heart, and breast, and womb, receive us in the eight auspicious emblems in thee, receive us in all thy body, from crown of thy head to the rim of thy toe-nail.' They were gentle and stern, kind and relentless, these ancestors, and their touch on her skin was cold with age yet burning with some passionate faith. For one dazzled moment she was unafraid and ready to receive them in her head, and heart, and breast, and womb. Then, suddenly something seemed to snap in her. Rebellion clutched her, and she sprang out of bed on an impulse. She snatched the family tree from the iron chest and tore it to pieces. Instantly the ancestors dissolved in the night, shadow into shadow!

She woke up, perspiring, and lay tense awhile, the dream vivid in her mind. Then she snuggled up to her husband and pressed her damp face on his shoulder. Strange dream, she thought, quietened by touching him. As though there's a rebel in me. Is that not its deep meaning? As though I hate to give myself to the Big House. But I must. This life is my own free choice. There's no other way.

Her arm went round Jayadev. Her face lay on his body, burrowing, finding repose. She drew a long breath, content. He was stirring a little.

You are all I need for my happiness, my husband.

Heeralal was leaving.

'Names. *Didi?* How will you collect them? There are no English papers here that are any good. Don't worry.' There was a huskiness in his tone as he spoke. 'I'll send you half the funny names I get every month.'

'Sweet boy!' Her eyes half smiled through her tears. 'I have a surprise for you. Look.' She lifted the lid of his steel trunk and showed him a familiar notebook — her own collection of names. 'Yours,' she said. 'The little blue book will remind you of *Didi* when you're about to forget her.'

Heeralal's eyes gleamed with pleasure as he watched her replace the book in his trunk. Then shame hit him.

'Oh, no, keep your book, *Didi.* How absurd!'

'Listen. Let the book be in your safekeeping. Enter names on its pages as if you were giving them to me. See?'

How could she tell him that his *Didi* was no longer the light-hearted girl he'd always known?

Heeralal was thoughtful. 'I have an idea.' He opened the trunk and picked up his electric torch. 'Take this. You are afraid of the dark.' Heeralal looked at his precious possession, a dry feeling in his nose.

Mohini accepted the gift after a little more pressing. Time was up. Ganesh, the cartman, discreetly coughed at the doorway to announce his presence. Heeralal would travel in his cart with the master, who would escort the boy to the railway station and put him on the train to Calcutta. Bindu's mother was to have a cart all to herself.

Heeralal had bowed to the mother and received her blessing. Now, the first time in his life, he bent to touch his head to his sister's feet.

'No!' Mohini drew him into her arms. '*Bhai*, see that Old Mother writes to me every week without fail, else I'll be miserable.'

'I'll get her the stamped covers and write out the address for her,' he said reassuringly. 'Why, I'll post the letters by air mail.'

'Air mail to Behula?' Mohini smiled, gazing at him, the back of her throat aching. 'Listen. Don't get down and run wild on station platforms when the train stops. I'll have no peace of mind until I hear of your safe arrival.' Her voice trailed off on a shrill note and she sniffled.

He, too, sniffled. '*Didi,* I told Jayadev *Dada* about your night fear of crocodiles. He listened with interest. He'll be very watchful, he said.'

'Tell father his Mohini has everything she needs and she couldn't be happier. And tell him, *Bhai,* to send me by post some 3-ply white wool, a half-pound. I'll knit a new sweater for his next birthday.'

Tears long unshed spilled out of her eyes. Heeralal's face worked, he thrust a knuckle into his mouth, turned and fled.

thirteen

'FRESH BLOWN LOTUSES die of shame! Even I, a woman and an old one, find myself gaping with wonder at such beauty. The very image of the young goddess, Uma, when she waked Siva out of a trance of meditation!'

So spoke the barber woman some months before Mohini's arrival in Behula village. She squatted on her haunches, holding in her lap the outstretched white leg of a girl whose red-bordered sari was tucked up to the knee. She rubbed the shapely foot with a bit of pumice stone to remove a stiff corn.

'Fit, indeed, to be a princess,' she went on without flattery.

She thought to herself: 'Some good fairy has given this girl beauty beyond measure, and some bad one has hit her with an unspeakable curse. The waste!'

The barber woman was an age-old functionary of the village. She pared women's nails and removed their corns. She added grace to young feet by painting the sides and the toes with red lac dye. She rubbed the gouty limbs of old women with homemade herbal oils. With free access into every household she saw all, and heard all. She was repository of all village gossip, and, like her husband, the barber, she carried the news of comely maids and handsome grooms. Together, like others of their tribe in the thousand years past, they had a monopoly; they were the undisputed brokers of the local marriage market.

The sight of Sudha always hurt the barber woman's pride. She could find no groom for the one maiden fit to be a king's daughter. One by one the other maidens of Behula were wed: snub-nosed and squint-eyed, pitchdark and with protruding teeth. Even Jamuna, who had limped badly after a fall from the top branch of a mango tree in her childhood, was married. But for Sudha's exquisite beauty there was no use. It was as though she had some horrid black stain on her face, her body and her spirit, as though she were a freak.

The barber woman dealt in people and knew the bypaths of the human mind. It was no wonder, therefore, that she had more sense than other village folk, more understanding.

Sudha listened to the strange compliment with a musing smile. This barber woman and the mother of the Big House were the only people with whom she ever felt at ease. There never had been any intimacy between her and the girls of her age, for she held herself aloof, enclosed in a hard shell of her own making. Sudha was oversensitive because of her fate and had nursed a feeling that the village girls scorned her, shunned her as something abnormal. She, in return, fiercely scorned all of them. Absorbed in herself, she grew fast, shorn of all tenderness — her early love for her adoring grandfather, who was responsible for her tragic fate, soured. She grew lopsidedly, scornful of human values, asocial, frigid yet darkly passionate. It was a growth in darkness, not in light, in the cramping space of a cold cell, in emotional bondage.

Now, her rose bud mouth opened with pleasure and showed the neat pearl tips of her teeth.

'What news?' she asked, for the barber woman must hand out gossip as part of her service.

'Man of full seventy!' said the barber woman while she removed the last of a corn. 'Crazy to marry — crazy. His third wife dead barely two months, she who was like Lakshmi Devi.'

'The money-lender?'

'Who else? And he has set his age-stiff heart on our Paru. You know how it is with Paru's father — neck-deep in debt to the money-lender, his three fields tied up in strong chains. The old man will release him for one price: our Paru's hand, her marriage flower.'

'Give and take,' said Sudha, impassive. 'The money-lender sits on a mountain of riches. How long can the old bones last? Paru has a bright future.' Sudha's grey-green eyes set wide in round white face had a quality of hardness. The barber woman ignored the cynical talk.

'A strange thing has happened,' the barber woman went on. 'The village lads, the ones called "ruffians", won't permit this union. They say they will kidnap the money-lender on the marriage day and hold him and duck him in a pond till he's swallowed a bellyful of water and forgotten his father's name!' The barber woman paused a moment, dropped the girl's feet with a quick move and reached for her right hand. 'The nails need paring. Yes, that's what the ruffians threatened, and the money-lender heard it and in hot panic rushed to the Big House and claimed the young master's protection.'

'What then?' the girl asked with quick interest.

The barber woman was silent, her eyes peering over the hand she held in her own, suddenly absorbed.

'Strange!' she cried in violent surprise, leaning forward.

'What did he say?' the girl demanded. 'He promised help?'

'The wonder!' the woman drew her brows together in an intent scowl, the case of her large brown palm holding the small and delicate hand of the girl. 'Surely that looks like a "wheel" —'

Sudha withdrew her hand with an impatient snap.

'Tell me. He promised help?'

'Show me, please.' The plump silver-decked arm reached out quickly and recaptured the girl's hand. 'Help? No. The young master refused to interfere. Why, he even seemed pleased with the hot-blooded rascals! He seemed to be laughing at the old man. The village elders have received a shock and go about with bowed heads.' She paused and then went on: 'Wheel, for sure, and conch and — oh, goddess, is that not a palanquin?'

'What do they matter?' Sudha was scornful. 'Wheel, conch, palanquin! Why talk?'

'Still other luck signs!' cried the barber woman, fascinated. 'Lotus, elephant. Oh, goddess!' Her face was excited. 'Many a time I have held this hand, and I never before saw them —'

'You wouldn't look for luck signs in the hands of the most luckless person on earth,' the girl said coldly.

'What superb irony to have them!' She stared in wonder at the criss-cross of lines in the pink whiteness of her palm. 'They don't mean a thing — conch, wheel, lotus, palanquin.' The soft lines of her mouth tightened with disdain.

The barber woman thought for a moment, then, she gazed in a curious way at Sudha. Her voice was a loud whisper, as if she were telling a secret. 'Surely you have heard? You are in the Big House often enough —'

'What now?' said the girl and she held her breath.

'The mother seeks a bride for her son who's at last willing to marry. She wants a girl with all the eight luck signs. Hard to find.'

There was a long moment of incomprehension, and then a vivid flush mounted to the girl's face, suffusing it from neck to ears. She did not speak. Instead, she forced a broken laugh.

'You too make fun of me? You are just like the rest?' She bit her lip fiercely.

'Listen. The other three signs are not easy to read. They're revealed only to expert eyes. No one in Behula knows them truly except the mother, for she herself bears them all. Sudha, girl, why not let the mother see your hand? Perhaps it will come to nothing. And, perhaps —'

Sudha trembled. The barber woman gave her a kindly look.

'Why not come with me? I have business in the Big House. We'll walk up together.'

'Yes, yes,' Sudha murmured in a daze. Suddenly she reached out and grabbed the barber woman's hand in a sort of terror. Her mouth opened, but she did not speak. In silence she rose to her feet.

They walked along a winding pathway through the fields. The sky blazed with light. Wind hissed in bamboo groves. Sudha walked in a trance, and the barber woman spoke no word. She knew the girl's feelings. Imagine, a maid with the rare luck signs, here at our own doorstep! And she, Saturn's Eyesore! The wonder of it! Wheel, conch, lotus, elephant, palanquin — oh, goddess!

Sudha saw a vision. Out of the dust of a hundred despairs rose the new mistress of the Big House. She, the most luckless one on earth, spurned, trampled on, holds the very life of the village in her grip! The young master who haunted the virginal dreams of all fair maids of marriage age — her husband, her own! A light shone in her eyes as she followed the lines on her right palm once in a while. She could not find the luck signs, but their names ran through her mind — wheel, and elephant, and lotus, and conch.

The mother had just risen from her noonday nap. The barber woman called out at her bedroom door and stepped in at her bidding. Sudha, with sudden shyness stayed in the corridor. She could not stand up because of her heart's hurried throbbing, so she sat on the white marble floor, her slim white arms wrapped around her drawn-up knees. The splendours of the Big House hung bright in the vision — the riches, but above all the authority, the power over people. The mistress of Behula village, a goddess of destiny, to be loved or hated, adored or feared, but never scorned. Sudha tensed. Her breath quickened. She lifted her hand, damp with sweat, and scanned the lines in her hand in a dazed way.

'Come, then,' said the barber woman.

There was cold unbelief in the mother's face as she took the girl's hand, but her listless look changed swiftly.

'You see them?' said the barber woman, noticing the new expression.

The mother nodded. 'Yes.'

Then her large, calm eyes grew troubled. She raided her glance to the girl's face, a face ashen and full of suffering.

'Tell me, Mother.'

Sudha's voice was a dead whisper, as though something hard had swelled up in her throat. As she looked it was as though the mother had a glimpse of Sudha's soul.

The mother thought rapidly. Sudha and Jayadev. The prospect of their union was a sudden blow that took away the mother's breath. No, it was impossible. Somewhere behind this girl the shadow of a lover lay. Untrue? Even so, no maid touched by such a stigma, false though it was, could be mistress of Big House. Never.

The mother made a swift decision, but pity stirred in her. She would not hurt the luckless Sudha any more than could be helped.

'Not all the luck signs,' said the mother, with a veiled expression, her voice level. 'One is wanting, just one.' She felt wretched because of her lie and lowered her face in heavy shame.

For a moment Sudha sat stunned her eyes flickerless, dead. Then her body began to shake like a leaf, her face to work like a child's and she lay on the floor sobbing bitterly, hysterically. The mother, watching this picture of misery, felt her eyelids sting. A woman could not grieve more for a lost husband or child. Poor girl! Sudha with all the luck signs in her palm could not be mistress of the Big House — ever.

The days passed. Jayadev married a city girl. And this story Mohini soon knew, for the barber woman talked. The days passed. Sudha sank into herself, more, more. There was no chance ever again for normal life. Her roots were twisted and warped.

Once in a while she would stare at her palm, scan the lines and murmur to herself, 'One sign wanting? Just one?'

fourteen

HARDLY HAD A month passed when Mohini sensed the mother's deep longing.

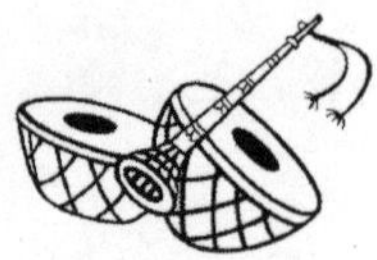

The days were pressed with work. In the harsh light of noon Behula grew drowsy and nestled to rest, but Mohini was still at work. The mother had given her a pile of old, white cotton cloth and a reel of red thread.

'Cut and stitch these into thick little quilts a yard apiece, and embroider them at the corners with the conch, and lotus, and wheel, and mace. It is well, daughter, that you've such skill with the needle. Make plenty of these quilts, for he will need them all. Even if he wets one every hour of the sun and stars, there will be enough.'

'He?' Mohini asked, puzzled. 'Who?'

'Your child, who else?' The mother's calm face, softened. 'Let this marriage be blessed with fruit early.' Her wistful voice lowered a little as though from secret fright.

Colour crept to Mohini's face. Not in her secret-most dream had she yet seen her child. The mother approved her shame.

'Our ancestors in heaven are joyful when a son is born to the house on earth. The family name will be carried for one more span of life on earth, and at the funeral anniversary of the departed sacrificial water should be poured.'

So the schoolgirl of yesterday was swept into maturity. As she sat stitching her baby quilts in the dozy noon hours, the idea of a baby filled her heart with wonder. Would he be dusky or fair? What if he were only a girl? She would love to have a girl, even though the mother longed for an heir to the house. What fun to make these baby quilts. As you worked on them, it was said, a baby would be on his way to you! Let the mind be filled with thoughts of a child, and the young, healthy, fulfilled body would surely respond.

Mohini was unaware of the full depth of the mother's feeling until one day Meera came and saw the quilts. Meera, the glib-tongued girl who had laughed at her underclothes, was now Mohini's best friend. They called each other — young village women drawn close in friendship often gave each other a common fancy name — Honey Pot.

'O-lo, Honey Pot! Now you know you must get a child. You have seen the horoscope.'

'Horoscope, Meera?'

'Your husband's. As though she knows nothing! You don't truly? Oh-lo! Of her own heart's longing she lays a snare on the sky path to catch a baby fairy.' Meera was a light-hearted girl, fat as a pumpkin, some jest or other always on her tongue.

'Tell me about the horoscope.'

'Such horrid —' Meera caught herself up and bit her lip.

Mohini felt her heart quicken. 'Meera, tell me.'

'Oh, sister, what is there to tell you? Nothing.'

'Meera —' The mouth had a worried droop.

Meera nestled against Mohini, and put an arm about her neck.

'Listen, then. Your husband's horoscope says unspeakable things which you are not to hear lest you worry. He will not live long after his twenty-eighth year, so it says.' With a quick look at Mohini, Meera hurried on, 'Oh, don't be alarmed. The horoscope also says if he gets a child he'll have the normal span of life through the little one's "father-luck", the new influence wiping out the old. Fate's scrawl on the baby brow will be stronger than the scrawl on his own, be sure. That is why the mother has long been anxious for him to marry and have a son. You see, this horoscope is as true to her as a divine word. It was cast in the Holy City by a great astrologer who had been a teacher and revered guru of her husband. You know what that means.'

Mohini's heart was beating heavily, but not with fear. Her eyes were large with wonder, and she knew an overwhelming elation. Out of her would come the means to save her husband; her child, born with the insignia of father-luck, would flout death! Pride and a passionate joy ran through her blood, and she felt a sudden heaviness in her body, as if she were already bearing the supreme gift of life. She was fate!

In the next breath she was laughing at herself for her easy credulity, her fear and her elation. Fantastic! The ways of nature were not so simple that you could foresee a man's life history in the relative position of stars at his birth hour. She, a modern high-school girl, knew at least that much.

Even city folk, Old Mother, and many like her, and men as well, pinned their faith on the horoscope, loth to permit a marriage unless the stars of the girl and her would-be husband were in favourable conjunction. Sometimes this led to tragedy. Mohini remembered the fate of Seeta, a girl she had known at Shibpur. Seeta loved her second cousin whom she had known since childhood. In a mood of desperation Seeta revealed her heart to her mother. There could not be a better match, for the boy was well-placed, both were of the same caste and social status, and no dowry had to be given. But as luck would have it, the stars came in the way. It appeared that if Seeta were to marry her cousin she would be widowed in her middle years. So the parents looked for another groom and forced the woeful Seeta to marry him because this time the horoscopes indicated a happy fruitful union. And what happened? A month had barely gone when Seeta's husband was killed in a street accident. This horoscope!

Then there was the luckless Sudha, a living symbol of the madness of things, her life wrecked by a man's crazy faith in stars. A fair and fragile girl, with faultless features. The years added to her beauty and to its impassiveness. All because of a stupid fate. She had no friends, no company. She was in her twentieth year, and there would hardly be a chance for her to wed. She was wed to knowledge, said mother. As if that could ever make a woman content! Better far if she had kept her blacksmith friend. Better far if she had married him. How could she live forever with cold, dead books?

Perhaps she could get Sudha as a bride for her cousin Dhruba, Mohini thought. That would be good, a fitting bride for a romantic poet. Search the city from corner to corner, and you wouldn't find a more comely one. Joy even to look at her face. But Sudha seemed to hate her, Mohini thought. Once an intimate of the Big House, Sudha had hardly set foot in it since Mohini had come. When they chanced to meet, Sudha spoke only a formal word or two and kept her face rigidly averted. The reason was plain, but was it a reason? And the mother was afraid that her three years of good work on Sudha might be wasted altogether.

In spite of her reasoning, Mohini yielded to an urge rooted deeper than reason and gave all her spare time to quilts, stitching and embroidering them. When one pile of cloth was used up, Mohini cut and stitched not-so-very-old cotton saris, and the mother, watching with frank pleasure, gave her a warm, approving smile.

'Clothes are not safe in this house from the pirate hands of my daughter. Why, there are enough quilts already for three little ones!'

So the days, in an aureole of glory, were full and she was breathless with her work. In the grey dawn Mohini rose and walked to the Rook's Eye to cast off the night's languor. Her body thirsted for the pool, for its softness on her sleep-warm limbs, as she floated with ease the way Meera had taught her. Then, with her sari dripping and rustling, her hair a black stream at her back, she set out to pick flowers for the worship chamber, heavy scented jasmine and bright marigold. She swept the *puja* chamber with a feather broom and crushed sandalwood, and lit sticks of incense. The *puja* over, she visited the cowshed and threw grain to the swarms of pigeons. Then she hurried back to hand out the daily measure of rice and kitchen supplies. Work folk on her husband's estate received a morning half-meal of puffed rice with molasses. To waste no working time, they sent their children to the Big House to bring the daily ration to the fields, and Mohini gave them a bellyful of hot rice and pulses — her eyes filled with a soft light as she watched their hungry mouths.

When, after noon, the metallic sky paled, friendly young wives visited her, and women from the farms came to pay respect to the mistress and seek her advice on a hundred matters. And the young mistress played her part with authority and dignity. Even the old ones touched their heads to the ground at her feet in salutation. Bright young men often came to her husband to discuss books, ideas, problems of the day — one or two were regular pupils — and sometimes they had meals in the house. When Mohini appeared, they took the dust from her feet — the teacher's wife was an object of reverence. Weeks had to pass before the girl with her city breeding, could accustom herself to this old-fashioned homage.

In all the busy hours of the day she would have her husband's company only for brief stretches. He would be in the pavilion of study, reading or writing, or working for the estate, and even if he came in for an hour, he was an eager teacher, not an ardent lover. He was creating his Maitrey! (Futile striving, Mohini knew. As she strained to give herself to his will. So tiresome. How achieve something beyond your power?) And after evening worship he returned to his work, or received visitors.

And a longing for him lay upon her at all hours. Did he not, too, long for her? Why else would he make excuses to come to her? Many times every day, as she was engaged in household tasks, he flouted the village code of propriety by going to her. He might be needing a document from the iron safe, or a few rupees, or perhaps he had a question to ask. But he might just as well have sent his old accounts clerk, Ramsadan Babu, or someone else, on the errand. Why would he go to her unless he had an urge? And though he always walked up to her with swift steps, as if in a hurry, he would linger to watch her work, and pay grateful tribute to her deft hands. He was loth to leave her, and even as he dragged his feet away, he turned round to give her a smile, a tender glance. Yes, the busy scholar with so much work in his hands was restless at heart for his young ignorant wife.

Your satellites? Somir? Ananda? The awakened woman in her curled lip mocked the romantic maiden. That odd game of make-believe. What a child she had been, fussing in her innocence over cardboard figures, building a toy-house in the air. To learn love, to feel love, through the literary feelings of poets and story-writers was fantasy. A hundred books could not stir in a woman the impulse that one moment of experience could arouse in a flash.

And then as though to deny her maturity, she fancied herself back in the yellow-washed house at Shibpur at a study desk, poring over a Bengali novel. Again, she was stretched out in a wicker chair on the front balcony, knitting wool coats, watching the hours of noon slide along the street until Old Mother came up with a cup of hot milk. ('I hate milk, I want tea.' 'Drink this up, girl, and then I'll bring you a nice cup of tea. And a biscuit. There!') Presently, from the street's bend, came the familiar sound of a cracked horn — two long-drawn hoots with which father joyously announced his return. What a home-loving man father was.... And as dusk fell, the little car took the family through crowded Calcutta streets (the ten thousand faces, the buses and trams racing by, the colour, the vivid life!) to a cinema or a park or the house of a friend.

Next, she was in a hushed room of All-India Radio, facing the microphone, pouring out her favourite folksong, a religious lyric that might also be the song of a lovelorn maid:

Lives and lives have I beheld His grace.
  And the eyes are not soothed,
Ages and ages have I held Him to my breast,
  and the heart is not cooled....

Old Mother loved her songs and sat at home by the 'chatter machine' listening, and though her face showed pleasure and pride (of that Mohini was sure), she wrinkled it in disapproval.

'Holy River! Even a rough in the bazaar, a scamp or a cutthroat, can buy a machine for 50 rupees and it is as though he buys our girl's voice. Oh, goddess!' She would say.

Mohini's heart ached with a pleasure that was half pain as she let her feet and her busy hands slacken, suddenly weary of her household duties.

The face of the village and the country around her, Mohini had explored already. She had toured the village in a palanquin only because the mistress of the Big House was not allowed to walk in public. Behula was a study in green, with endless bamboos, huge banana clumps, tall fingers of toddy-palms. Ponds were tucked everywhere: smooth swans' ponds, mirroring the bending bamboo grooves, gay with white and pink lotuses, lilies; shallow ponds strangled by green, gleaming water hyacinth, purple-flowered and pretty, but a deadly curse; stagnant ponds, evil smelling, malaria breeding. Around each pond, the central feature was a loose cluster of mud-walled cottages topped by conical roofs oddly perched one over another as an extra shield against the heavy monsoon downpour. In these lived the various caste groups: Brahmins, near-Brahmins, the professional castes — blacksmith, barber, washerman, milkman — and the largest group of all, the peasants, both Hindu and Muslim.

Outside the village Mohini had seen the strips of pathway edging yellow waves of sun-sodden paddy; the swift cut of the scythe at harvest time. She had heard the songs at corn-gathering. She had savoured lungfuls of the fresh earthy air of the meadow of Man-Lion named for the stone image of a god. For uncounted centuries the image had stood there guarded by the hanging roots, python fashion, of a great brooding banyan. From here Mohini had seen the weavers' huts at the end of the meadow and the little settlement of the untouchables beyond.

There was little else to see in and around Behula village. The river, Meghmala, three hours away by cart, she had not seen yet. There were vast swirling waters, picturesque sail-boats. Boatmen crooned their sad, soulful songs, and sometimes a hundred yards of clay bank, nibbled by the tide, came down with a tremendous boom-oom, like gunshot, so she had heard. One festive day her Honey Pot would take her to the river with a party of young women, she had promised. They would bathe and swim and eat the watermelon growing profusely in sand and silt. It would be a welcome change, Meera said, for the women to frolic and leave the men behind to do the housework and feed the babies! A chance anyway to fly, one whole day, the colourful kite of gossip!

If only your husband would take you to Meghmala, just once, one part of Mohini whispered with longing. They would go out in a rowboat under the bright *Purnima* moon and she would sing to him, her voice full and free. But fancy the mistress of the Big House appearing in public with her husband unless there was a special reason which the whole world would have to understand! What if the river was deserted? The blue sky had eyes and ears! And to sing openly like a peasant woman or like a city actress would cause a titter to fly from mouth to mouth. Behula would be shocked. Men of the Big House had always spent leisure apart from their women. So it had been for centuries past, and so it must be for centuries to come.

Marriage had its hurts even apart from all the harshness of an orthodox way of life. The very moment of fulfilment ached with defeat. Her husband, she could not help realising as the days moved on, was different from her image of him: he was melancholy with thought, concealing himself behind barriers of reserve. The dark spaces between a man and woman have to be lit with sympathy and comprehension. Reveal thyself! her eyes begged. She was bewildered. She needed more, or, much more of him than he gave. She ached to know all that he was, all that he had been. What had his childhood been like? What thoughts and feelings had marked the years that carried him into young manhood? Who were his friends? What is your work, your dream of glory, scholar of scholars? I know so little of you! But he was trapped inside himself, expressing almost nothing of what he thought, and felt, and needed when he did speak.

She had to be content to hear his story from the mother's lips — the mother enjoyed speaking of her son. Meghmala had flooded the countryside and taken her husband while he bravely fought to rescue his stricken people. She, then pregnant, was away on a pilgrimage with her baby girl. When she reached home, she had brooded:

'Why didn't I stay here so that I could die with my husband? What good was my pilgrimage?'

And she had answered her question, 'Siva wanted to protect the candle flame to this House, my son who is to come. My widowhood is the price of his life. If he also had gone with the flood, who would be here to sprinkle the sacred water for the thirsty mouths of the forefathers in *swarga?*'

When this son came, she had bent her life to one purpose: to make him worthy of his father's name. So the child grew up a recluse, cut off from life. While other boys of his age played games and climbed trees and made war on their disapproving elders, he sat hunched over his books, reading grammar and logic. Boyhood passed, but life, even at the University, brought little change. It was almost an extension of his boyhood and a strengthening of his single-minded aim.

'Why must he return to the village and obscurity, he who has been a jewel of the University?' his friends had protested.

The mother had hated their suggestion. She had kept her anxious glance on the wooden sandals of the dead father: so much had been carried away in the maniacal rush of the river, but the wooden sandals had remained in the house just as their clop-clop-clop when he paced his study rooms had stayed in her ears. These sandals were a legacy for the son — a continuity, a link in the chain of the old order lengthening from century to century.

One other aspect of Jayadev she saw from the mother's talk. Crisis had once tested the real man in him, as it had tested his father. When, in the peak year of the war, the grain profiteers had cast their evil nets over the people, the master of Behula had given his stern command: not a palmful of paddy was to leave the village. Agents of the rich merchants had first pleaded with him, then threatened him with ruin. Who was he to stand against the sweeping tide on which men of his own order drifted with profitable ease? It was strange how, in that hour of decision, the dreamy quiet-eyed philosopher, fresh from the University, revealed a steel core. He went from house to house. He called assemblies in the meadow of Man-Lion and spoke to his people. Soon after, the great man-made hunger spread swift devastation over Bengal. Behula was safe until the starving peasantry of neighbouring village began to pour into it in endless streams.

Mohini could see them because of the pictures burned into her memory: the living skeletons of men, women and children with dead eyes and balloon bellies, tottering from street to street, lying down exhausted. She could hear their hollow whining wail; *'Ma! Ma-go-a-ma!* A sip of rice-water, pray, *ma-go-o-ma!'*

Jayadev had risen to his full height. A true son of the father who had faced danger for the people and given his life. Yes, Jayadev had called for volunteer workers and built a thousand palm-leaf shacks for the destitutes in the open meadow. He had given free meals to all who needed them. When his barns were empty, he took out all his money in the banks and bought grain from the sharks in cities. He sold for cash many rich jewels that had been in the house for centuries. The mother, tight-lipped, saw the iron safe being depleted but she, too, gave her son the full strength of her spirit. The Big House must stand by the people in their hour of need. Impoverished, it would yet live. Failing in its duty, it would perish by the weight of its inner defeat.

The famine had passed. The Big House had become more than ever a legend.

This was Jayadev's story. Mohini loved it.

Mohini would have loved to tell him her own history, too. What if it were worth little? Self-stripping was her need. She was hushed, her mouth full of unuttered words. Jayadev seemed to have no curiosity about his wife's past, and, as the weeks went by, he seemed more and more indifferent toward her. He was rushed for time, preoccupied, mindless of her presence, and he called her Maitreyi no longer. He had given up teaching her. What a blessing that she need not try her teeth any more on stiff Sanskrit, yet it hurt her deeply.

If only she could know what was happening in her husband's mind. It was as though all at once work had ceased to be his anchor. The pavilion of study was an empty shell.

Jayadev, in fact, was filled with his bride. The ascetic in him, thrilled by his first emotional contact with a woman, seemed overwhelmed, helpless, lost. Lost? No! Jayadev girded himself for a struggle. He could not afford to be distracted. He must stay poised in the *yoga* of a single-minded aim — 'still as a flame burning clear in a windless place', as the Holy *Gita* said; he must carry through his immediate task. How could he pause and give himself to his private life at this great moment of history when India, proud with the freedom of which he had often dreamed, must reorient her national life on a new social basis? He, too, in his way had his contribution to make to India's developing struggle for social freedom, the fountain of all true freedom. This in his heart he believed.

'Neglect your work, be less intense,' he would say to himself, 'and never would you recapture your vision. Having reached your aim, having dedicated your vision to your people, you would be free, free to be fulfilled with — no Maitreyi, but Mohini, just Mohini.'

If only she were his Maitreyi, his fellow traveller, he had often thought wistfully, they would have worked together in complete harmony. What bliss! Jayadev soon knew it was a romantic fancy to ask so much from a girl of eighteen. He pressed his lips together and laughed at himself. What a childish fancy. He had quickly outgrown it, but he nonetheless regretted his lost illusion.

A man closer to life, more attuned to reality, would have achieved an inner balance with little strain, fulfilling the claims of both his mind and heart. But Jayadev, detached from the world, shrank from life, afraid of his own awakened spirit with its needs and demands. He closed himself in a safe cell of delusion.

But he gave Mohini no hint of what went on inside him. He had his feelings behind a tranquil mask, and wrapped himself in silence.

His apparent coldness and neglect bewildered and hurt her deeply. It was as though he had no need of her except physically. And physically satisfied, he withdrew into himself, into another universe. Had he no love for her, no deep feeling at all?

Why would he not lift his eyes and take notice when she had made herself pretty for him? One evening, while he sat writing in the lamplight, the elsewhere look on his face, there was a burning in her for his admiration. She flew down the balcony to the room that was hers alone in the west wing. For an instant she broke into her old joyous gait. She put on a sari of blue Benares silk with silver threadwork, and adorned herself with her pearl bangles, necklace, earrings and a gleaming tiara. She wore *kajal* and lip rouge. Her face, a lighted lamp of gold, illumined the mirror. And the words that the tongue could never shape lay in her heart and lent their tenderness to her face: I hunger for thy love.

Up the dark balcony she passed like a woman walking through the night to keep a tryst! I hunger for thy love.

'Remember this sari? I wore it for my Flower-bed night.' Her eyes and voice were lit with memory....

'Pearl goes well with my complexion, *nah?*' Bangles tinkled impatiently on her arms.

There was a long pause and something in her trembled 'I — I do not exist for you?' Her voice was very low. As if caught in her throat.

He looked up. He could have reached her by flinging out his arms. Instead, he looked at her with unseeing eyes. His rapt face lowered slowly.

Still she waited, waited with a choking rush of dismay, silent, her face pale. She could have trampled on his books. She could have screamed. With desperate will she tightened her lips, turned and fled.

A curious thing was happening at that moment in Jayadev's mind. Mohini had spoken to him; he had half-listened, without answer. How rude he was. He grew unhappy, put down his pen with a sigh, rose and walked off, still wrapped in the repose of contemplation, to the west wing.

'What's wrong?' His eyes saw, as though hit by a harsh light. He gazed, bewildered, at the scattered jewels on the floor. 'Won't you tell me?'

Mohini's face burned. Hot words died unspoken on her tongue. With a jerk of her head she rid her throat of pearls.

He looked at her and came quickly forward. He put out his hands and took her face between them, searching beneath the lines of her anger. His eyes were unhappy with realisation.

'I hurt you terribly, Mohini, didn't I?'

Glance in glance, she softened a little. She shook her head with violent calm.

'Then what is it? You are so annoyed —' His hand, caressing, moved along her cheeks, lips, eyelids. 'Tell me.'

'Why ask? Rush back to your work.'

'My work stands between us.'

And the realisation hit him that it was not his work alone. The Big House stood between them. The unaccustomed ways of life oppressed her and he who had imposed them on her must face the result. How could he have thought she had adapted herself in the space of months?

'Absorbed in work, I lose sight of all else. Work becomes my obsession. One cannot live effectively in two altogether separate worlds, but one must. Else —' he broke off, paused, then cried in an intense way, 'Give me your sympathy. Help me. Let my work be done soon, that I may be free, free.'

She looked up, her brows knit, and in a murmur she spoke: 'Help you — with my sympathy?'

'You have the power to draw me from my purpose. You could destroy my creative dream with a word.'

It was a language the meaning of which she could not reach, but she caught the passion in his voice, she gazed into his tense face, and knew he was restless, truly needing her help. All the hurt was forgotten in that instant.

'I have been childish. You're not laughing at me?'

She sat down on the floor, collected the jewels, looking for the pearls that had slipped from the broken string.

'Why didn't you tell me — just once — I was the prettiest girl you'd ever seen?' She looked up and her eyes smiled but her mouth pouted faintly.

He stooped down quickly, and drew her into his arms. 'Prettiest — and no jewels could add to your grace.'

'True?'

'True.'

'And Sudha?'

He looked surprised. 'What about Sudha?'

'Where have you seen such beauty?'

Her eyelids were lowered.

He laughed in answer. 'There's no one like you.'

He pressed her hard against his body and his mouth on hers made her gasp.

False, that chill fear of hers. Sudha meant nothing to him. Sudha did not count. Mohini gazed at her husband with the radiance of faith.

~

'Beware of the green snake in the grass,' the barber woman had said at noon today in the thick whisper she used for conveying a deep secret.

'Snake?' Mohini had asked.

'That girl. That Sudha.'

'What has she done?'

'Nothing. Only beware of her. A trampled snake bites madly.'

'What have I done to her?'

'Nothing. Only beware of her. A trampled snake to make a sweeping movement, all this could have been hers. Sudha could be mistress of Behula village. And what is she? You know. In her is a madness. No wonder. She could destroy Behula village as well as herself, with her anger and hate.'

'My fault?'

'Her doom — it's due in part, to you, so Sudha thinks. If they hadn't found a girl with all the luck signs, the mother would have been content to have the next best, Sudha thinks. She lives in that idea, fans it and makes of it a fire to heat herself up.'

'She does?' Mohini's voice was strained.

'Do not despise her. Poor Sudha. Behula has made her what she is, in her life and in her mind. Pity her, yet — beware.'

Mohini had laughed, though her heart had thumped twice.

'I see your meaning. But you don't know my husband. Even an *apsara* from Heavenland would fail to break into his meditative trance.'

The greying head of the barber woman had nodded in quick agreement.

'True. True. An *apsara* from Heavenland would fail. But a *dakini,* with dark witchery? Who knows?'

Yes, a *dakini,* too, would fail, thought Mohini, with her replenished faith, a *dakini* with the darkest witchery.

~

'Mohini,' came her husband's voice, 'let's go away for a while. I know how you feel. So lone and unhappy.'

Go away? That would be lovely. A spell at home, then they would travel together, he and she. They would see India, not the sights alone. She would see with his eyes and know the true India. But —

'Your work? What about that? What about your fame?'

'Fame? That's not what I care for. I have *you* anyhow.'

She pondered awhile, nestling close to him, her face over his shoulder.

'If you slacken, what will people say? They expect so much from the great scholar —'.

'They can do without me. There are scores of others to carry on my work.'

But the head on his shoulder shook decisively.

'No! There's none like you.'

He laughed because of her faith in him, then his face turned grave.

'Mohini, listen then. My writing is no more than a prelude, and the sooner I get through it, the better. After that my work moves to another field. I want to make Behula a model village — socially. Our political freedom is worth little without social uplift. (I hate the word!) That means struggle. If we win, as we must, Behula will be an example for all Bengal. In this difficult undertaking you, too, Mohini, have your part.'

She looked up quickly, crying, 'I?' and gazed into his eyes with wonder.

He did not answer at once. In the impulse of the moment an idea lying half-formed in his heart had taken shape. Mohini could be his Maitreyi, not in the intellectual field but on the more dynamic path of action. The sudden realisation thrilled him.

'When the moment is ripe you'll come forward, Mohini' — he gave her an eager appealing look — 'won't you?' and he rushed on: 'To start with, the women of Behula must be taught how to read and write. They need the first elements of knowledge. There's work for you. Sounds too unexciting? But there's no hope until ignorance, that arch enemy of our people, is laid low. Our plan will unfold itself as we get going. Mohini —' the appeal was still warmer — 'won't you?'

'Yes, yes,' she mumbled, 'why not?'

She felt small and incompetent. She, a sort of school teacher, with her little learning?

'We'll have Harindra with us —'

'Harindra?'

She had never heard of him.

'When I was in Calcutta for our marriage,' he explained, 'a young surgeon, just out of college, came to see me. He belongs to our village but has been away for years. We had a long talk. He knows all our problems. His ideas agree with mine. His keen interest, his perception and depth of feeling — I was surprised. It is luck, indeed, for Behula that he has made up his mind to come and live in the village, so that he can work for its progress.'

'He will stay with us?'

'He will stay with his father, the old *Kabiraj* who practises the Indian system of medicine in its antique purity. An iron pillar of orthodoxy! Harindra won't find him easy to live with. Anyhow, Harindra will be here in a month — I have a letter — he will set up a dispensary.' Jayadev paused and added softly: 'A bold, selfless youth. Harindra has true fire in him.'

Mohini was gazing intently at her husband. Yes, there was true fire in him, too, deep beneath his calm. And the truth flashed on her that he would be unhappy, parted from Behula. He stood rooted in its earth drawing his strength out of it. What right had she to drag him away for a selfish reason? How could she trample on his plans and his dreams?

Visions of travel died in her eyes. She would not see places, he and she together, not for a long time anyhow. Sadness entered her heart, yet there was a great joy too. Had he not revealed himself at last? Was this not the beginning of a truer understanding between them, of a new, deeper relation?

How hard to be an idealist's wife! If only he were like other young men! No! How compare him with others! He was far, far above them all. He belonged to the people. What right had she to claim him for herself alone? She had the power to destroy his work — what higher compliment could he pay her? And in paying it, had he not vested her with high responsibility, lifted her to a pedestal? She, too, appeared to be an idealist!

An idealist? She? But the quick light in her eyes was quenched in a moment and she sighed. She would much rather have the commonplace things of life, like other girls. She was not made to be an idealist. She couldn't bear the strain.

But she could. She must. Her husband needed her help. How could she fail him? In the great task ahead she would play her part. She would be his true partner in feeling, in faith, and in dream.

fifteen

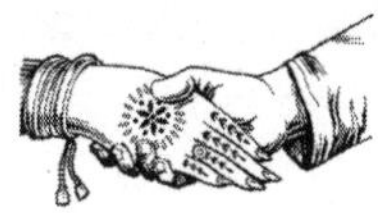

At home in Calcutta they were not altogether at peace about their child. The serving woman had handed out her tale, some truth, some fiction: the little mother had nothing but herbs to eat. The tongue pined for fish with a riverful of fish almost within sight, and this the season for roes, the bellies of fish fat, and white with roes! The little mother was worn with toil. There was no sleep for her at night for the scream of jackals, *hua-hua-hua,* the hiss of pythons, the wolf prowl, of bands of robbers yelling *reh-reh-reh!* The sun was a bare man-height in the skies when the little mother must be up and doing. The women of Behula mocked her city clothes and the mother-in-law was a tigress.

Old Mother spoke to her son in utter misery.

'Rightly you said in those days, "Let her not be sent to a village. Let her stay in the city where, in spirit, she belongs." I live in an old world but those folks are of a world far, far older. Why expect our girl to be like them? How can a plum tree grow pears?'

His eyebrows worked up and down with worry but he restrained himself in order to soothe Old Mother's grieving heart.

'Look, Mother. Jayadev has an article in the current issue of *Maya.* You have read it? What scholarship, what style, what brilliance —

above all, what a broad outlook and what vision. No, a man with his enlightened mind and wide sympathies could never make his wife unhappy. He has the true legacy of the past, an inner health, a source of graceful living, and to that he has added our modern culture. Gift upon gift. No, Mother, do not heed that garrulous cook-woman who wears a waist-chain at her age. *Wolves, python. Robbers.* An imaginative mind, indeed! Mohini has nothing to complain about, you can see that from her letters. She's not a schoolgirl any more, but the proud mistress of the Big House!'

Old Mother wiped her eyes with the back of her hand.

'A girl crosses the doorsill of her childhood home, cuts the ties of blood and the air looks empty without her. Still, write and ask our Jayadev to bring the girl back to us before the coming of the ten-armed goddess. They can stay for a month and go back when I have fed her some delicacies. Mother Ganga knows how my fingers ache to rub her fair skin with a little mustard oil and do up her hair.'

~

Yes, the young mistress of the Big House took deeper colour from her new life everyday. Slowly she fitted herself to the rural design. Her sprightliness, her quick girlish laugh, she easily subdued. The mother was a ruthless teacher.

'Cheap trinkets are not becoming,' she told Mohini with a pointed glance at her braceleted arms. 'Why not wear gold?'

Mohini, in silence, had slipped off her favourite glass and painted lac bangles.

Once when she was in a mood to make herself pretty she wore a sari of gay-coloured silk and the mother said, looking pointedly at the sari, 'Plain cotton woven in our village handlooms is more becoming than mill-made muslin. There is dignity in simplicity and quietness.'

She was precise, well-meaning, relentless. The bare expression of her will had the force of command.

Old Mother had compromised with modernity and her struggle to uphold the orthodox way was without passion. But the mother of the Big House was stern, adamant, like iron. Old Mother was of the old and of the new; this mother had nothing in her nature that would allow change.

Besides, there were no end to prohibitions. You shouldn't use powder and rouge; they were for actresses who had to make their faces shop windows. You shouldn't wear a sleeveless blouse, or one that was tight across the bosom. Your hair mustn't be done in a thick, single braid, waist-length, or twisted, plaitless, in a soft coiled mass low on the neck. You must follow the old, heavy style of oiling and dragging the hair back in many slim plaits all woven tautly together in a flat pancake under a gold-mounted comb.

Bored and fretful one hot July afternoon, Mohini walked out of the house into the spacious stretch of garden among the tress — mangoes, guavas, figs, their abundant foliage shading and cooling the sun-burnt grass. A *jamrul* with its plum like, luscious fruit, sweet and rose-scented, caught her fancy, and she stood gazing at the spread of its branches, her hand held against the sun's glare. It was a slender, leafy tree, forking off as though by design to give many foot-holds, making it an easy climb. On a sudden impulse Mohini pulled her sari above her ankles, tucked it in at the waist, took a quick look around to make sure no one was about, and stepped up to the tree's lowest footing. Slowly she climbed to a bunch of *jamrul* which she snapped off. She sat on a smooth branch, with the trunk as a back rest, dangling her legs, squaring her shoulders with proud satisfaction. She dug her neat white teeth into the painted fruit skin with a sort of love and rapture. Down below lay her cloak of dignity, abandoned, on the grass. No fruit had ever tasted so sweet! It was the fruit of *jamrul* she ate, but something more too, the fruit of release, the fruit of freedom! Contentment filled her spirit. If only she had Heeralal to share this pleasure with her!

Once — it was a year or so before her marriage — father had taken the family to a health resort, Kalimpong, a night's travel. Woodlands and a narrow threadlike stream wound over smooth pebbles between banks of sand and rock. Heeralal loved to climb trees. Deft and sure. She was clumsy and afraid. One day, half-way up a tree, Heeralal had looked up to meet the baleful eyes of a monkey hidden in the leaves at the top, and, chill with fear, he had screamed and come scrambling down in a flash. He panted. For all his brave manly talk, he had looked up and shouted at the monkey and made awful faces. Mohini at the foot of the tree had had a good laugh.

As she unrolled that picture from her memory a spill of laughter rolled from her lips, and the juice of *jamrul* strained the curve of her chin. She dangled her legs, eyes alight, and laughed.

Then, all at once, she saw another picture in her fancy, she saw the mother waiting at the stairhead.

'Why didn't you ask a servant to get you the fruit?' asked the mother who had watched from a window. Her voice had a ring of surprised pain. 'No mistress of the Big House in the past thousand years would have climbed a tree — ever.'

But, uncaring, Mohini went on laughing. She plucked a green fruit and flung it hard in the air, a direct hit at the cold, unwelcome picture of her fancy!

In that instant, joy grew cold in her heart. She remembered her *dilruba,* cracked and useless. She would sing no more. Yesterday evening, as she played on it, mingling her voice with its melody, the mother had stood at the doorway, listening.

'These modern songs make no sense,' she had said curtly. 'You have such sweetness in your voice, why not use it for religious lines? Bengal has no lack of them.'

Then she had walked off, and the next moment there was the sound of a smash. Mohini, in sudden anger at such a senseless restriction, had thrown her *dilruba* against the wall. It had bruised the face of a mural goddess, and the lyre was cracked.

'Why don't I die?' she had asked passionately, between sobs.

She could remember another day when she had cried like that, the day she had been an anxious bride in the palanquin. Then, she had had Heeralal with her. She had had his warm presence to give her comfort. Today she had no one.

Her natural resilience had lifted her from dejection. She had given herself to an ancient house and its age-old traditions, and she must subdue her temper and her turns of mood. She would not be beaten even when she felt bruised. Her reward was in hand: dignity authority, trust.

Dignity, authority, trust would please a woman, but as a setting for her life, not as the main theme. Never could they satisfy her. All the same, one passed through an inner change, an expansion. An easy carefree girlhood with its lack of form, with its odd conceits and fancies, was slowly forgotten, tucked away somewhere in memory. One gave in more and more to cast-iron codes, to an old-world design for living.

This sadness came upon her once in a while, and it lay heavy on her heart.

The evenings unlit by a moon in the sky were oppressive, almost unbearable. The Big House was a pebble clutched in the iron black fist of night. Dim kerosene lamps scratched the darkness tiredly. Dull bursts of cricket chirp, *jhinn!* with frog songs for variation, deepened the immense, listening silence. Then, the ancestors of the house brooding on the high walls slipped down and trod the long corridors back and forth, the *clop-clop* of their wooden sandals echoing from wing to wing.

Mohini sat stiffly in her room. She could hardly breathe. What comfort was there in the knowledge that she could order the huge splendid silver chandeliers that hung in every room lighted? The house would be less forbidding, less haunted by its benevolent masters of the past, but who would understand such festive illuminations? The mother would be annoyed. The whole village would come wondering to the gates of the Big House, and what explanation was there to give?

There was one more dark spot in her life — Sudha. 'Beware of Sudha!' the barber woman had said. All at once Sudha had unaccountably made up her broken contact with the Big House, with its master in particular. She was his pupil again. She sat in the shade on a stone bench near the pavilion by herself, seemingly immersed in her books. Once in a while she rose, walked swaggeringly to her teacher to seek a meaning, an elucidation. Sometimes she called to him, 'Listen —' Perhaps there was no answer, so she repeated, shrilly, imperiously, 'Listen —' When he came down from the pavilion in response and sat besides her, and started to explain — he would speak a long while in his absorbed way to make a point simple and lucid — Sudha held her full glance on his face with a strange air of possession. Now and again, she would lift her eyes to a room in the west wing, Mohini's room — the curtained window commanded the garden — and she would wear a look of proud satisfaction. 'This part of him is all untouched by thee, vessel of ignorance, this part anyhow belongs to me alone,' that cold, scornful gaze said.

And Mohini in her room felt lonely and miserable. Her faith in her husband was unshaken, yet she hated to see Sudha touch the scholar in him. Sharp jealousy pricked her heart. Clear enough, Sudha played the game of intellect with a dark purpose. Why — why would she not leave him alone?

If only she could unburden herself to her husband! But how could she speak against Sudha? Her outward ways were proper enough. It was his duty, no more, no less, to teach Sudha, an eager pupil. What was there to complain about? Especially when she had failed him in this respect?

Every month a fat book parcel came to her by post — magazines and light fiction. How well father knew her taste! Mohini looked forward to this gift, and to the ten-rupee note he sent her in an envelope, the same allowance as of old. A large amount of money lay at hand for household needs, but Mohini loved these few rupees.

One spot of light in the Big House was Ranjan, a boy of eight, a relative of Jayadev. Ranjan had lost his mother some years back and his father, an official in town, had married again. Jayadev saw how the boy was neglected at home and had asked to have him in his charge till he grew older and was ready for the University. The father had agreed, which was luck, indeed, for the boy.

Ranjan passed at once into Mohini's care. Small, spare, delicate Ranjan had a gift all his own — he played lovely tunes on his homemade reed pipe and sang well in a thin sweet voice:

To the house of forms
  Comes He, the formless.
He, the image of joy!

And again, liltingly:

Wanderer!
  Take some bucketfuls
From the stream of life,
  Wanderer!

Mohini, delighted by his voice, had once said, 'Ranjan, how did you learn to sing? Who taught you?'

'I never learnt it, *Didi,*' he answered. 'No one taught me. Song grows inside you just as sweet juice grows in fruit.'

Yes, that was it — the very sweetness of his being gave Ranjan his gift of song.

Ranjan hung around Mohini, eager to help with household tasks.

'Ranjan, go out and play,' Mohini would urge him. 'Go and see the village. Make friends. Do something, boy.'

Ranjan wandered awhile in the garden, chasing bright-winged moths, watching the squirrels, throwing stones at an evil-looking lizard that sat on a tree, glaring, as if it would pounce on him. But he was back too soon in the house, at Mohini's heels as she moved busily about. He was like a lonely puppy that asked to be petted.

'Ranjan, boy, go and make me a list of fruit trees in the garden, all sorts.'

Paper in hand, he rushed away. To be of use to *Didi* made his heart beat with pleasure and pride. But he would have loved it more if *Didi,* too, had come out to watch him.

The fruit trees were all counted. Then, banyan, and *neem,* and *asvatha,* and others that gave shade. He counted flowering shrubs: *Hena, Kunda, Kamini,* oleanders. 'What now? Lists of birds, insects, moths, squirrels?' thought Mohini, laughing. Or she might give him a tape and ask him to measure the grounds, acre by acre in every direction!

But his companionship was a gift for her, too, and she enjoyed telling him stories. Stories — Rajan seemed to live for them! It would be good when the comics came. Mohini had already written to Heeralal and asked him to send copies every month. Meanwhile, she had to count on her own memory.

'King Vikram goes for the *Jewel of Sinhal* today, doesn't he, *Didi?*' Rajan looked up excitedly from his evening meal. 'Good fight, *Didi?*'

'Grand fight,' Mohini, squatting close, gave him a reassuring nod.

The thick dusk draped the sky, and was lighted by a glitter of tinsel stars. Mohini had finished her day's work. Jayadev was away as usual in the pavilion, with visitors. Ranjan had had his meal early and before bedtime it was story time! In two months Mohini had exhausted the tales from the epics, *Ramayana* and *Mahabharata,* and was now telling the boy adventures of the legendary King Vikram.

'You eat next to nothing, Ranjan, that's why you don't grow as you should. You must finish the rice.' Neglected at home all these years, no one could have made him eat his fill. He needed to be coaxed, such was his nature.

'Didi, I'm full to the throat,' the boy gave her a pleading look.

'Ranjan —'

'No room even for one mouthful, *Didi*. What can I do?'

'I won't tell you a story ever, boy, unless you eat well.'

'Didi, what if I burst like the frog that swelled because of its pride?'

Mohini laughed. 'You tiny, shrimpy frogling!'

'Didi, what if Vikram gets hurt? What then?'

His lips were open. He held his breath.

'Vikram always does the right thing, doesn't he? How can he get hurt, then? He fights only to help others who need his strength, never for his own selfish needs.'

Ranjan pondered this.

'Didi, you don't have to eat to be strong!'

'What now?'

'You have only to *fight* to help needy folk. Look at Vikram. He doesn't eat like an elephant, does he? He fights for others and gets stronger and stronger.' Ranjan's face beamed with this discovery of truth. 'Tell me, then!' he demanded.

'Clever one!' Mohini reached out a hand and touched the young, proud face with love and pleasure.

Yes, life was brighter with Ranjan in the house.

Five well-guarded barriers King Vikram has to cross to reach faraway Sinhal where the peerless maid, 'The Jewel,' lives. His heart is set on her. First, on his way through the deep woods, he is challenged by a huge giant, as tall and thick as a mountain, wielding an iron mace in his tree-like hand. The second is a forest fire, which gives an intense heat, and the flames reach the sky. The third barrier is a tract over which fly millions of big, hungry, carnivorous birds whose beaks reduce a man to bone in the flick of an eyelid. Next comes a gateway guarded by a fearful demoness as fond of human flesh as the birds of prey. Finally, on the hinterland of Sinhal, the air is of such a quality that it turns a trespasser instantly into stone. And even after this last barrier, near the gateway of Sinhal itself, wild elephants with long tusks roam about by the thousands.

Ranjan listened and his eyes were wide. Goose pimples showed on his arms.

'*Bhai*, now go to bed. I must be off. Time, soon, for the evening meal.'

'*Didi*,' begged Ranjan. 'Just one more story, *Didi* —'

Mohini watched the wistful face and smiled. 'Listen,' she said.

Vikram is as good as he is brave. A holy man once gave him the secret of leaving his own body and entering a dead one, so that it comes to life. The king's barber, knowing the gift his master has received, wants it and is ready to kill himself unless Vikram shares the knowledge with him, so the good king, out of his kindness, gives away the secret.

Vikram, hunting in the forest one day, kills an antelope with an arrow. 'Why don't I test my knowledge?' he wonders. And he speaks the charmed words. At once his body falls dead and the antelope comes alive.

The barber had followed the king closely. He reached the scene and saw the lifeless body and the tall antelope standing by. At once he knew what's happened. Evil grips his heart and he, too, uses the charmed words and quickly enters his master's body and then, vile traitor, aims an arrow at the antelope. Vikram wakes to his peril and dashes away.

So the barber poses as King Vikram and returns to the palace with the unsuspecting retinue. He is now eager to meet the queen who, he has heard, is a young woman of great beauty. As he steps into the inner apartment, a pretty serving maid receives him and the stupid barber takes the girl in his arms, mistaking her for the queen!

The queen is amazed. Is this man with Vikram's physical form an impostor? She asks him questions which the barber fails to answer. Finally, she asks him a riddle she has learnt from Vikram himself.

'It has feet, and face, and form, and goes with you as often as you walk about in the sun, but it can never eat or drink. What is it?'

'Your shadow' is the obvious answer, but the barber was stumped. The queen's suspicions are confirmed, and she hurries out of the room and quickly locks the door lest the impostor escape.

Meanwhile, the king, wandering about as antelope, sees a parrot drop dead, and he decides to take its form. He enters the tiny body and flies off to town. He reaches his chief minister's house, finds him, and since as a parrot he can talk, he reveals all. The minister, aghast, takes the bird forthwith to the broken-hearted queen.

How can they undo the tragedy? The king in his wisdom has a plan. A dead sheep is brought into the palace.

'If you be the king,' the queen tells her captive, 'you can surely enter the dead body and make it live.'

'Test me,' answers the barber eagerly.

The door is unlocked. Out comes the barber who sees the dead sheep. He uses the charm at once, and at the same moment, the king, perching nearby, leaves the parrot's body and gets into his own.

Ranjan clapped his hands, thrilled. 'How clever, Vikram! He sends the wicked sheep to the butcher for its meat, doesn't he, *Didi?'*

'Oh, no,' said Mohini. 'Vikram is good even to an enemy. He brings the barber the body of a dead man so that he can be a man again.'

Ranjan did not like that. *'Didi,* I want to be brave like Vikram but not so good, oh, no!' His tone was firm.

Mohini patted his cheeks. Her eyes were bright. She felt very happy.

'Didi,' said Ranjan, 'if I be brave like Vikram and good also, will she come, she —

'Who?'

'She, my mother —'

Mohini drew him close, and pushed back the hair which always drooped on his forehead.

'Ranjan,' she said, 'I, too, lost my mother when I was very young.' She paused and cleared her throat. 'If you are brave and good boy, *she* will be happy. She can see you and hear you, and she knows your thoughts and feelings.'

'All?'

'All, Ranjan.'

Ranjan pondered this and smiled faintly, content. Then a sudden fear came upon him. *'Didi,* you won't go away — like — Mother?'

Her voice was warm. 'How can I, Ranjan?' Oh, he meant so much to her, this little boy.

And it happened as she told Ranjan stories, sitting on a low green divan by his bedroom window, that when she wearied and paused in the telling, a dream would come upon her, a secret dream of motherhood like a wisp of tenderness, a yearning ache. When she fell silent, Ranjan never bothered her. He nestled to her and was still, as though he understood her mood, but he was reliving the story.

Frustration fretted her. It was as it had been in her girlhood, and nature denied, nature starved by pallid circumstance was stifling. Brimful, she had to spend her emotions or cease growing, and there was none on whom to spend them in full except the tiny one who did not exist, her dream child.

Mohini imagined this beauty and joy, and created her child. The silent compulsion of the Big House had forced some blossom within her to ripen fast enough to bear rich fruit.

sixteen

One cannot live effectively in two altogether separate worlds, Jayadev had said one day to his wife, yet this need for two-fold living was inherent in his work. Thought had to be related to action. Abstraction had to be resolved in human terms. The philosopher had to step out of his temple of silence and lead his people across the valley of conflict and discord to end social slaveries.

Social salveries were cactus growth that would renew themselves over and again unless the roots were cut, roots that were deep in economic bondage. Ever since the dread days of the famine Jayadev had been aware of this. A hungry man could not be free in spirit.

The battle for economic freedom, however, was in full swing and ten years hence there would be no landed gentry to live on peasantry. India was fast moving that way. But then, would the people, fed well, be free in spirit because of their new physical state? The answer was plain. It was the crux of India's problem.

It was the test and crisis, too, of the Big House. Would the Big House topple into oblivion with a hundred others like it? Had it not been distinguished from others as a true friend of the people? Even when it crumbled to dust, as it must, the Big House could live by progressive leadership.

Would he, master of the Big House, step out of his shrine of contemplation, his cosy sanctuary, and take over this immense task?

Jayadev shrank into himself. His was the world of vision, not action. If only he could have a private corner of his own where he could read, and think, and write, and so pass the days of life. But he had no right to be feeble. He must play the role assigned to him.

Youth had now unfurled in the village the banner of the times. It was a little banner but the elders of Behula, in anger and fear, ached to pull it to pieces before it was made larger. It and the new spirit had the approval and the blessing of the master of Behula. That awkward affair of the seventy-year-old money-lender and the young girl, which had been thwarted, was not to be forgotten. What business had the 'ruffians' to stop the marriage with a threat of violence? Was there to be no individual freedom in Behula? And the master of Behula had been unmoved. It was as though he had *approved!* Preposterous! In the twenty generations past such an act of abject treachery was unheard of. Where would it all end?

Treachery, indeed. Jayadev, the repository of tradition, had reached a decision, and his way was the way of Harindra and the so-called ruffians.

He was a symbol no more. The Big House must fight. The village lived in its enormous shadow. And the Big House had not room enough for progress and decadence alike. Youth looked to it for leadership. It was time that the Big House made its final choice plain.

What an emblem of conflict was Harindra's own life! His aged father, the *Kabiraj,* had been practising old style medicine in Behula for a half-century. Harindra, brought up in his uncle's home in Calcutta, had, with his father's consent, read in a Western-style medical school and taken a degree. The old man was well aware of the material benefit of such training — a *Kabiraj* had no real future — so he wanted his son to get into service in a city hospital and earn a high, steady salary. But Harindra had other ideas and plans. He came home, a full-fledged surgeon, resolved to set up a practice in the village. His father was disturbed, shocked, his professional pride was bruised. Worse still, here was a challenge to the indigenous system of *Ayurveda,* the system that had prevailed for a millenium, enriched by the genius of the great physicians, Charak and Susruta. Cities had gone over to the new medicine, cities deserved no better, but its onslaught on the country, strong as it was, might yet be absorbed. To think that his son should be a carrier of the alien contamination! The old man's heart burned. What madness had come upon him that he had sent his son to town and let him study at a medical school where they cut up live rats and dissected corpses?

What boldness for a son, a mere stripling, to ask his father to give up practice because of age! Age! He, at seventy-two, wore no spectacles and had not lost a single tooth while Harindra at twenty-four needed a pair of glasses over his nose. *He* walked miles to answer calls; Harindra had to ride a two-wheeled contraption, a bicycle. *He* walked with his head bare in the hard September sun; Harindra must have a broad-rimmed *topi* to shield him, and once, when he went out without it, what a headache he had had! A doctor trained in the Western way!

'There are many good drugs in our *Ayurveda* system,' Harindra had said to his father. 'We know them, we use them, not the home products but those made in modern laboratories. What's wrong in using in the fight against disease the best that East and West have to offer? Medicine knows no race or nationality, Father! No greater blessing for our people than the sulfa drugs.'

'And the knife? The needle? Your best weapons, aren't they?' His father's voice was heavy with sarcasm.

Harindra smiled. 'Our people have great faith in the knife and the needle. You'll be surprised. I had a call one day last week from an elder, a friend of yours. It was just influenza. I gave him a mixture, but he shook his head and said, "Harindra, let me have the needle." "This is no case for the needle," I told him. But he begged, "Harindra, just one prick of the needle, and I'll be on my feet. I'll pay your fee, so why not go ahead?" I said, "Since you know so much you may as well tell me what medicine to use." And I gave him the names. "Which one would you like?" I asked him.' Harindra, as he told this story burst into a laugh, amused, and sad.

But the old man's face was livid with anger.

'The contamination,' he cried, and his voice shook. 'Even the aged have caught the contamination. *Bhagwan! Bhagwan.*'

He turned around quickly and shuffled away. How could he deny the fact that even the elders of Behula with their scorn for Westernism had, in this respect anyhow, gone the way of all others?

There was no cause for wonder. The rot that had seized the very soul of the elder of elders had to spread. The Big House, the citadel of stability which had preserved for centuries the old values and ideals, had passed into the keeping of a stripling trained in alien ways, filled with the disruptive spirit. It was no secret that the young master of Behula lent full support, moral and material, to Harindra and his kind — Harindra and his kind, for the doctor was not playing a lone hand. He had drawn about him the 'ruffians,' guiding their seeking minds, and he was ready to perform what he called a social operation. The impudence!

'They say, Jayadev, you're helping the fellows called "ruffians" in their mischievous work. True?' the mother asked him sharply one day.

His cool, clear look rested on the mother's face.

'What have they done? They are out to destroy fever mosquitos; they demand that ponds and grounds be kept clean, that shallow pools of water be filled up, so that mosquitos lose their main breeding areas. They even volunteer their services free to the owners of ponds. What could be more fair?'

'But they *demand!*'

'They begged, they pleaded, they prayed, and were laughed at. Now they demand.'

The mother was silent awhile, then she said, more sharply: 'They've a social programme, as they call it.'

He smiled. 'That programme is not very dreadful, Mother. To start with, they won't let an old man remarry unless he chooses a widow.'

'How marry a widow against social sanction?'

'Let the man who wants to marry become a reformer!' His smile broadened. 'The ancient books approve such a union, my research tells me. Later, degenerate ages stripped the widow of her human right. Today, a dependent widow's lot is bad enough often. She would be better off even as an old widower's wife.' He waited a little before he went on. 'Look at our — er — ruffians next item on the programme: no girl under sixteen may be wed. We have a law fixing the minimum marriage age at fourteen. To step up a bit is not so very revolutionary? In ancient India there were no early marriages. The pressure of circumstance, the repeated waves of alien invasion most of all, reduced the status of our women almost to the helpless chattel.' His eyes twinkled. 'You, too, don't like early marriage, do you, Mother?'

He waited for answer but there was silence, so he resumed, 'The ruffians want to end untouchability. You won't approve of *that*. But who are you to stop a world force? All untouchability — they are different sort under different labels almost everywhere — is being brought to an end. Mankind had a new charter of equal rights for all.'

'What do they say, the untouchables?' The mother was scornful. 'Do you know?'

Yes, he knew. But some months were to pass before he had the painful realisation that the knot hardened by centuries would not yield to a mild sword stroke. The untouchables — *Harijan*, people of God as they were named — were furious. They would not be wiped out, they would fight for their existence, they said. Harindra pleaded with their *mandal*, Muchi the cobbler. 'You'll cease to be untouchables but you'll be people, like the rest of us.' The head man shook his big, shaggy head with some violence. 'We are no fools.' The 'scheduled castes' as a backward class had many special rights and privileges granted by the government. In the expanding democracy they formed a separate electorate and sent their own men to popular councils. A vested interest! What would happen to the leaders in district towns if there were to be no untouchables?

'Don't you go about giving our folks ideas,' the cobbler warned Harindra threateningly. 'What if our own low caste folks lift up their heads to the higher among us? What if a scavenger claims to be a leather-worker's brother and equal?'

Yes, the castleless had their own hierarchy of caste. They had their priesthood. If there was no equality among themselves, how could they be equal as a class with other people?

One moonless night Harindra was returning home from a call when a man rushed out of the dark and emptied a bucket of water on his head. The water stank. Harindra's fist struck out, and the man fled with a shriek.

Harindra was trembling with rage as he strode into the pavilion.

'What folly to try to help such people. Why should I waste myself? I am going back to town, Jayadev-*da*. I'll set up a practice in town.'

Jayadev's face was cut in stone and for a fleeting instant the graven sternness made him look like his mother. Then he relaxed, reached out and held Harindra's arm.

'What has happened to you, *Bhai*, is all the more reason why you must help these people. Don't you see? Are there people anywhere so very helpless because of their lack of growth? No, Harindra, you can't run away. I know you won't.'

Harindra stayed on.

More trials came Harindra's way and along with it, unexpected triumph. His old mother fell sick with pneumonia. The father treated her but she grew worse.

'Give me a chance, Father. We have a specific for this disease, a sulfa drug that cannot fail,' the son begged him anxiously.

In vain. The old man was a firm rock. And Harindra, helpless, sat by his mother's bed night and day, biting his lip in impotent rage.

'Take this, Mother,' he bent over her and held out the powdered drug. 'Open your mouth, Mother.'

But his mother lifted weary eyelids and gazed deep into his eyes. She read him, but she smiled and shook her head: 'For shame, Harindra! How can you insult him?'

As the powder dropped from her son's limp hand she reached out and pulled him close. She held him a minute to her bosom and said, 'Promise me, never to try to give me anything without his knowing.'

His face burned. There was a tense silence.

'Promise me, Harindra,' she repeated, in a soft, caressing voice.

'Mother, I promise.'

At last the old man woke to the peril. The patient was dying. There was nothing he could do. He sat very still, his head between his thin brown hands as though in deep contemplation. Then he rose and tottered to the sickbed. He lifted a gnarled hand to his son's head in a prayerful gesture.

'Take charge, Harindra. I am beaten. Do what you can.'

The son, shaken out of a daze, stared at his father, at the shrunken figure of his dying mother.

'Too late,' he cried grimly. 'You've killed her. If only sense had dawned on you three days ago, even two days —'

The old man fell in a heap at his son's feet and clasped his arms imploringly.

'Harindra, save your mother. Don't let her leave us, my son.' Tears ran down his face.

'I —'

'Harindra hurry, my son. There is no time to lose, not one moment.'

'I will try,' Harindra said.

'Harindra,' the strong light of hope and faith burned deep in the age-sunken eyes. 'Your sulfa drugs, the specific. Son, use them full strength. Use all your skill. Use the needle. My son —'

The miracle happened. The mother's life was saved.

Youth's unfurled banner added a proud cubit to its length.

Jayadev rejoiced. Was this not a triumph for the Big House itself?

seventeen

Meantime, in the Big House, a sweet intimacy built on their common dream linked Mohini with the mother. It was as though they were two conspirators filled with one secret. Everything else, the movements and gestures of workaday life, was a covering shell. Mohini with a shy thrill felt the mother's exploring glance on her now and again. The mother's love was fraught with danger! One day she held the girl's face by the chin and gazed wistfully.

'The nostrils are fine, Daughter, and faultless in shape, only they look bare without a diamond,' she said. 'It is strange that the revered Old Mother did not bore your left nostril when you were a child. Perhaps she hated to hurt the tender skin. Now it will hurt more, for the skin has toughened. But what can be done? A young woman must look her best.'

The dark threat from a sunswept sky! Village women bored the nostril to wear a stud. In the city it was quite out-of-date, laughable. To fancy it would improve your face!

'Here is my own diamond.' The mother opened her palm and help out a flashing, gold-set stone. 'An heirloom. Now it's yours.'

'May be it's five hundred years old?' Mohini gave an uneasy smile, trying to find a way to refuse the gift without annoying the mother.

The mother answered her simply, and gazed at Mohini with fond eyes.

'Not so very old. My husband's grandmother wore it for many years, and she gave it away for joy at the birth of a son's son. I wore it until the day the sky broke and came down on my head. Now, daughter mine, it is yours. At your age why be ashamed to deck yourself prettily?'

Mohini was distressed, silent. Her lips curved, a little amused, a little cross.

'The barber woman will come on the morrow to bore your nostril, daughter. Meanwhile, gather the thick cream from a bowl of cooling milk, and rub it on the left wing of your nose to make it easy for the needle.'

The threatened nose twitched in unconscious protest.

'No, no, Mother,' the girl moistened her lip and cried in a small tight voice. 'Let the barber woman wait.'

Mohini gulped and took a deep breath. Something had to be said. Mohini was thinking hard.

'You see, Mother,' she spoke with quick invention, 'this nose is dedicated to Kali. As a child I used to catch cold too often and had breathing trouble, so Old Mother vowed away my nose to the goddess to win her protection. This nose in all my life may never be decked. Pity. Such a beautiful stone!' she added, blushing.

The mother nodded gravely with understanding.

'Foolishly I accused the revered one of neglecting her duty out of a soft feeling. We should not fear to do what is right even if it twists our heart. How I misjudged and wronged Old Mother!' She paused and when she spoke again her voice quivered with emotion. 'Do I not know how she longs to see you? And you, to see her? What is to be done? Daughter, let the scrawl of destiny be ever in your mind. Eighteen months are gone, time hurries by. Let the gift of motherhood soon be yours, soon.' Her eyes closed for a minute and her hands folded at her breast as she bent in prayer to the ever-living symbol of godhead, the wooden sandals piled with flowers on their throne of gold.

~

So the nose was saved, with tact, without open revolt, but not all her personality. The Big House cramped her, squeezed her in its grip, and she reacted in a curious way. She escaped often to the garden, to the far corner where she climbed to her tree-perch. The tree became her refuge against negation. Here, she expressed her right to be herself. The mother spoke one day.

'Is it proper to be up there?'

Mohini's answer was clipped, precise. 'I like it.' This was her one mutinous move, her rigid self-assertion. The mother was bewildered and anxious. 'But why, of all places... so undignified... people would laugh....'

And Mohini's simple but final answer: 'I like it.'

In so many matters of real significance she had yielded, denying herself, absorbing the heavy strain into her spirit. And this one symbolic act of revolt cancelled out all that submission. Up on her perch she was beyond the reach of the Big House, she was above the restraints of everyday living. She was integrated, and free, free to read, think, feel and dream.

'Hoo-ee-oooh!'

The blood-curdling yell made Mohini almost slip. She clutched a limp and trembled. A shout of boyish laughter followed, and Ranjan, who had sneaked up behind *Didi,* appeared.

'You let out that yell?' Mohini was almost incredulous. Her heart was still beating.

'Hoo-ee-ooh!' Ranjan repeated it.

'Don't!'

Mohini clapped her hands over her ears. Perhaps it was his idea of Vikram's battle cry!

'Didi...' Rajan said.

'Yes, boy?'

'Ashu asks to come into the garden. Won't you let him?'

'Ashu?'

'My friend Ashu. He's twelve. He can set a crow trap better than any other fellow. He can go down into the water and you think he's drowned and he floats up like a fish —'

'Let me see Ashu, then. Where is he?'

'At the gate. And Hori, *Didi?* He can —'

'Ask Hori to come.'

'Didi, Gopal?'

'Gopal, also.'

'Montu — Jhoro — Jeeban — Robi —'

Mohini laughed.

'Let them all come.' It was good to see this shy boy growing up, happy with friends.

The youngsters walked in, taut and silent with excitement, while the fat gate-man, Roghua, who with his back up-curving moustache and his thick bamboo stave guarded the Big House, glared helplessly. What challenging glances the youngsters flung at their old enemy! It was a great moment. Once, after a heavy thunder shower, Ashu had manfully scaled the compound wall, eight feet high, filled a cloth bag with ripe mangoes that had dropped on the ground, and scaled back over the wall. A heroic feat, and Ashu was almost a legend!

'Who's who?' smiled Mohini, gazing at the strained young faces. Ranjan told her. 'Take all the fruit you like,' she said, jerking her head at the trees. This had a magical effect. The boys were up on the trees in a flash. When they returned, waistcloths bulging, the strain of the first encounter was gone. She, the mistress, was no stranger. One of their own — almost.

'Didi,' Ashu addressed her with familiarity, 'the Western alien's back from the moon? We'd like to hear —'

'Back from the moon? Who, Ashu?' Mohini was amazed.

Harindra came to the Big House often these days. The mother had known him since he was a child, and she had high regard for the old *Kabiraj*, her house physician. With Mohini, Harindra who had an easy manner, had an informal, friendly relation. *'Bau-didi,'* he called her with respect, using the name for the wife of one's elder brother.

'If he takes the trouble —'

'Harindra will love it. What a hold he has on our village youth! And all after a few months' contact. Amazing! These boys of yours will adore him no less. Why didn't we think of it before?'

He was smiling, with another thought. 'Harindra's gone to the city; he'll be back this evening. I have a surprise for you —'

'For me?'

'You'll never guess.'

'Not books,' she said doubtfully.

Books had ceased to be a surprise. He had been bringing her books, light fiction, not the heavy literature with which he had once tried to educate her. He knew now how novels made her evenings less tedious.

And that evening there had been a big surprise. A new *dilruba* lay on her bedroom table.

'Where did it come from?' she had asked her husband in great amazement.

He had smiled and answered, 'Some good fairy must have sent it. Some good fairy who loves to hear you sing.'

And he looked at her with such tenderness that she could have cried. He was not altogether cut off from her, not quite in another universe!

'Tell me,' she said. 'I hate guessing.'

'Try, Mohini,' he coaxed. 'Think.'

'I look so funny when I think too hard,' her mouth pouted a little, 'so Old Mother used to tell me.'

'Old Mother told you?'

'Old Mother used to say, "Mohini, don't put on a serious air, girl, your face isn't made for it. You look your best when you're happy, and gay, and laughing. Don't think too hard." '

And as she spoke, she saw Old Mother and heard her soft voice with the break in it. She felt the touch of the child-slim fingers doing up her hair ('Such hair — why make it a bird's nest?') and the ache was heavy in her heart.

'A gramophone, Mohini. I've asked Harindra to bring one,' he spoke quickly to change her mood. 'All your own songs. And the latest records, two dozen. Harindra —'

'When will it be here?' Mohini cried with a rush of pleasure. She had lost none of her agility at shifting in the space of a breath from one mood to another.

'Any moment,' said Jayadev, joyous in her joy.

He looked very young and eager, younger and more eager than she had ever seen him.

Next day, while she was busy in the kitchen, Meera arrived.

'Sister, you've set a grand example. We womenfolk of Behula village have all decided to sit in trees. When a baby screams, so that your eardrums ache; when a husband flies into a temper; when a mother-in-law nags you so — get out of the house and up in a tree. A good sanctuary!'

Meera nudged her friend and shrieked with laughter.

'Meera,' said Mohini excitedly, 'come with me.' Mohini spoke to a servant before she and Meera walked out into the garden. They sat on the grass while the servant carried out a small red gramophone and a box of records.

'Song machine!' cried Meera with pleasure.

Mohini put on a record.

'Why, sister, it's just like your voice! *You,* singing? You, truly?'

'I,' said Mohini, proudly with a nod.

Never before had she felt so rich with achievement.

The great news spread fast, and in the noon hours the womenfolk came crowding up to hear the young mistress sing out of the red box. They loved this treat. What rare fun to compare the two voices, human and machine! So young, and so great a singer. The company had captured her voice at a great cost that all the world might hear it. The glory! A worthy mistress of Behula. None like her in the hundred villages around. Their own, their joy, their joy and pride, and she was so human, without any of the plumage of the rich, whose distant look bespoke that they trod the blue pathways of the sky!

Mohini felt very happy. The gramophone was more than a machine: it was a new eye with which to see the village; it was a way of communion.

Life, once so empty, was now full. It was not all play, however, because the women pressed her with questions on all manner of subjects, eager to know, and to learn.

Then Mohini had an inspiration. Why not prepare talks? Her visitors would love to sit around and listen, and it would be easier for her. Talks on India — the past and present, cities, rivers, peoples of the world, the wonders of nature and science, animal life. There was so much to tell them. She would need books to supplement her own knowledge. Yes, she would speak to her husband.

It was an exciting idea, and it worked. The class assembled in the cool shade of a great banyan in the garden. A newspaper came every day by post, and Mohini read out bits from its columns. She read aloud passages from books and short stories from magazines. She showed her pupils pictures. Through all this material she revealed, as best she could, the nature of life. And she revealed the face of the motherland. How she loved this work!

The older ones dropped out of the class in a day or two, with fond remarks and complacent smiles. The earth moves round and round? Why aren't you dizzy then, dizzy as a top? All the world knows the earth rests on *Basuki's* head and when he, the great serpent, wearies and shakes himself the earth quakes. What makes day and night? The sun god retires from the sky world, and goes back home to his spouse in Heavenland, and there's darkness. Is that not a simple fact? — Talk of caste? All men are born equal? Then why did the Creator bring forth the Brahmin out of his mouth, the Vaisya from his navel, the Sudra from his feet? Tell us *that.*

So the old ones spoke, but they hastened to add, 'Let the young mistress have her fun. Let her tell fancy stories to the girls. She, our pride and joy, has the right surely to amuse herself.'

But not all the old peasant women were like that. There was Ratan's mother, now past sixty, and the wonder was that at her age she was seized by a longing to know the shapes of letters, to learn how to read. Spellbound, she listened to Mohini, the teacher.

She would wag her head with the hair twisted at the back in a small grey bun and exclaim. 'True! True!' and cast prideful eyes round. In a thick whisper she would say, 'You hear her? What knowledge! Listen well, ignortant hussies, and fill your empty stomachs. Let not your minds trot about lest you miss a golden word.'

And her eyes roved this way and that, watching for bemused expressions, chasing minds that trotted.

So, around the conservative code of the village, Mohini built something of the city — in spirit. Rooplekha, if she knew, would have been amazed. But it was give-and-take. The wall of isolation breached, the grateful women took her into their hearts. Mohini was asked to their festivals, some of which had a deep meaning, others were merely picturesque. In the city the festive days slipped by half-noticed. They were valued mainly as public holidays, a respite for the work-stained spirit. But the village celebrated them all with faith and ritual, as though the birth anniversary of a god was the intimate concern of Behula. Mohini at once loved the legends, the lore of the Hindu god-world. Until then she had heard only snatches of it from Old Mother. At many festivals a professional story-teller would present to an eager audience the particular legend for the occasion, building up vivid pictures by word and intonation and song, creating suspense, calling forth laughter and tears. The story-teller's art, cultivated with assiduous care, handed down through the centuries from father to son, was the joy of the whole rural community. Those who could afford the story-teller's fee sponsored it and the others crowded up to listen. It was their time-honoured privilege to come unasked and to fill their ears with tales from the epics or myths from the *Puranas* wherever they were being told.

The ceremony of brother anointing was a day to be remembered. It was a simple ceremony of good will, which happened once a year. All the boys in Behula were looking forward to the occasion. Ranjan had never been anointed, for he had no sisters. Ashu was the most excited of all. He was the only son in the house, with four sisters to anoint him, and he was prepared to adopt Ranjan as it were for his brother.

Ranjan had the secret wish *Didi* would anoint him. It was hard to think she was not truly his elder sister. He was too proud to ask her, though, but the day before the ceremony *Didi* settled the question.

'Ranjan' said Mohini, 'tomorrow's the anointing day, don't you know?'

'Ashu's invited me,' Ranjan answered quickly.

'Ashu?'

'He has four sisters.'

'You will go, of course. But there will be a ceremony in our house, too. Tell your friends. They must all come.'

'All?' Ranjan beamed.

'Why not? Only you must tell me how many friends you have, so that I can be ready for them.'

Ranjan in a rush mumbled the names. But he lost count and said some names twice.

'Make a list, Ranjan. Write down the names. Then go and tell your friends to come early tomorrow morning.'

There were twenty-four names in Ranjan's list.

'Not too many?' he looked at *Didi* a little dubiously.

Whom could he leave out if *Didi* asked him to shorten the list? Even if he had only four or five true friends, the others, playmates, would love to come and be anointed.

'It's all right, Ranjan,' *Didi* assured him. 'Go and tell them. It's *your* party.'

And the boys chattered excitedly. 'What could we give her with our *pronam?'* asked Jhoro.

'Let's trap a myna. If she fancies song birds.'

'Or a rabbit, if she'd like a pet.'

'Why not make her a bead purse? We could string coloured beads together and weave them —'

'She loves blue lotuses. Each of us could give her a lotus — a fresh one with a long stalk,' suggested Ranjan.

'Why not?' voices cried in approval. 'If she loves them —'

Edging the Man-Lion meadow was a pond where blue lotuses grew. Three of the boys were to set out before sunrise and pick a large basketful. They must take care not to be caught — the lotuses, rare in Behula, were prized by the pond's owner.

The Big House looked festive. Even the gate-man, Roghua, concealed his accustomed glare. As the boys filed in, he averted his face. Long strips of carpet lay spread on the inner verandah floor. An auspicious brass lamp on its tall pedestal sent up a flickering flame. Mohini, her face fresh after her bath, sat facing a boy at one end of the row they made, and she anointed his brow with sandal paste and touched his head with grains and fragrant grasses in the familiar gesture of greeting, chanting the words:

Lo, I deck my brother's fair brow,
    I cast barbed thorn at Yama's door!
Oh, brother mine, I deck thy fair brow,
    Thou art truly an image of gold.

And she picked up her conch and blew three joyous blasts. One by one she sat before all twenty-four boys and spoke the charmed words as she anointed their brows, as an elder sister should, and she blessed each boy with a gift of two silver rupees. Then came the sweets. Each boy had a big trayful.

The huge blue lotuses the boys handed her in return were indeed a shock. They came from Harindra's pond and Mohini knew how he cared for them. The pool stripped of its glory — she put the thought away. Were these not gifts of love?

Behind the joyous boom of her conch was a stilled longing. How she missed Heeralal. How she longed to mark his brow. He had waited with eager expectation all other years for this day.

It had always been a day of material benefit for both, Mohini remembered, her lips curving. She and Heeralal had a financial deal. The pocket money father allowed him never lasted long enough, and Heeralal was nearly always short of funds. He coaxed loans from his *Didi* who knew how to save up her allowance, a few *annas* now and then, but these mounted up fast. On the day of the ceremony Old Mother gave the girl five rupees with which to bless her brother. A blessing, indeed, for both! Heeralal paid back his debts and started fresh.

Mohini went to her room and sat facing the wall. She dipped her little finger in the sacred paste, and recalling the face of her brother marked the bare wall in the customary way as she spoke the charmed words and blew three joyous blasts for him. And she was soothed.

eighteen

THE STAGE WAS set for a battle royal. Tension was at a high pitch. Behula, divided as never before in all its history, had reached a crisis. A crisis of outlook had become a crisis of emotion. A boulder overgrown with the moss of shabby centuries had been shifted a trifle, and the earthworms, exposed to the light and air, wriggled violently.

Siva's pond, now commonly called Crocodile Pool, was the scene as well as the symbol of the deepening strife. It belonged to an old shrine at the very centre of the village in the Brahmin Lane. It was bigger than any other in Behula and when, years ago, the river Meghmala had burst its banks, an enormous crocodile, black with age, rode the swirling waters, it was said, till it saw the temple when it turned and swam in through the door. The flood receded but the crocodile stayed on in the pond. Every night while the village slept, the temple priest swore, the aged crocodile crawled over the bank of the pond, and through the wooded grounds to the stone god in the shrine of the temple, and lay immobile, its eyelids closed, worshipping. The presence of this devotee of Siva — a Brahmin in a prebirth, apparently, doomed by his *karma* to brute form — lent sanctity to the pool. Surely it was not accidental that suddenly the vivid hyacinth blossomed on this water and spread rapidly until it had laid its heavy bright green carpet over the whole pond. Bathers could no longer interrupt the meditation of the devout one! The mud banks had crumbled and the stagnant water from the pond had seeped over to make a swamp where mosquitoes dropped their eggs in spoonlike masses. Malaria could find no better breeding ground.

Harindra spoke to the temple priest. The pond must be cleaned up, the edges cut and deepened, the hyacinth removed. This would be the starting point of a campaign to rid the village of a deadly pest.

'What madman's talk is this?' cried the priest in anger and surprise. 'To annoy the devout one now disguised as an animal! To make a vulgar commotion in this holy abode!'

The priest was a large man with a white beard, Siva's trident painted in red on his forehead.

Harindra smiled amicably.

'Uncle,' he said, 'do you think I have no sense?'

The priest stared with suspicion lest, unwary, he had slipped into a trap. Young Harindra was not to be trusted.

'We'll get the saintly one, our Father Crocodile, a new abode where he will be happier. We'll have servants to tend him and feed him big chunks of goat flesh.'

'Siva! Siva!' said the priest, invoking the divine name. 'Goat flesh! He, a devotee of the ascetic god. Harindra, you are a fool, my boy. Alien learning holds your spirit in its slimy corruption. A worthy father cursed with such an unbeliever for a son!' He paused a moment and his voice lowered with curiosity. 'Where is the new abode, pray?'

'Listen to me, Uncle, before you lose your temper. We'll take this creature of faith to the zoo in Calcutta city where he'll lord it over a pool inhabited by many others of his tribe, and he will be free to speak the name of Siva and make saints of them all.'

'Siva! Siva!' the priest's face was convulsed with horror. 'Go, Harindra. Do not cast your polluted breath, ever, in this temple yard. Go!'

'Listen Uncle —'

'Siva! Siva!' And the priest lifted his hand to the consecrated tuft of hair on the crown of his head as though to draw strength from the contact. Then he turned round and sternly walked away.

Two or three days later, Harindra was in the Big House seated on a strip of carpet at the kitchen threshold, while Mohini stood and watched a group of peasants eat. They were the men who worked on the estate, planting the fields each season with new rice. In seedtime and harvest they were entitled to meals from the master's kitchen.

'Bau-didi,' said Harindra, 'there are exciting times ahead. The priest won't listen to reason. I have hit on a plan.'

'Tell me,' said Mohini, 'Khanto,' she addressed a cook-woman sharply, 'Govinda needs another helping. His leafplate's empty and he's still hungry. Why don't you see?' Then she turned to Harindra's with a quick smile. 'Tell me.'

She sat down on another strip of carpet.

Harindra lit a cigarette, leaned back against a pillar and spoke of his plan. One night, just before dawn, he and his comrades would assemble at the shrine with picks and shovels, and attack the pond's hyacinths. They would work hard and make a good deal of progress before the priest saw what was happening. He would shout, and rave, and call forth the thunder of the gods, but the party would work on in silence. Then, of course, the priest would rush off to the village to get help. The party would carry on in strict non-violence until forced to withdraw. Later, another night they would make a similar surprise attack until at last the pool would be free of the strangling plants. A small boat would be needed which Harindra was having built to order. There was danger from the old crocodile, but the brute could be kept off with spears and staves.

'What do you think of it, *Bau-didi?'* asked Harindra, as though anxious for her approval.

Mohini was excited to have Harindra's full confidence as well as with his plan. Jayadev was not to be told, for in fairness the master of Behula should not be a party to such illegal work, Harindra felt. Besides, the moment was not yet ripe for Jayadev to come out of his sanctum and join the forces of progress in an open clash with reaction.

'*We?* Why blame yourself?'

Her eyes were soft with compassion.

'I must. It's a collective responsibility. The village has wronged her — none of us individually — so all must pay.'

All must pay? *All* couldn't marry this girl? Her hand flew to her mouth, ready for a laugh, but she restrained herself. What would Harindra think of her? So childish, when she ought to be serious. Her face became grave.

'Listen. If he speaks to her,' the words came warm to her lips, 'then, maybe, Sudha will relent. I'll ask him. Yes?'

'Yes, yes,' said Harindra, but he felt an unaccountable pang. 'Let Jayadev *Dada* speak to her.'

He smoked in silence for a moment, then after one deep draw at his cigarette he stubbed it out on the floor and pulled himself to his feet.

She stood still; watching him as he walked away, sadness again in her face.

So the day for the attack on the hyacinths in the pond drew near. All preparations were made, but a curious accident made them needless.

The old priest one day walked from door to door after dusk, asking, 'Son, have you seen my Bistu? He's been missing all day. Night deepens and he has not yet come home.'

No one seemed to have seen his six-year-old grandson for many hours. As the priest trudged the village paths, the cry on his lips was a cry of anguish from his heart.

His daughter had come with her child for a month's stay. How look her in the face with Bistu gone, lost? When he returned home alone, the wail of the wretched mother made him shudder.

'The pond, father, it's the pond. The pond has taken my Bistu.'

'The pond.'

That was the obvious explanation. The old man felt his knees sink and he buried his face in his hands. There was nothing to be done.

The news aroused the village. Harindra heard it and rushed into action. Scarcely a half-hour later, his little two-oar boat was afloat on the pool while his friends as well as others started to uproot the hyacinth whose deep roots perhaps held the little lifeless body in their fatal grip. Scores of lanterns came from the Big House. Every household sent its lamps until the dark pool gleamed with light. Harindra carried a flashlamp. While a hundred hands attacked the hyacinth, long fishnets, brought by fisherfolk dragged the pool from end to end.

The old priest had locked himself up in the shrine praying to the stone god.

The bereaved mother lay crouched in the mud and shrieked. 'Bistu, oh my jewel of jewel, Bistu *reh* —'

One thought lay in every mind. The aged crocodile — even if he was a vegetarian and a saint — had the child in his fat belly. There was not a bone left for the funeral rites which would release a soul from its earth bonds and make it fly heavenward in happiness and peace. What a fate for a Brahmin boy and the grandson of Siva's priest!

Dawn came and the sun peered over the horizon. The tired men were breathing hard, staggering with weariness on the pond's edge, when a voice called out in sudden alarm.

'Bistu! It's he!'

There was a moment of cold horror. Someone had seen the child's ghost. It was earth-bound, never to be released, and must haunt the pool for all time.

But other voices took up the excited cry: 'Bistu! It's he!'

All heads turned stiffly. A sleepy boy was coming on donkey-back, held by an old peasant who walked beside the animal.

The peasant explained that he belonged to the neighbouring village, Sonarpur. He had seen the boy tramping, exhausted, across a mustard field at dusk. The peasant had brought him home and fed him. The boy could not explain where he came from. He lived by a pool, that was all he knew. So the peasant had no choice but to put him to bed. At dawn he had borrowed the donkey from a washerman, set the child up on its back and come to Behula to make enquiries.

Bistu had been out trying to catch moths. He was so intent on his hunt that he took no notice of where he was going. When it was too late, he had to retrace his steps. That was his story.

'I ate fish!' the boy cried in a sort of triumph to his mother as she held him clasped in her arms. She gazed misty-eyed at him and the tears of joy ran down her cheeks. Fish was forbidden food.

The priest had come out of the shrine and had stood very still, his eyes riveted on the pool now rid of the hyacinth. It was steel blue in the soft sun. Harindra read his thought.

'So the devout one, our Father Crocodile, is a figment of fancy!' he said, his face merry. 'You knew?'

The priest glared at him and broke into a loud angry laugh that made his beard quiver.

'Fool!' he cried. 'Have you not the sense to see what is plain and simple? The devout one has made himself invisible and moved elsewhere. In his new abode the hyacinth will bloom and spread its green coverlet. Soon we shall know who's favoured by his holy presence, soon.'

The owners of ponds, listening to the priest's words, trembled. A pond has a hundred uses for the household besides the fish, the rich harvest of fish. Who was to be hit by the dubious luck of the devout one's favour?

Harindra felt the chill in their hearts and he gazed off toward the horizon, as though he could see the dawn of a new day. He smiled and spoke with a sort of joy.

'Never again shall the hyacinth grow in Behula village. The myth of the devout one along with a hundred other myths is dust for the breeze of a passing age. We march ahead, we progress.'

But Harindra was not deceived. Chance had put off the battle to a future time, about a different matter, but the clash had to come.

It was to come over an issue far more vital — over the fundamental right of a man or a woman to choose a mate outside his or her caste. Harindra had intimation of the bitterness it would cause. He was aware of the electric shock that would first paralyse the village, then stir it to mad fury — he, a non-Brahmin, marrying a Brahmin girl and defying a timeless social practice. Inter-caste unions were not rare in the cities — there was a law that sanctioned them. A government official entered the facts in a ledger, but there was no priest to chant *mantra,* and no gods were invoked. Villagers, however, would not stand such sacrilege, not yet, not a citadel of Brahminism, anyhow. Not Behula.

Not Behula? Harindra drew a long breath. He would marry the girl he needed, needed with the deep hunger of his spirit. Let Behula do what it could. His heart swelled, and he felt a swift surge of power. He would break Behula. In this fight with reaction he was not alone. He was much more than Harindra. He was the New Free India, strong because he was aware after dark ages, because he hated all chains.

Then, all at once, his exaltation snapped like a chord strung too tight. How could he be sure that Sudha would marry him, would accept the challenge of the future? Had he built his house of hope in thin air? Once or twice he had caught her looking at him intensely and when their eyes met, how her pallid face reddened! Once or twice she had given him a strange smile, so fleeting that it might have been only his fancy. One day, when she had fully recovered, and he had no reason to visit her as a doctor any more, she had cried out in dismay. 'So soon am I well? If only the fever —' She had cut her sentence short and hung her head in shame. But he had treasured the glance and the smile and the impulsive speech. He had lived in them.

Was she just grateful that he had saved her from typhoid? The idea depressed him. Yet what more could he reasonably expect? They were strangers to each other. They had been seldom alone together. He still called at her house often, drawn by an urge he could not suppress, to be received by her uncle. He listened to the old man's chatter, while the one for whom his eyes hungered was hid by the walls. She came perhaps for a moment to offer him a spiced betel due to a visitor. But how could she know his feeling? And what if she knew?

A woman as ingrown as life had forced her to be would make no swift response to emotion. Coldness was her shield against pain. But if her defences fell if she were aroused —

Harindra felt excitement at the prospect of waking her out of herself, of rousing the woman in her to her destiny. The adventure of her!

Circumstance and perhaps temperament had cut her out for a social rebel. Only a lead was wanted, a direction. Sudha, aware of her strength, would be a revolutionary force.

He was exalted again! Harindra felt his heart swell.

nineteen

The tree of marriage, now almost two years old, was still barren.

Mohini rose at daybreak one day with languor in her limbs and walked heavy-eyed through her tasks. In the *puja* room she felt very sick. Instantly the lynx eyes of the mother were probing her. There was joy behind her calm mask. Hurriedly, she fetched a bamboo chip and stuck it in the girl's hair-knot like a pin, to ward off the powers of evil — the first few days of pregnancy are ringed with peril. She took great care of the girl and would not let her bend at the hips to stir the low cooking pots or lift the heavy rice bowl from the oven. Swift, secret looks passed between them.

Suddenly, like a river released from ice, the mother released her joy by telling story after story of the family. The family chronicle was endless — a pageant of men and women wresting values out of life. There were men who had built up the House, men unspoiled by wealth, seeking knowledge. There were women who had attained the eight-fold virtues, and some of them had voluntarily cast themselves onto their husbands' funeral pyres.

A little shrine close by the pavilion still shielded the century-old memorial of the last *sati* of the house, a stone slab with the print of a woman's hand in faded vermilion.

'Hark thou, boy or girl,' the mother said in her heart (the fables reached the ears of the unborn child), 'such is thy inheritance. Let the glory of all yesteryears enter the spirit. Let the strength and grace be echoed in thee. Hark thou —'

A week later, Ranjan touched the chip in her hair when the sari had accidentally slipped off her head.

'*Didi,* what's that for?' he asked in wonder.

'Oh, that?' she said, shamefaced, snatching it on an impulse and breaking it to pieces. How could she tell the boy?

When the mother saw her hair, she was speechless with shock for a while. She gave Mohini a searching stare and, her face marble, she dropped the unexpected words pitilessly, 'Are you barren, then?'

Mohini stared, and it was some moments before the blow found its mark. She clenched her hands and pressed her lips together.

The mother stood immobile for a minute, brooding, before she spoke.

'Vow to the goddess of births that you'll give her a nose-ring set with pearls when she fulfils your wish. If the nose-ring is not enough, then you must give her something more, something of yourself. You'll cut the skin of your bosom and give her the blood in a lotus-leaf bowl. I, too, shall give my heart's blood and pray for the gift of a grandson.' She paused, a grave statue, and then the words came with a knife edge, 'We'll visit the shrine in three months, if need be.'

'Heart's blood?' Mohini was tense. Anger burned in her. What wrong had she done to need such crude penance? She would never submit to this. Never. The mother had been taking too much for granted. The mother —

Suddenly, she was afraid of the mother. Inside that graceful frame was some metallic hardness, some lining of steel. The mother, who had never spared herself, would never spare those dearest to her.

This mother, widowed in her twenty-fifth year, had gone many a time to perform the hard *kalpavasa* austerities far upcountry at the confluence of Ganga and Jamuna. She had lived one mid-winter moon in a leaf hut on the river's edge, eating nothing but a palmful of fruit and a little milk, sleeping on a leaf-bed through the windy nights.

This mother, a young sweet-faced widow, a picture of wonder and pathos, had cut off her hair, only after she had overheard a chance remark one day at a pilgrim shrine.

'See the glory of her hair. What length! What richness!' This eager tribute to her beauty made her burn with shame and that day, scissors in hand, she cut her hair. Years later, yielding to her son's pleas, she let the clipped hair grow a little, but never more than a palm's length, never below her shoulders.

This mother, even in her first year of widowhood, vowed away her right hand to Siva, begging the god's protection for her fatherless son.

Fortunately, Meera came along as Mohini read new warning into these familiar stories of the mother's self-denial and self-chastening.

'Barren women, so I hear, Meera, make a vow to the virgin goddess and get cured. True?'

'Why,' declared Meera, who was then bearing her third child, 'Many have been cured. That's a fact. Not that they've all kept their vow. Look at our police officer's wife who was childless for a year after marriage. Alarmed, she prayed to the Devi and vowed ten silver rupees to her for the great gift. Soon after, she was pregnant. "O, Devi," she pleaded, "where can I get so much money? I'll give you five rupees. Absolve me from the rest." But still she doesn't pay. She waits. In childbed, she prays, "Devi, how spare five rupees with a new mouth to feed? Take two." Still she does not pay. When the child is born, "Devi," she says, "what need have you of two silver rupees? If you must have them, why not pick them up from somewhere? All the rupees in the world are at your feet." And the strange thing is, she does not displease the goddess. She even bears a second child.'

'The Devi is not often deaf to prayers?' Mohini said after a silence.

Meera, knowing her friend's heart, groped for words of comfort.

'Listen, sister. Go back to your city home for a month and rest your troubled mind. We'll miss you; we'll be lonely without you, but, for your sake —'

Go back home? Mohini bit her lip because of the overwhelming sadness in her heart. Unawares, she had put her roots deep down into the new earth. Life in Behula had been hard at first, even drab and tiresome, but she had conquered the strain and had built a life for herself with a great brightness, a life of fulfulment. This was her real home. She had learnt to love it. She loved the Big House with its empty rooms and long marble corridors, its lovely garden and cool greenshaded pool, its odour of refined oldness. She even loved the ancestors on the walls, for they were her own people; they belonged to her, as she belonged to them. And her husband — how bear to be away from him so long? From Ranjan and the boys? The peasant women her eager pupils, on the threshold of new thinking — how could she let them down? Why must her life be upset because of that horoscope which pursued her like a curse? Must she submit to stupidity, as Sudha had once done? Her eyebrows knit with anger, but her voice was controlled.

'If there's no truth in *his* horoscope, Meera, how do the stars in it in conjunction with mine make a "royal union"?'

Meera gulped. 'To speak the truth there is a paradox,' she said. 'Stars for good and evil fight on the astral lines of our lives and until the battle is over fate is undecided, so the belief goes. Who knows whether it's right or wrong? The most evil of all evil stars is Saturn. Look at Sudha. She, too, has the luck signs on her person, all except one. But she is doomed to remain unwed. Saturn holds her in its grip.'

Mohini knew Sudha was no longer doomed. Sudha's luck sings were not to be wasted. Harindra loved her. Would Sudha know his value, Sudha with her bitter nature?

'Poor Sudha!' Meera spoke with pity. 'Every day she grows in beauty like a king's daughter. There is no end to fate's mockery.'

Mohini spoke to her husband with false gaiety.

'What sort of second wife would you like? Tell me. A wingless fairy like our Sudha? Brittle and labelled, "Glass — with care." No, she isn't the right sort. You need a woman who'll sacrifice herself, cease to exist, make no demands on you.'

'Mohini,' he cried, 'what bitter talk! You are unhappy.'

'Answer me. This is serious. You must have a child whose luck will save your life. I can't give you one.'

He laughed aloud. 'I see. It's horoscope. It amuses you, doesn't it?'

She looked at him. After a bit she said, 'Amuses me, indeed!'

He read the meaning of her voice.

'You don't believe it, do you? You have sense enough,' he cried.

'Who knows?' It was a half-whisper.

'We're fighting ignorance and superstition, aren't we! We're fighting the false clayfoot gods. They've had their day and now they must quit,' he spoke gravely. 'Or else the true gods will elude us.' He gave her a tender smile. 'I tell you, I'm not going to die soon, Mohini, and I don't need a child whose luck will save me — what a fantastic idea! — from the malice of the stars. Mother makes herself unhappy because of her crazy faith.' He saw her face darken and added, 'Does she make you unhappy, too?'

'No, no,' Mohini denied this at once. 'Why should she?'

How could she complain against the mother? It would be easy enough to defy the mother's will, anyhow. 'Mother,' she would simply have to say, 'I can't do this, don't you see? He disapproves. We're fighting ignorance and superstition, he says. Those false gods. Lest we lose the true ones. Yes, so he says. Why not speak to him?' How those words would anger the mother!

But she never spoke those words. A brooding conflict was growing inside her. Opposite influences clutched her. Her enlightened girlhood was still a part of her fibre. She heard a voice as though her father was speaking.

'Have courage,' it said. 'Do not bow down to such insult. You are the New India. The old orthodox ways have been our yoke, have enslaved us. Let us be free.'

And Old Mother's thin lips trembled as Mohini imagined her answer.

'How can we live without our past? Time is our earth, the earth which feeds our roots. Faith will not be denied. Give yourself to the goddess with grace, if not with faith.'

With grace, if not with faith. That idea made her pensive.

~

In these tense unhappy days Mohini more than ever before yearned for her husband. She had great need to lean on him, to take shelter in his strength. But he failed her. He had his own problems. He was breaking down under the pressure of work. He grew depressed, irritable. His shoulders had a tired droop. He realised with heavy pain that the thesis on which he had toiled was a mirage of his intellect. It was a mass of false effort; it lacked real substance. To have frittered himself away so! Mocking laughter would be his reward.

Jayadev could not bear his defeat. Mohini, he felt, had failed him in this crisis of his spirit. Sunk in her own gloom, she did not see the darkness of his mind.

Mohini felt, on the other hand, that she had given him all he needed of her, that she had submerged herself in his life. Why would he not stand by her in her suffering? Why would he not see what she felt? There were moments when she could trample his work into dust! But he was shielded by his reserve, unreachable. Her anger bit into her and lay deep in her flesh like a splinter.

Two sensitive people who could have sustained each other were beaten and plunged in misery. And the mother, who could have sustained Mohini, was distraught with her obsession and made the girl suffer more. 'You are the doom of this ancient house,' her accusing glance seemed to say. Never, except once, did she lose the calm look that fitted her face like a mask, but she seemed to cry out with cold scorn nonetheless, 'You are barren. You are barren.'

Then, one day Mohini and Jayadev both yielded to their brooding. Mohini was working in the *puja* room, thick black circles under each eye, languor in every limb, and she felt the mother's exploring gaze on her. How she hated that scrutiny she knew so well! The blood burnt in her cheeks.

Anger overcame her modesty and she cried out, 'It isn't what you're thinking, Mother. I am not going to have a baby. I never will.'

The mother was staggered. This was a blow for which she was wholly unprepared. She, too, lost her control and struck back at Mohini in ruthless rage. 'What evil destiny made me bring you into this house? Your barrenness will curse it for all time. You will take the life of your husband, you will —' her voice broke with emotion, 'you will put an end to the Big House. Those deceptive luck signs — scrape them off your skin with a knife. Do not bear the shame of so much falsehood.'

And she walked away.

'I am needed only to bear a son.' Mohini clenched her hands as the mother's words rang in her ears, and she cried, 'Just as well I am barren, just as well I am barren.' And even as she calmed down, her hands clenched again, and her eyes were bright. 'I won't have a son who is to be a limb of the cold, heartless Big House.'

Nausea welled up in her throat. She tightened her jaw and clapped her hand to her mouth lest she give way.

How she longed for the warmth and solace of her city home. She got ink and paper and sat with the tears thick on her lowered lashes as she wrote long letters to Old Mother. She poured out her wretched tale. When she had filled many sheets of paper an oppressive load seemed to lift from her heart, and she could breathe with some ease.

But she never mailed these letters. She kept them locked up in the iron safe a day or two and then tore them to pieces. How could she let her dear ones know she was unhappy?

She had been away two whole years from Shibpur. Her people would never see again the light-hearted girl who sang and laughed so readily. She was changed beyond recognition. Were they not often unhappy on her account? Many a time this past year they had begged that their girl be sent back for a month, but the mother always answered, 'Wait awhile till she is a mother. She will go back to you proudly, then.' And to ease the shock of this refusal Mohini said in her letter sent at the same time, 'I musn't go home just yet. My mother here is helpless without me. Oh, you can't imagine how well I play the mistress of the Big House! But that's half the story. I tell the women of Behula village how to read and write — even to sing. During the noon hours I hold classes for them under the aged banyan in the garden. Can you believe it? The women love and adore me! Then, Ranjan and his young comrades, I have told you about them —' Father would be proud of his girl, and Old Mother's smile would be somewhat forced. 'Do I not know my child? Give her a book and she'll become a scholar. Give her a spade, and she'll be a gardener. She knows nothing but work, work, work. The rest of the world sleeps through the noon hours, but she image-of-joy, used to sit on the balcony, skilfully knitting warm wool coats for all the household.'

Mohini, image-of-joy, lay back on a divan in the rich splendour of her room at the Big House and asked herself, 'Why is this body barren?'

She sat up in a fit of restlessness, unbuttoned her jacket and let her hands follow the slope of her breasts, down across the curve of her stomach, as if by exploring she could learn the answer. What's wrong with you? This body is smooth and tight, fairer and fuller than in my girlhood. It looks like all the others, who have children. Meera, Renu, Bimola — had their first babies within two years after marriage. What's wrong with you then?

'Why don't I die?' she said to herself with a bitter rush of passion.

She laughed through tight lips as she remembered how, for one whole week, she had been sure of her child.

'What if he's born with buck teeth, Meera? Like Ranjan's friend, Ashu?' she had asked.

Meera had laughed and answered: 'You're an ass, Honey Pot. Are babies born with teeth? Gaze at the moon an hour or so on bright night while you sip a bowl of cold milk. Then your child will be born moon-fair. I tried it. Look at my Lalu.'

Even though Lalu was not moon-fair by any stretch of the imagination, Mohini had followed her advice, and night after night had stood on the terrace, her eyes drinking in the beauty of the moon, her mouth sipping a bowl of cold milk.

Fool, fool! Nursing wishful fancies just as in the old days. The mother had to shake her out of it by telling her she was barren. Fool, fool!

And the quilts, the mass of baby quilts she had stitched. Her lips tightened. She jumped from the deep divan and returned with a pile of quilts and her scissors. She seized broad stitches of the embroidery in her scissors and clipped away the auspicious conch, and mace, and lotus, and wheel.

That, strangely, seemed to quieten her. The scissors slackened. Heart's blood? She had given more to this house than *that,* much more. She had given it her body, her soul and her dream. Let there be this final surrender. Then she would go away.

Go away? This was no place for a barren woman. All Behula was pitying her, scorning her. She was the doom of the Big House, the destroyer of an ancient line. Even the peasant women who came to her, they, too.... How could she have failed to notice? How could she have been so insensitive? Her odd castle in the air! Like those odd castles of her girlhood fancy. Had she not grown at all, then? How could she face the women, preen herself as their teacher? She would be less in their eyes than the least among humankind.

Go away... go away....

Her head was aswim; there was misery in her belly, and nausea rushing up in her throat. She was as sick in body as in spirit....

twenty

The wooden wheels of the cart creaked on the rough road; the axle chattered and groaned.

'Tchuk! Tchuk! Do not sleep, good folk,' Ganesh cajoled his oxen.

Mohini and the mother sat under the cart's thatched awning, their backs against cushions, their legs folded.

At noon, the day before, Mohini had reached the kitchen yard after a dip in the cool Rook's Eye when a cowherd boy came bursting through the back door.

'Mother!' he panted. 'Oh, Mother!'

'What now, Rakhal?'

'Oh, Mother! Creeper —'

'Where?' asked Mohini, unimpressed. Creepers, as snakes were often called, were a familiar sight in the village and nothing to be excited about.

Rakhal's narrow chest heaved so hard that for a moment or two he could not speak. Finally, he gasped more than spoke, 'Creeper — Master — creeper — he bit Master's leg —'

Mohini grew rigid. The servants had now come crowding to the yard, silent and tense with concern. The mother emerged from the kitchen.

'Where? Speak!' Mohini's voice was shrill, her eyes, big and staring.

The cowherd wept aloud. 'Meadow,' he wailed. 'Creeper — Master's leg —'

With a scream Mohini flew toward the gate.

But the mother lifted an arm and commanded, 'Wait.' She turned to the awe-struck servants. 'Let the *palki* be rushed to the Meadow. Let a man go racing to Harindra.'

'Mother, we must hurry —' Mohini shrieked.

She could see her husband lying helpless in the hot dust, the venom spreading in his blood. Soon it would be too late. Her eyes were wild with panic.

But the mother spoke quietly. 'The *palki* must go empty, that it may rush. We must wait.'

'We can walk — run —' Mohini's strangled voice was full of hatred.

'It is not becoming.'

Mohini was staggered. She could hardly trust her ears. She stared at the mother and felt violently sick. Her breast felt empty, as though her heart had stopped. The mother met Mohini's fear-haunted glance and suddenly the calm full beauty of middle-age drained away from her face and left it incredibly old.

'I too suffer,' she murmured through tense white lips. 'With every moment that passes, something dies in my blood and bones.'

Mohini could not bear her stricken look. She turned her eyes away. Her head swam. I must not faint, she thought desperately, clutching for support, fighting down a fit of weakness. The dread vision of him dying, dying, and she unaware, lying in a swoon. Like carved images, the two women stood at the gateway, mute, in a stupor. At last a figure appeared around the bend in the road, and moved toward them, fast. It was he — he! And the palanquin was way behind. The women trembled. Suddenly, the mother could not restrain herself. With a cry she rushed forward, rushed out to the road, Mohini at her heels. A hundred yards on she stumbled into her son's arms and held him clasped to her breast.

'Jayadev!' Her voice was a whisper.

He spoke rapidly, though out of breath. 'Easy, Mother. It was a *dhaman* snake, a big yellow brute at least two yards long, quite harmless. I trod on its tail. The snake bit in self-defense. Yes, I've been running hard to come tell you — the worry you've had.'

The arms that held him shook and held tighter.

'Jayadev, how do you know?'

'I cried out. Herdsmen came rushing. They looked for the snake, found it in a shrub and smashed its head with bamboo staves. Then, it appeared that it was an old *dhaman,* poor thing.'

He turned his head and gave Mohini a wide boyish smile, a smile she had not seen for ages.

Meanwhile, all Behula was rushing madly to the Big House. News had gone like a flash. Women beat their breasts and wailed. *'Hai, hai,* Mother goddess, for what sin dost thou strike us with such a disaster? With the last of the House gone, what will happen to Behula village? Oh goddess, *hai, hai!'* Men strode up in tight-lipped silence, bewildered, anguish in their faces.

Later, when the mother was alone with the girl, she spoke intensely out of deep emotion.

'This is Fate's ultimate warning. Fate will strike again — to kill. We have one last refuge, one final hope — the Devi in the shrine. We can afford to wait no longer. Tomorrow, early, we'll leave for the temple.' Her face took on a determined look.

'Yes, Mother.'

'Do not breathe a word to him, else he will not let you go. We'll slip off in the cart.'

'He will not know. We'll slip off in the cart.' And after a slight pause, Mohini added, 'Then, I'll go away — home. In a week's time —'

The mother nodded and all at once her face revealed an unknown warmth. 'Yes, girl. You have suffered much. You'll not be away long?'

'Who knows?' Mohini tried to smile, but her mouth drooped, twisted.

That was the way it happened that they rode down the village path at dawn.

'Tchuk! Tchuk! Do not sleep, good folk.' Ganesh cajoled his oxen.

The mother was telling her beads, her lips and eyes closed. This was not so much an act of devotion, Mohini knew, as of self-discipline. The spirit's athletics! The measureless patience developed by this ritual of the telling of the beads hours on end, at dawn and again at dusk, year after year without a break, was a basic preparation. Boredom was exorcised. The sternest duties slipped into the day's routine. That was the secret of the mother's calm. That was why pain oppressed her so little, pain in her or in others, of the body or of the spirit.

There was a sudden lurch as the wheels struck a pot-hole and Mohini, thrown against the rough side of the cart, cried out, hurt. The mother opened her eyes and leaned over. Her fingers touched the girl's bruised head with a tender caress. Strangely, she broke her stern ritual of silence and spoke.

'My daughter!' she cried with concern. 'Close your eyes. Lie still a minute. There!'

In those days, Mohini, intensely sensitive, was ready to weep with thankful joy at the least gesture of kindness to her. Her eyes were fastened on the mother. How the mother had changed almost overnight. Where was the serenity? The sculptured face was graven with lines, with the pinched look of anxiety. The clipped black hair had strands of grey. The eyes, once so cool and clear, were haunted as though with a ceaseless dread.

In that instant Mohini was very close to the mother whose trust in the horoscope was complete. It was a trust learned from her husband, who was vested with sanctity, who was infallible. And the warning had come — the last warning. What strength she would need to keep from breaking down! It would be a wonder if she did not hate her son's barren wife as the real instrument of the Big House's doom.

What if the horoscope were to prove false and he lived through his fatal year?

What if he lived a normal life span? To die sonless? The mother's eyes were raised to the sky-world where the family's forbears dwelt. They were no mere shadows but deathless symbols of a spiritual heritage.

Deathless symbols of a spiritual heritage — Mohini was startled by that new idea. Was that the inner meaning of your *pitri-purusha,* their true value? Were they symbols of the continuity of culture as the household gods, images in clay, stone, brass, were symbols of God?

Her eyes opened and she watched the roadside touched with dawn. This was the time of year when a special homage was paid to the ancestral spirits with 'Lamps of the Sky'. Long bamboo poles were made fast on rooftops or high up in trees and the tips, like fingers pointing skyward, hung at night with bright, shaded lamps, symbols of reverence to the unseen beings. Now, at dawn, the lights were lost. The Big House too had put up its lamps, one for the eastern sky and one for the western, one for the northern and one for the southern and a last one for the zenith. But where was the need for this gesture? The mother had much more to render her son's ancestors than sky lamps; her heart, so cold to the living, so insensitive, was alight for the dead, a steadfast flame.

Yet, Mohini told herself, perhaps she judged the mother too harshly? Perhaps she saw the wrong side of this old tapestry of tradition and missed the design? Duty and compassion were not at odds in the mother; the key to the design was sacrifice which was a right and privilege, not a duty alone. If necessity pointed to a co-wife, it was your proud privilege, not a punishment, to perform the welcome ceremony for the new bride, waving lit lamps before her face, touching her ears with honey! This much was certain: the mother in the prime of her youth would herself have arranged her husband's second marriage if fate had made her barren.

How wrong to fancy the mother was without feeling, insensitive! Here she was, resolved to give her own blood to the Devi — not that it would count — as an example, an encouragement. Mohini remembered an incident in her childhood when, hot with malaria, she had furiously refused the quinine mixture. 'Drink it up, childling, it's not so very bitter. Look, I'll take it too,' Old Mother had coaxed and had each day for weeks gulped some of the medicine.

Mothers were like that, thought Mohini, smiling with tenderness. For the last miserable weeks she had hated the mother. It was so easy to love, so hard to hate. Let there be some sweetness between them before she went away.

~

'Hurry!' Jayadev thrust his excited face out of the palanquin and urged the panting bearers to more speed.

This was the hour he usually sat in the pavilion of study, recording the ideas he had during the night. Strange how ideas would creep up while the mind rocked between sleep and waking. These thoughts had to be recaptured and given substance. The day's work had to be charted.

But his hour of meditation had been interrupted. Up the pavilion steps Sudha had come, Sudha who was never seen in the Big House any more.

'Am I to have as a new pupil, an old one who forsook me?' he asked jestingly.

Her eyes lay cool on his face. What power was there in him that held her caged? Sudha, who did not know herself, could not see that it was not Jayadev but the master of the Big House she loved. If she possessed *him,* she would possess all. And how she would be avenged then!

'What do you care?' Her voice was brittle. 'You have someone better to teach.'

He watched her face redden and he gave her a friendly laugh.

'Mohini? She isn't like you, Sudha. She was made to be the mistress of the Big House. She is absorbed in people, not ideas.'

There was a pause. Her throat felt stiff. 'I hate books, I have ideas.' Flecks of fire sprang to her eyes. 'You never knew. I have always hated knowledge and loved life. You never understood.' She lost her voice again, but at last, with an effort, she managed to say, 'But I haven't come to tell you that.'

Sudha, at sun-up, was returning home after bathing in a pond when she saw the familiar ox-cart of the Big House pass by. She had given a careless glance inside. Amazed, she had looked again. Where were they going at this hour, those two women? She had stood awhile, watching, wondering. Till the cart was out of sight. One or two explanations seemed possible but she felt unsure. She must know. She turned quickly and walked down the road to a cluster of earth huts.

'Mother of Pantu!' she called at the door of one hut. 'Some dung-cake kindling please.'

A woman of perhaps thirty came hurrying out.

'Two scores will be enough?' she asked.

She was the wife of Ganesh, the cartman, and she earned a few coppers on her own by selling dried cow-dung cakes for fuel. For many hours of the day she walked about in the meadow where cattle grazed, collecting dung.

Sudha counted the flat brown dung cakes. As she handed the money she said casually, 'I saw the cartman on the road. He's up and about early today.'

The woman nodded. Her eyes betrayed her excitement. 'I'll tell you, only you, but keep your lips sealed. Don't breathe a word to a bird or a beast, even. The cartman told me in deep secrecy. They're going to the virgin goddess, those ladies of the House.'

Sudha was startled.

'Virgin goddess?' she said.

'The young mistress —' the woman let a meaningful gesture serve for words.

'She must give her blood, then?'

The woman nodded. 'She must. How else appease the hard-hearted virgin? But do not breathe a word even to bird or beast.'

Sudha was pensive as she walked back home. She lit the kitchen fire and set an earthen rice-bowl on the oven. It was while she peeled the sweet potatoes for a dry curry that the strange thought struck her: Let Mohini not make the offering lest the Devi fulfil her wish. The thought, sudden and significant, took her breath away and she carelessly cut her finger.

She sat still, watching the blood stain the clear lines of her palm. Then her eyes flashed; her lips were grim.

'Let mine be the offering, let it reach the Devi in the temple. Mohini shall not give her blood.'

In a great hurry she picked up the heavy rice-bowl and set it on the floor. She stepped into her bedroom, and stood before a small wood-framed mirror hung on a wall. The heat of the kitchen had made her face rosy and wet with perspiration. With her sari she rubbed her face hard till it freshened and the bloom deepened. She smiled with pleasure at herself, at her soft eyes and yearning lips.

A minute later she was out-of doors walking up the path to the Big House. She looked covetously at the sprawling old building as she hurried towards it. If only she could have exchanged the grace of her face for one luck sign in her hand, just one! The gift of her beauty was so much less than that fateful scrawl. It was strange that all the luck signs had not helped the mistress of the House with her fruitless womb. She was not a womanly woman, an abnormal woman who would throw the village into desperation and distress.

What then? Sudha had an image of Mohini haunting the House as a widow in white, unadorned by jewels, her hair clipped short, hated by everyone. A spot in her ached with a tender feeling. Mohini was always so kind to her, so gentle and sweet. When Sudha had had the fatal sickness, Mohini had come almost every day to see her and brought flowers and fruit. She had sat by her bed, caressing her hair with a loving hand. How could she harm anyone so very kind? Last Tuesday when she was returning home from her rice fields where the wage labourers were hard at work harvesting, her feet ached, her limbs were warm, bathed in sweat. Mohini came along in her blue palanquin. When it was abreast Sudha, it stopped. Mohini stepped out on the road and walked to Sudha. 'Going home?' she asked. 'Ride in the *palki,* sister.' Sudha had hesitated and Mohini had taken her arm; she smiled and drew her gently along. 'Come sister. The *palki* is as much yours as mine.' How could she stab such a gracious woman in the back! What would she gain in any case were the House emptied of life and joy? She would still be doomed to be Saturn's Eyesore. It was madness to plan that the Devi go unappeased.

Go back home, Sudha, go back, but her feet drew her onward. Ahead lay the tall, iron gates and beyond, in the pavilion, was Jayadev. No Mohini, no mother in the house, only Jayadev. Sudha walked in excitement. What would be the harm if she saw him, for she had suppressed her mad urge to reveal anything? Soothed by that belief she paused a minute before an oleander shrub, plucked a bunch of the red flower and pinned it to her hair.

'What is it?' Jayadev asked anxiously. His face was grave. What had happened to this girl? She had been the problem of the village and of the Big House. Then Mother had reached out for her and had set her firmly on her feet. He, too, had helped. Was all that effort wasted?

'I've not come to tell you that.' She bit her lip to stop its trembling. Something inside her had snapped with a violence that made her gasp. What did he care for her? He belonged to Mohini, body and soul. And with that bitter thought she identified herself with the suppressed, asocial woman society had shaped with heedless hands.

Let destiny have its way; let Saturn smite the village with the light of its Evil Eye; let the suffering that had long been her lot be the lot of all.

Cold anger hit her voice as she spoke.

'Do you call this manly? For your sake she bears this torture. She cuts her bosom to the Devi. It means nothing to you?'

Dumb with surprise, Jayadev had to think over her words before he grasped their meaning.

'What?' he cried, springing to his feet. 'What's this you say?'

A strange joy rang in her hollow laughter.

'As if you didn't know! Manly, indeed!'

His face grew very pale. 'It can't be true. Tell me about it, hurry,' he commanded gruffly.

She hesitated a second before the mounting wave of her fury took her in its grip and made her speak in a rush.

'They set out for the shrine an hour back, your wife and mother. By this time — no, the preliminary ritual may not be over yet. Soon —' And having spoken the unspeakable, Sudha, in the next breath, could have bitten her tongue.

Jayadev paced up and down the pavilion, arms folded on his chest. Why wasn't he told? Sharp resentment against his mother rose in him. *She* was responsible. Jayadev felt the blood in his temples. As though he feared to die! As though he must buy his life at the cost of Mohini's suffering! And to what purpose? That stupid horoscope. That evil power. As he thought, his pace became more rapid and restless. He had lost sight of Sudha, standing very still, her face ashen. Suddenly, he reached a decision, rushed out of the room, and called out to Roghua, 'Order the palanquin. Quick!' he had to rein in a strong urge to rush away on foot, not to waste a moment when a moment could mean failure.

He turned back for an instant. 'Sudha,' he called with quick warmth, 'don't worry. Mohini will not be hurt. I'll be there in time. Go home, Sudha.'

How good of her to come rushing to tell him. He was grateful. If only — the thought saddened him as always — Sudha could have a normal happy life, like other people.

Sudha stood frozen and in horror watched the *palki* speed off, as though carrying *him* to his doom. Malice, some ruthless compulsion had made her speak. Excitement subsided into despair, tears burned in her eyes and spilled out in big drops. She slumped, exhausted, on the floor, staring at the hundred lines in her palm. The madness had left her heart, and she was inexpressibly wretched.

The manuscript on which he had been intent lay open on the desk. She reached out and pressed it to her breast as though to still its agony.

Ranjan, meanwhile, could find no one in the house. He had rushed to the gate, breathless.

'Roghua, where's everyone gone? Where's *Didi,* my *Didi?*'

Roghua was straddling the gate lion. His fat proud body was poised while he broke crisp tobacco leaves in the hollow of his palm. The lion's back was his favourite perch, but he could enjoy it only on rare occasions when the housefolks were all out. Roghua looked forward to such a chance as this.

Ranjan grabbed one of Roghua's thick knees in both his hands and shook it fiercely.

'Why don't you speak?'

The gate-man knew the facts, but true to his calling, he concealed them from the boy.

'Gone for a joy ride in ox-cart and palanquin,' he said.

He slipped some tobacco into his mouth. His eyes and his fat, black moustache seemed to show his enjoyment.

'All? Leaving me? Leaving just me?'

Creases lined the gate-man's face as he chuckled.

'Better ride the king of the beasts,' he said soothingly. 'Ride the other one. *Huaaa-mm!*'

He rolled his eyes and gave a tremendous roar, like a lion.

Ranjan felt his throat tighten; his mouth worked strangely. He turned and was gone like a dart, while the gate-man yelled after him at the top of his voice.

'Don't be up to mischief while the housefolks are away. Come back.'

But before he could put his short legs down and heave his belly around to dismount, Ranjan had reached the far bend where the three roads crossed.

The palanquin swung across the village, across the meadow. Once in a while Jayadev urged the bearers to speed. His fists clenched and unclenched; his eyes flew ahead and ate up the white furlongs ahead.

His mind was with his wife, torturing herself. For his sake. Had she a half doubt that the horoscope's prediction might come true, after all? That was it. His heart ached for Mohini. The melancholy that had of late settled on her face, the bewildered, haunted look in her eyes. When had she lost the gift of vivacity, so becoming an adornment? Pallid, and nervous, too — the bang of a door, the harsh hoot of an owl in the dark would startle her. He had wanted to speak to her about it, but somehow he hadn't. She needed a change, that was plain. She had stayed too long in the country without a change. A month or two at Shibpur, and she would be her old self, eager and bright-eyed. It was good indeed, that the trip was being arranged. He would take her home and stay with her perhaps two or three weeks — then he would return, for his work must soon be done. The sense of futility that had for some time troubled him had passed off and he knew his goal was close. His work completed, his mind free, he would be back with Mohini, and nothing would come between them. They would travel, just the two of them. Mohini had a keen longing to see places. Strange, how little he knew her. But the joy of discovery was near.

This task at hand — the clash with his mother with her iron will and misguided faith — would be difficult. What, he wondered, had happened to the ancient quest of the Hindus, the quest for *satyam, sivam, sundaram* — Truth, Goodwill and Beauty? The core, the spiritual content had been choked by centuries of evil overgrowth. Misguided faith burned like a great lamp of oil that gave little light but a great deal of smoke. It was this smoke which was pouring over India, this smoke which made the Big House stifling. Jayadev had long known that the conflict between himself and his mother must one day take real shape. It, too, was part of the wider conflict. Today was the beginning, and Jayadev, was unhappy because of his love for his mother and his respect for her feelings.

It was just after noon when Jayadev saw the tall temple of the virgin goddess, its brass-pointed spire glinting in the sun at the edge of the village named Vermilion Hill. Once more he urged his palanquin bearers to speed. He might be too late by the flicker of an eyelid.

The goddess stood in the dark inner sanctum, a life-size brass creation, with a full handsome face, plump limbs and balloon breasts. Her gold cheeks and brow were smudged with vermilion; her bosom was thick with chains of marigold. Mohini squatted before her on the damp floor strewn with blossoms and lighted by earthen lamps, praying, repeating the *mantra* after the temple priest. A lotus-leaf bowl lay in her lap.

'Not that,' the voice was sharp and imperious. A hand seized the bowl and flung it aside.

'Jayadev!' the temple priest cried out in surprise and Mohini, startled, burst into tears.

The spell was broken by the mother who was alarmed but self-possessed.

'What brings you here, Jayadev? No evil news?'

'Mohini mustn't insult herself,' Jayadev cried. 'I won't have it. To appease a cruel goddess in this primitive way!'

Stern-eyed, the mother faced him.

'Barren women have always given their blood to the Devi. What's wrong with it? Why this fuss?'

'We are not slaves of the stars,' Jayadev answered. 'There is no room in the Big House for crazy beliefs. The village looks to us for ideals and a way of living. The pattern we set is not our private affair; it carries the strongest social sanction.'

'I know your mind. Heresy holds you. Old beliefs, old morals, old values mean nothing to you. To have a degenerate for a son — for what sins in my past lives am I now punished?' She closed her eyes, struggling to control herself. Suddenly, sternness and pride left her face and she was a helpless woman, pleading. 'Jayadev,' she begged, 'this petty penance would do no harm anyhow.'

Mohini saw his face flush and his eyes shine. Her heart was pounding painfully.

'Values, Mother? There are values beyond your grasp, since you'll always try to reach them with your reason, never with your feelings. Life has punished you.' His glance rested on his wife. It returned to his mother whom he now addressed thus: 'Blind belief shapes your thinking; blind belief cannot make a sentiment.'

Mohini felt a thrill. Through a mist of tears she watched his excited face. The mother, too, stared at the face of her son, newly revealed and strange.

He grew calm and thoughtful. He smiled a little sadly, and said, more gently, 'Let's not be terrified by what seems to you inevitable. Are we not greater than our *karma?*'

The mother knew his secret strength, his inner core of steel.

'Do as you wish,' she said, crushed with despair. 'An old woman who has overstayed her time on earth would not expect to shake you from your purpose. Only this much' — defeat and wretchedness made her voice sound like heavy sobbing — 'this much I beg of you: in your quieter moods, my son, turn your mind to your revered *pitri-purushas* who dwell not in a dim sky-world but deep within you, seeing all, hearing all, and saddened now by your decision to end their life which has gone on for a thousand years.'

~

On the way back the ladies took the palanquin, Jayadev, the cart.

Jayadev was pleased with himself. He had rescued Mohini from her ordeal, and he had seen the changing grace of her face: startled, pale with alarm, tearful, proud, triumphant. He had been amply repaid. Barren? Was it not enough that she was alight with beauty, giving a touch of it to all with whom she had contact? Her presence filled the Big House, which throbbed with the lotus of her love.

He stared ahead at the palanquin fast bearing her away, and he felt a hunger for her face and her voice, for her smile, her fragrance and warmth. His heart was full of tenderness.

Barren? And if the child came, after all, as he must? A wistful smile grew on his face. Better, perhaps, if his son were to wait awhile, a year or two, so that the horoscope was wholly disproved and discredited. *His son!* His smile faded. Around the image of his son the battle of the Big House raged in full fierceness. A sudden regret came upon him, like a shock, that the old order must pass, that his son, his heir, would not know the ease and graciousness, the power and godlike prestige, the splendour and grace of living that had been the inheritance of the Big House for a thousand years. Jayadev, regretting the bounteous past, ached for his unborn son, who was caught in the flux of a fast-moving tomorrow.

What then? Would not the young, too, have their own proud inheritance? Were they not to be a living torch of the new age to come? Great and exciting days lay ahead. India, free to build up her destiny, was not yet truly free. She was like a prisoner held too long in a dark cell. Unchained and released suddenly, she was bewildered by the light. But the stupor would pass. India would renew herself, and her strength would be the strength of the young — not more, not less.

Yes, Jayadev told himself, his son had no need of the Big House, of a House of the past, for he would have his own proud inheritance.

A furlong up the road, Mohini sat very still in the palanquin, utterly spent. Exaltation was swiftly followed by depression. Her husband had wakened to her existence and fugitively cared for her awhile. This was one such moment, but he had no real need for her. She was still only a pet, a habit, a physical convenience, a moral obligation. Mohini sighed deeply. How it would hurt her to leave in such a dark mood, and how it would hurt her to stay on. Her hands fretted in her lap.

She turned and assessed the mother without compassion. One good thing had come from this pilgrimage: the proud mother had been thwarted. Nothing like this could ever have happened in the Big House — a son challenging his mother for the sake of a mere wife, or for the sake of a sentiment. Mohini's glance was intent on the erect figure, the stony face, the closed eyes and the long white fingers on the rosary. The mother, firm and calm as ever, was telling the beads again.

Mohini misjudged her, for the mother was not calm. She had been deeply shaken. This was the end. The Devi insulted and enraged. Mohini and Jayadev doomed. Each day, each hour ate up his allotted span of life. He had flouted his mother and hurt her cruelly — all Behula would hear the story — but it was a trifle compared to the fact that fate had set its final deadly snare and there was no way of escape.

He would be twenty-eight in a year. There was one year left for his son to be born — a year, a speck of time.

If only he had never known of this trek to the temple! Or if he had been a half-hour late! But whatever had happened, it was the work of the stars. She guessed immediately it was Sudha who had rushed to tell him, Sudha, who loved him in her secret heart and therefore shunned his very shadow. What need had Sudha to tell him? Sudha?

The face grew tense. New light shone in the mother's eyes as they opened wide because, suddenly, she knew why Sudha had told.

Sudha hated the young mistress of the Big House. Sudha hated to see her fulfilled. Out of spite she had made her plan. She knew how Jayadev would react if he heard of Mohini's penance. He would never let Mohini give her blood to the Devi in the temple, and so Mohini would remain barren. What if Jayadev died? Sudha's possessive love knew nothing of selflessness. She couldn't marry him, therefore let no one else be happy with him, no matter what happened.

The mother felt her head spin. What a well of bitterness was the heart of this outcast girl! Society had done this to her, and her hate, was deeper than common malice. It grew in the bitter flow of her blood. Self-preservation made her predatory. She who could not live for others had to live for herself.

'Fast, fast, race the gale,' chanted the *palki*-bearers, road dust in their mouths and sweat in their eyes, 'fast, fast —'

Then the idea, the terrible idea, came upon the mother with a shock that nearly stupefied her. What if Sudha could have *her* fulfilment? What if Sudha could bear the child of the man she loved so fiercely?

Visions filled her eyes as they closed again: Mohini gone to the city; two conspirators — Sudha and the mother. Sudha would make her battle with every art of seduction.

Would he yield? He had been unhappy about the cruel persecution of the innocent Sudha. He would even have wed Sudha if the mother had willed it. Out of his compassion for Sudha another feeling might grow.

There could be no lovelier temptress, and the tremendous force that Sudha could become might sweep him off his feet. He was really bred in the cynical ways of the city, its fast life, its bland acceptance of vice; he had the city in his ideas and feelings, in his bones.

The mother's very soul shrilled in outraged protest. It was a loathsome thought — a mother planning to drag her son into the mire. A perversion! How could she be so degraded?

He would marry her because he was honourable, and his life would be saved. And the life of the Big House, for another generation.

She, a mother, dragging down the unstained image of her son into filth!

Trapped in her wish dreams, the normally stern realist made light of the basic problem: her son was not the kind who fell readily for women.

The desperate mother, carried away by her fear, clutched at a straw and made it an anchor. There was no other way. Sudha would not fail, and, graced with all the luck signs, she would be a bride of the Big House, its hope, its destiny.

'Give me strength for my mean task. Out of evil good shall come. Out of mud a lotus shall grow. Let one curse counteract another. Time rushes by. There is no other way,' she prayed.

Mohini was startled. Tears were falling from the mother's eyes. Never before had Mohini seen her cry. How worn-out, how exhausted she looked. Even in her bitterness Mohini felt a stab of pity. She felt the tears hot and prickling in her own eyes and averted her face.

twenty one

Life had been moving fast in the Big House. The mother had her plan and not a moment was to be lost in putting it into effect. Mohini would go away with Jayadev, but a telegram an urgent call, would bring him hurrying home. Then Sudha....

Sudha would have her chance. The mother had sent for Sudha and spoken to her with humility, in misery and burning shame. Sudha had gasped. Stupefied, she had stared at the mother, unbelieving. No reality, no dream could be more fantastic. Her face flushed and her eyes lit up at the astounding turn in her affairs. She lifted her palm in a habitual gesture. Had the lines changed? Was she not to waste away, unwanted? The gifts of life, which every woman needed, would all be hers? For her, the battle of the Big House planned by the mother in such meticulous detail, was a battle for Sudha's triumph. Her brooding jealousy had a razor's edge; her wounded ego had made her cruel.

'No, Mother,' she shook her head. 'How shameful! What madness! How could you ask me? *You?*'

This was Sudha's moment. Had the mother not denied her once and broken her heart?

And the mother said in her heart: 'Today I pay for my deception. I pay with my honour, with all that is dear to me, with my very soul.'

'What has Mohini done to me?' Sudha cried with a sort of breathlessness. 'Mohini?'

Only the mother's suffering eyes spoke.

Sudha had had enough. She stopped pretending she was shocked.

'He is no clay to be shaped by a woman's will,' she said in a low tight voice. 'What do I mean to him?'

The mother clutched Sudha's arm. 'You have power.' She was deceived because of her desperate need.

'His life hangs on your decision, Sudha.'

Sudha without replying, lowered her eyes, and the mother smiled. But it was as though she wept. She lifted her hand to Sudha's head in a gesture of blessing, turned quickly lest the girl see her tears, and almost ran away.

Sudha stood motionless with her vision. She was his pupil again, with him always, his companion, his shadow. Out of that close communion something vital must grow. She had power, the mother had said, power! Sudha clenched her small fists, her mouth was grim. No man could scorn her. But even as she reassured herself, Jayadev's image was supplanted by the image of Harindra, that bold impulsive young man whom the elders of Behula disliked and feared. He had tended her with the infinite care of a doctor, but he was more to her, much more than a kind and skilful doctor. Where in this unheeding world was there another man so kind, and patient, and gentle? He had sat for long hours at her bedside when her life hung on a thread. Her life was a gift from him, indeed. Later, when she was well and he came to see her uncle, and he came often, Sudha would stand by the inner door listening to his voice, to his loud laugh with its joyous ring. She could deeply feel his presence and it gave her a strange restful happiness. Face to face, he would look at her not as some other men had often looked. His eyes were frank and respectful yet tender, filled with some longing. The evenings when he did not come were for her drab and wasted.

'If only our Harindra were a Brahmin boy,' her uncle had murmured a few days ago as though speaking to himself 'then I could have him as my son —' His sad sunken eyes looked at her face in a helpless way.

'Son?' she had asked with a start.

'Fate places a supreme gift at one's door and still it is out of reach.'

'Uncle, I don't understand.' But her heart was beating fast.

'Harindra spoke yesterday.' Suddenly the old man awoke from his absorption and his glance sharpened. 'Sudha,' he said, frowning to cover his emotion, 'go and light the kitchen fire. Tonight I'll retire early.'

'What gift of fate, Uncle?' Sudha persisted.

The old man was suddenly fiercely angry.

'Sudha, get along.'

Sudha had no need to ask. She knew.

But Sudha in a panic blotted out all visions except one — the one that would be her instrument to power. The egotist, more than the women, needed satisfaction.

Mohini saw no shadow of this threat, and the Big House, wrapped in gloom, took no notice of the changes in her: the persistent sourness in the mouth: the sickness that routed her out of bed while her head swam. But she forced herself sternly to bear the hundred disorders of a barren woman.

Besides, something had happened to Ranjan. He seldom went near her or spoke to her.

'Ranjan,' she coaxed him as he sat turning the pages of a comic. 'I'll read you a story. Rokfist Rogan? Don Winslow?'

Ranjan kept his eyes on the comic and refused to answer.

How could he forget that *Didi* had not taken him to the Devi's temple?

'What now, boy?'

'Nothing. I'm looking at the pictures.'

Didi read his face with anxious eyes.

Ranjan snorted, which was a sure way to annoy *Didi* who had cured him of the habit.

'Ranjan, why not come to town with me?'

Ranjan made a scornful face. 'I hate town,' he said.

With one hurt look at Ranjan, Mohini turned and left the room. Ranjan did not need her any more. Why should he? He belonged to the Big House, to its stern coldness. What right had a stranger to take him away to *her* world?

The day before the scheduled journey to town, Mohini fainted. She was directing the cook as usual when the light died in her eyes, and she slipped unconscious to the floor. Perhaps it was the stuffy kitchen or the long and increasing emotional tension.

Harindra saw her half an hour later. He invited the mother out of the room to speak to her. Afterwards, when Harindra had gone, the mother stood as if electrified, pressing her hands to her breast as though she could still the mad violence of her feelings. When, at last, the painful pounding of her heart quietened, she rushed off to Mohini's bedside.

It was a strain for her to pitch her voice low when she wanted to shout in pure passion, in joy for all the world to hear, 'Daughter mine, you are pregnant!'

Mohini felt her blood stop, then flow in a rush to her neck and face. She sat up fiercely, overcome by a new wave of sickness and cried, 'Must you make fun of me? Must you?'

'Make fun of you, Mohini?' The mother's voice shook. 'This is true. True! Harindra told me, Harindra.'

'No, no!' Mohini groaned. 'I don't believe it. I am barren.' She was trembling violently.

'Harindra told me, Harindra,' the mother repeated. 'There's no shadow of doubt, he said. You are in your third month. You must have known this, girl. Why didn't you tell me? So many days of jubilation have been wasted in heartbreak.'

Yes, she knew, but she dared not believe it. She could bear no more mockery, so she had hidden her secret from everyone, even from herself.

'And what if —' said the mother, a quiver in her voice, 'Mohini, what if you had not fainted?' She paused. 'Daughter, don't go away. Stay till the child is born,' she begged Mohini.

But Mohini could not answer. She lay exhausted in bed, shocked by the news, her face burning in the pillow, a sudden sob shaking her from head to foot. The mother sat silent at the bed head. Lovingly she caressed the girl's hair and let Mohini's excitement spend itself.

As the mother sat and slowly regained her calm, a fury of shame ate at her. The ruthlessness, the awful meanness with which she had planned this girl's doom! How could she ever lift her eyes again, if Mohini knew? And if Jayadev knew, would he ever forgive her? What madness had grown out of her anguish, and how she had tortured both Mohini and herself. The mother of the Big House had transgressed the basic moral laws as though they were meaningless. Was her son's life or, for that matter, even the life of the Big House worth saving at such a price?

But this agony of spirit cleared her vision, and for the first time, she could see her son clearly. His ideas, his point of view, molded by the new spirit in the land, were different from hers and opposed to them, but they were, nonetheless, true ideals. Right or wrong, he had honest faith in his set of values, his set of tools for improving life. How could she have misjudged him so completely or think him debased? In that moment of insight the mother almost understood her son and, through him, the new revolt, the restless spirit of the new dawn.

And Sudha. How Sudha would despise her. She had striven to lift her to a noble pedestal, and for a mean, selfish reason.

The mother winced. She had a furious desire to hurt herself, to bang her head on the stone floor.

And then she was again engulfed in her joy of knowing there would be an heir to the Big House, a son for Jayadev, a child for Mohini.

Mohini calmed down, but she lay with her eyes closed. Suddenly she felt tears on her cheek.

She opened her eyes, startled, sat up and whispered, 'Why, Mother?'

Dread choked her, so that she could hardly breathe. She wasn't pregnant? It was all false?

But the mother said, 'I am so happy, girl,' and smiled a bit and kept on crying shamelessly.

Mohini lifted her limp hand and put it in the mother's. So she lay, fear eased, her heart almost content.

'Mother —'

'Yes, child?'

'I didn't have to wait for the Devi's favour. Long before I went to the temple — the time I had the bamboo chip in my hair —'

'No, no, girl,' the mother interrupted, concerned that harm might befall the fruitful womb. 'You don't understand. The Devi has always known your heart's true desire. You promised her a nose-ring set with pearls, remember? Your will to penance was real; that, too, the Devi knew. The act itself is nothing — a symbolic gesture. The goddess is not duped by the veiled face of things, she looks deeper behind the veil.'

Who but the Devi had willed that Mohini fall ill on the eve of her journey? How else could the mad mischief she had planned be averted? The mother shuddered at the thought that fate hung on such a slender thread, and if it had snapped, there would have followed a tragedy whose end could only have destroyed them all.

Mohini closed her eyes again. How could you oppose or undermine such faith? Let mother have her blind trust in the goddess if it makes her happy. Let the credit for the child go to the goddess in the temple and let the goddess have her nose-ring set with pearls.

Suddenly, Mohini yearned for her husband, yearned to be alone with him, to ask how he felt when he heard the news? To ask whether he would ever again be able to neglect his wife? To ask him to guess whether it would be a boy or a girl.

And just as suddenly and unexpectedly he was there, softly pushing open the door, slipping in, his face beaming. The mother stood up, smiling.

Before she left the room she pleaded again. 'Mohini, do not leave us yet.'

But Mohini answered sharply. 'I must.'

'You are so weak, girl —' the proud mother suggested humbly.

Mohini lay still, gazing at the mother. Her eyes and lips softened and the tightness in her heart eased. It was not in her to nurse a violent anger.

'Weak? Oh, no, Mother. I never felt more fit. Don't you see from my face? I —' She stopped and her face was lovely with a new radiance.

'Take the boy with you. Ranjan —'

'Ranjan?'

'He is crying his heart out. His eyes are swollen. Poor boy, he won't eat. You can manage him, who else?'

Ranjan would go with her, Ranjan needed her.

At home in Shibpur she would not be truly away. The Big House lived in her, a part of her inmost self. At last, there was no discord. Life was music — a note of song for the Old Mother was in her, a note for Jayadev and his rebel gods, a note for the Big House and Behula village, torn and at cross-purposes for a while. Her life was music — the true quest of every woman, her deepest need.

Her eyes rested on her husband in a restful ecstasy as he stood at her bedside. And he, as though knowing what she felt, smiled down at her.

~

As the *palki* was passing the mango grove that almost hid Sudha's whitewashed house from view: Mohini looked at the house with pleasure. Sudha would at last be happy. Mohini felt a twinge of regret that she had not helped draw Sudha and Harindra closer together, had not made things easy between them.

Harindra had been too proud to ask her help in such a delicate matter. But how could she have failed him, when she knew his heart? As soon as she came back to Behula she would — Mohini made a firm resolve.

Drawn by the cry of the *palki*-bearers, Sudha slipped out of bed and crossed to the window to look out through the bars. There they went in the dawn, the two palanquins, bearing the mistress and the master of the Big House. Her glance lay on him, while her breath quickened with the picture of her satisfaction. Soon the tables would turn. The mistress, riding a joyous palanquin, would be stripped of glory. The earth would split open under her feet. And out of the dust of a hundred despairs the new mistress of the Big House would rise, who would bear it a child and save its imperilled life.

Even in this moment of exaltation she was discontent, her heart was heavy. Under her breath, she said a name, while unaccountable tears grew in her eyes. She suppressed them and stood rigid.

The cart was out of sight now, but she could see in the distance the face of the Big House, that vast instrument of splendour and power, shaping to her hands. Her body tensed with bitter pleasure and her small delicate fists clutched the iron bars of the window.

❑❑❑